PARASITIC

PJ Burgy

Printed in the United States of America

ISBN: 9798375028873

Imprint: Independently published

"SWÖRM", trademarked pjburgy

It is with great pleasure that I unveil this latest piece. Peel back the layers and look, view in its entirety the levels to which I shall stoop in my mission to spread joy.

As always, a heartfelt thanks is extended to those around me. Their patience is appreciated. For, you see, one tends to disappear for long periods of time when on a mission such as mine. When I return, they are there waiting.

Much love.

PJ   BURGY

Chapter 1

Olivia Nelson trekked across the deserted parking lot to the docks, her duffel bag heavy on her shoulder and the wheels of her rolling luggage bouncing on the heavily pockmarked blacktop. Circling gulls screamed, their calls high and keening. The roar of the ocean grew steadily louder, the air salty and warm. A few stray clouds stretched across the sky as a bright red sun rose behind her. She was glad she'd chosen to wear shorts and sneakers that morning. If she'd worn her originally planned outfit – a nice blouse, a skirt, nylons, and that hateful pair of uncomfortable pumps – she'd have been absolutely miserable dragging her baggage in the sticky humidity.

As soon as she neared the short wooden staircase leading down, she saw the boat – smaller than she'd imagined, older than she'd have liked. Descending onto the docks, she took a closer look. On the side of the rusty gray hull, Olivia saw the name of the ship written out in huge, peeling black lettering, 'LEUCOSIA'. In her head, she practiced pronouncing the word and pondered on the origin.

The waves crashed against cement barriers, the sound mingling with the conversations of half a dozen people loitering on the docks. They were in the slow process of leaving, by the looks of it. Each had their own piece of luggage in tow. The purr of a powerful car engine and the squeal of tires drew her attention back toward the parking lot.

A fancy sedan had pulled up at the top of the steps and a man in an expensive suit was getting out, walking down without a glance backward. Another fellow, dressed well – but not as well as the first – leaped from the driver's seat, and rushed to the opening trunk of the car. He covered

1

himself in luggage like a pack mule, slammed the trunk shut with his elbow, and clumsily followed the other man.

She stepped to the side to make room for him as the man in the suit glided past her, barking at his cellphone, his free hand cupping his other ear against the sound of the ocean and gulls. The breeze teased his short, chestnut brown hair. To Olivia, he looked like a young company man, out of his element on the dingy dock. He was lightly tanned, clean shaven, wearing black sunglasses. Tall, with an angular, classically handsome face and jawline, a loosened tie, and an ironed gray suit jacket – open.

He ended his call dramatically before noticing Olivia's presence, lifting his sunglasses above his eyes to gaze down at her with an almost detached sort of curiosity. Those eyes were a striking sky-blue.

Olivia looked up at him, her smile polite. "I'll bet you're the Samos-Barnes rep, am I right? Mr. Wilcox?" She waited for his subtle nod before reaching for a handshake. "I'm Olivia Nelson from Occupational Safety."

He did not extend his hand toward her. Instead, he glanced away briefly, searching the dock. "Where's Leblanc?"

"He couldn't come. He sent me."

"Who are you?"

"Um, Olivia Nelson."

"And why isn't Leblanc here?"

"Because he sent me, Mr. Wilcox?"

He rolled his eyes and turned on his heel, pulling his cell from his pocket. "That didn't answer my question. Whatever, I'll call him and find out for myself."

"All aboard!" the captain cried, the gulls answering.

Olivia walked up the ramp onto the boat, again listening to Wilcox bicker loudly on his cellphone behind her. Her chin lowered, she adjusted her duffle bag on her shoulder and dragged her luggage. Halfway up, two of the crew hurried her way, offering to help, their hands out and their brows knit.

Despite her protests, they wrenched her luggage from her and proceeded back onto the deck. She trailed them, hands at her sides and chin jutting in annoyance. Wilcox strolled past her, his assistant lugging his things up the ramp behind him. None of the crew jumped in to offer the poor fellow any help, though they did exchange sour grimaces.

Once she'd reached the deck, the same two crewmen holding her things led her down below to her cabin.

As soon as she'd settled into her cabin, her luggage and duffel bag tossed onto the tiny bed, she had a chat with Leblanc. His fatherly smile strained briefly as the video pixelated on the small screen on her cell propped up with a ketchup bottle on the cabin's dining table.

"I'm sorry, Olivia – I should have warned you."

"It's alright. He's everything I expected in a company rep."

"Samos-Barnes sent their best to twist my arm. Astor Wilcox is their new junior partner, but I met him before the promotion. He thinks we have some kind of understanding after the incident at their plant in Hillston, due to my determination on the case – which had nothing to do with his constant badgering, let me just say. Regardless, now Brett believes I'll cow down to his boy. They won't know what to do now, with you," Leblanc said. "Don't let him bully you; follow your gut."

"I always do."

"'Course – I have total faith."

"It's just, I've never been to a facility like this."

"You have your resources. Your training. You've worked warehouse accidents. They're very similar."

"They've been on land. And the machinery was… smaller."

"Same concepts, Olivia."

"I had driven those machines. I've never worked a giant drill."

"Well, you won't be concerning yourself with that."

She nodded bleakly. "No, I won't."

"The company is going to try downplaying the accident. Make it sound like it was the worker's fault. It's not the fine they're worried about, Olivia," he said. "This will be the third death at one of their facilities this year, and it knocks their stock prices when consumers shy away from their products."

"Noted, sir."

"You've got this." His image pixelated on the screen.

"I appreciate your confidence in me."

He brightened, the lines around his eyes deepening. "Sure, I'm confident in your abilities – you were trained by the best!"

"Sure, I was." She smiled softly.

"Kick him in the shins if he acts up. You can always claim it was a reflex if he throws a fit."

"Did that work for you?"

"Well, no, but then again, I didn't press my luck. Frankly, I'm a little disturbed by those company suits. Never had the courage to kick one of them. You might get away with it if you play innocent, but they know me too well by now."

"I'll let you know how it goes, if I end up shinning him."

"Much appreciated," he said, his image distorting again. "I've got to run, Olivia. Give me a call when you're at the site, will you?"

"Absolutely. Thank you for the call, George."

"Goodbye!"

She ended the call and glanced at the porthole window,

seeing only gray mist outside. The motion of the vessel at sea soothed her, lulling her into a constant sleepiness. Digging into her luggage, she withdrew a thick book and settled into her cabin bed to read before eventually dozing off.

The mess hall was on the smaller side, the unoccupied chairs pushed in against the handful of round tables. A few of the crewmen enjoyed coffee and eggs, talking loudly back and forth. Olivia entered and they quieted, looking at her as they sipped from their mugs. Feeling the weight of their gazes, she walked over to the counter to see the line chef's back. She had to clear her throat twice before he turned.

His bottom lip swelled, most likely stuffed with chew, and he smiled at her. She couldn't have guessed his age, his leathery skin lined and his hair light. Wiping his hands on his apron, he nodded.

"What can I get yah?"

"Eggs. Ah… scrambled, with cheese. Bacon. Please."

"Ayep." He went to work at the griddles.

A few minutes later, she had a plate and found a table to sit at, eating her breakfast and sipping her coffee. The crewmen did not attempt to hide their interest. One winked when she made eye contact. Olivia smiled tightly and pulled out her phone, pretending to be invested in scrolling through her emails. It was a relief to see a new email from Leblanc that she could actually read, focus on.

He'd forwarded her something by the looks of it. She scrolled down to the beginning of the chain to read the short message, unsure of whether she found it funny or insulting. An email from a rep at Samos-Barnes – a name she didn't recognize – questioned Leblanc's choice at sending Olivia for such a high-profile case. Leblanc had replied, stating that she was the right person for the job.

Lastly, Brett Chambers himself had chimed in, his three-word reply sticking in her mind as she read it, over and over.

'*Sure, she is.*'

Her shoulders tensed. Why had Leblanc sent her that? Was she supposed to laugh? Fume? Resisting the urge to reply-all, she simply closed the app and finished her breakfast.

Face warm, she began the walk back to her cabin. She made her way down the corridor leading to the stairwell and opened the door, slipping in. Down one flight, out another door on the next semi-circle platform.

Her cabin door within sight, she paused at the sound of familiar barking. That male voice was embroiled in some sort of argument and dropped to a hiss very suddenly.

Cautiously, Olivia took another few steps down the plain white hall. She passed the portal door to her cabin, nearing a junction ahead. Closer now, she heard Wilcox speaking, and, curiosity pushing her forward, Olivia pivoted around the corner of the junction expecting to see him there. He was not. Instead, she saw a janitor's closet, partly opened and dark. The cracked door swayed gently, a soft click-clack emanating from within at random intervals.

"Hold on now," Wilcox's voice came. "What did you say?"

Arms wrapped around herself, she tentatively approached the closet, pushed the door open, and stared in at an unsecured mop and bucket as they rolled to-and-fro with the motion of the ship. She let out a ragged exhalation.

Wilcox continued. "No, it's fine. I can talk."

Head tilted, she realized his voice was coming from inside of the very end cabin, the one at the corner of the junction. He was literally three rooms down from her and she hadn't seen him once. Turning her head, Olivia blinked at the shiny white paint on the wall next to her. She could hear him clear as day and felt a small pang of guilt standing there listening into his private conversation.

"Your secretary had me on hold for a long time," Wilcox said. "Right, it's Veronica. Whatever. She put me on hold and- what? What's that?"

Head low, she shuffled a bit closer to the wall.

"No, I mean, yes. You didn't reply to my email, and I left a message. That was yesterday and… Right." A long pause and then Wilcox sighed. "What did Leblanc say?"

The small hairs along the back of her neck bristled. Olivia licked her lips, bent toward the wall until her ear nearly touched the surface.

Wilcox cleared his throat. "She's young, yes."

Her face grew warm again.

"I suppose if you're into that type. Ah…" Another pause. "I didn't mean… I don't think that's what Leblanc was thinking, no. No."

From the other side of the wall, she heard his shoes scrape against the tile floor of his cabin and knew he was standing at the small kitchenette.

"It will be handled quickly and quietly, I assure you," he said. "I know. Right, yes. I'll say whatever I have to. Ah… Do what? Oh… I mean…"

She heard a soft, impatient tapping.

"Well, not that far, I'm sure… Jessenia would kill me if- ah, no, but… Yes, I… Really? I… Alright."

A low, gravely sigh.

"No, it's fine, I'm sorry. Whatever you want, Brett. I mean, if I have to wink or flirt, I don't mind that, but I'm… What? Right, I know. I see. I'll handle it, of course. Don't worry about it. Whatever it takes, I'll make sure we come out smelling like roses," Wilcox said. "Yes, I've got the blueprints."

She balled her fists and stepped away from the wall, her hair hanging in her face. In his cabin, Wilcox again apologized before going silent.

A low sigh escaped him. "Goodbye, Brett."

Olivia blinked, gaze lost and thoughts wandering through the one-sided conversation she'd heard. A loud crash frightened her. She heard it again, tensing. Inside of his cabin, Wilcox took out his frustration on a piece of furniture, either kicking or throwing it to the floor.

She hurried around the corner, making her way to her cabin. Pulling the key from her pocket, she unlocked the door and rushed inside.

When the boat reached Site Decimus, the captain summoned her via the wall phone in her cabin. Olivia readied herself, luggage packed, and went to the mirror in her bathroom to check her hair – long, dark brown, and pulled back into a tight ponytail. A bit too much skin was exposed above her right ear, and she adjusted her hair to cover the thin patch of bald scalp with the long, pink scar. Satisfied with her appearance, she slung her duffle bag over her shoulder, grabbed her rolling luggage by the handle, and left the cabin.

Above, a bright blue sky with a hot sun blinded her as she watched the salty wet mist drift on the breeze, and Olivia wished she'd brought a pair of sunglasses. A few seagulls drifted lazily in the air above the rig. Standing a few yards away from her, Wilcox waited in his dark shades, his black jacket open. No tie. A pale blue silk shirt, the top three buttons undone. Smooth black trousers. No driver to carry his collection of bags this time.

She subtly studied him, squinting, prepared to look away at any moment. He had his luggage hanging on his shoulders, a suitcase in his hand. So, he could carry his own things if he had to. He was obviously capable, wasn't built slight at all – probably worked out on a regular basis. For aesthetic reasons only, she assumed. Remembering what she'd overheard him saying a few days prior, she scowled. His nose crinkled from a bad smell she couldn't detect, and his head tilted her way.

Not wanting to get caught staring, Olivia instead gazed at the massive facility with its five stories, the scaffolding intricate between the metal bridges connecting the various stairwells. The tower of steel girders on the top level reached into the sky, bits of metal glinting. Dark blue water lapped at the base of the rig, the root of the facility disappearing into the ocean. A dozen small life rafts hung suspended from cabling along the lowest deck, clunking against the hull.

She sensed that he was looking at her and awkwardly turned to meet his eyes. Wilcox appeared to smile, the corners of his lips pulling back stiffly. Before he could speak, if he were planning on saying something at all, the metallic whine of the hoist grew deafening. From the rig's highest platform, a thick metal cable with a mighty hook swung down to the deck of the boat, the crewmen rushing to grab it.

Olivia's attention turned to the crew and their new mission. Her stomach sank as the men fixed the hook to a shipping container on the deck and opened the barn doors, exposing the seats and buckles inside. They gestured to her and Wilcox, calling out instructions to take a seat and strap in. She obeyed quickly, hurrying into the container with her rolling luggage and duffle in tow while the other man strolled leisurely, appearing disengaged with the entire endeavor.

There were multiple yellow utility lights stuck in the corners of the compartment that threw a sickly glow across every surface, the shadows confused and muddy. The crane lifted the closed container with both occupants safely strapped in and began to carry it across the gap between the boat and the rig, the rocky trip a bit disorienting.

Buckled into her seat across from Wilcox, she watched him lean back stiffly, head tilted up, his cheeks flushed. He burped softly, held his fist protectively to his mouth, and gave a weak undulation. She wondered if he'd vomit. The thought of being trapped in the stuffy container with a hurling businessman brought both a smile to her face and a crease to her brow as she watched his Adam's apple bob perilously. With some effort, she forced a straight face. Luckily, despite the green tint to his skin, he kept the contents of his stomach inside of him during the trip. Soon enough, the container set down on a pad on the lowest platform above the soft waves.

The door opened and a gray-haired fellow in a casual suit consisting of a jacket and jeans instructed them to exit.

Another man, tall and lanky, approached the platform from a connected metal bridge and raised a hand in greeting, the wind tousling his wild, curly hair. He shared an exchange with the gray-haired fellow as Olivia and a wobbly legged Wilcox stepped into the daylight onto Decimus.

As the crane reset, controlled by some unseen hands on the rig, the gray-haired fellow shouted over the sound of the machine, greeting them. He reached out and shook Wilcox's hand first, then hers, his grip strong, fingers thick and rough. "Mr. Wilcox? Ms. Nelson? Welcome to Site Decimus. I'm Larry Wert, Site Lead and Head of Operations. Need help with your bags, miss?"

"No, I'm good!" Olivia hollered, offering a polite smile.

"You sure, miss? They look awful heavy."

"I've got it, thank you!"

"This is Robin Frank, Site Safety Supervisor," Wert said, gesturing toward the tall, lanky man hovering close by as if waiting his turn. At the mention of his name, the lanky man strutted forward. "I asked him if he'd mind showing you to your cabins since he walks a little better than I do. It'd be time for supper before we got you settled in."

Olivia extended a hand again. "Mr. Frank, hello!"

"Nice to meet you, Ms. Nelson!" Frank smiled and nodded, shaking her hand exuberantly. He reached toward Wilcox next and did the same. "Sir, hello! Welcome aboard! Come with me, please!"

Olivia and Wilcox followed Frank off the platform toward the inner stairwell and walkway. She marveled at the metal bridges and steps leading up, down, and across the five floors above the ocean. The scaffolding above shaded them from the sun. They neared the elevator at the end of the bridge, and Frank – first to arrive – opened the doors, stepped in.

Wilcox had a little slip on the way, caught himself, looking crossly at the metal grates with the rubber padding.

"Careful, it gets slippery," Frank warned.

"I can see that…"

All three stood together in the elevator and the door closed.

She could see Wilcox in her periphery. He folded his sunglasses, slipped them into his jacket pocket, and sniffed once. Olivia noted Wilcox's tight smile when they made eye contact. Plastic. Forced. She offered him a polite nod, looked away.

Frank selected L5. The lights flickered, the compartment rattled just a little, and they were carried upward. The numbers on the panel lit up one at a time.

"Hope the trip was easy on you," Frank said, breaking

the heavy silence under the hum of the elevator. "Five days at sea feels like an eternity, doesn't it? We're too far out for a helicopter. Too far out for most things."

"It wasn't bad," Olivia replied. "I don't mind boats, long as the trip was."

"Got your sea legs, eh?" Frank asked.

"Spent a lot of time on a lake as a kid."

"Mr. Wilcox?"

He shrugged. "I adapt quickly."

"Good to hear. Right, so, I'll show you to your rooms. Did you want a tour of the facility first?"

Wilcox replied impatiently, speaking over Olivia just as she opened her mouth. "No need. I've memorized the blueprints."

She recovered quickly after a split second of obvious irritation at having been cut off and smiled sweetly toward Frank. "I'll take a tour after I drop off my bags."

"Ah yeah," Frank said. "I'll get Mr. Wilcox to his room first then. He knows where the mess hall is, the offices, the game room…"

"Yes, I do."

"Good, good, okay." The elevator doors opened on L5, and Frank led them out into a hall, the ceiling lined with smooth ducting, the walls painted white. He walked fast, legs long, gait awkward. "L5 and L4 are housing, and each level has its own showers. Got a nice little half-bath in every cabin, two beds per, bunk style. Hah, don't worry, you're in separate cabins! Not sharing! I knew you'd ask, yeah." With a wide grin tossed over his shoulder at them, Frank snorted. "You got scared for a second though, didn't you?"

Wilcox refrained from answering.

Olivia struggled to keep up with the two men, her roller luggage bouncing on the linoleum behind her. "I knew better, Mr. Frank."

12

Head tilted her way, Frank's grin faded. His eyes looked suddenly tired. "Figured I'd try a joke to lighten the mood. Oh well. The floor plan on L5 is pretty simple." He took them around a right turn, waved at the plaque on the wall at the junction. "There's a map and signs in case you get turned around."

"Noted," Wilcox said.

"It's nearly 1300 now," Frank said. "Plan is to meet in the L2 meeting room at 1500 so we can get down to business."

"I'm aware," Wilcox said.

Frank sighed. "Almost there, I promise."

Wilcox grimaced as he glared in through the open cabin door. She leaned over and snuck a glimpse inside, bubbling curiosity overriding proper decorum. The junior partner's cabin was spacious with two dressers, a large desk with a plush rolling chair, and two windows. He also had a big, single bed, the white sheets folded neatly on top of the bare mattress. He entered and shut the door, leaving Frank in the hall outside with Olivia.

Her room was one floor down on L4 and she noticed the size and quality disparity between their two rooms immediately. She had the small bunkbed setup, one window, a small bureau, and a tiny desk with a frail roller chair. Letting the quiet resentment roll off her back – *like water off a duck, girly-girl* – she received her key, dropped off her bags inside on the floor beside the bottom bunk bed, and stepped out again to lock her door. It was time for the tour and Frank seemed more than eager to start.

"Okay, so this is L3. It's where we spend our time when we're not working, usually. Got the game room, the mess hall, the gym, y'know – entertainment, so we don't go

13

completely bonkers all cooped up in here." Frank walked ahead of her, slowing to a stop, and turned to watch her catch up. After that, he maintained a slower pace, leading her to the mess hall first. "No cook in the kitchen, but you can use the stove and there's plenty in the fridge and pantry."

"Ah." Olivia looked in, spotting the large screen TV in the corner, the feed fuzzy and displaying an error message. There were two arcade machines to the left of the door, both unplugged with black screens. Three men sat together, having a meal at one of the six long tables.

One man was massive, his head shaved. Another was average built, hair pale, features sharp. The third man was short with dark hair and mousy features. They all glanced her way, seemingly fascinated with her arrival.

"Guys, this is Olivia Nelson, from OcSaf," Frank announced.

"Welcome," the dark-haired man said, raising a hand. "Bill Petry, Site Planning. Nice to meet you."

"Yuri Ursov, drill operator," the bald man spoke with a thick, strange accent.

The fellow with the pale hair and sharp features shrugged. "Joe Timmons, Lead RME. Maintenance Head. My team fixes shit when it breaks. Welcome aboard."

"Thank you," Olivia said.

"Come on." Frank waved toward her and stepped away from the open doors, nodded down the corridor.

He led her past the mess hall, showed her the rec room with the dart board, pool table, and ping-pong table. Five working arcade machines sat blinking in the corner next to a small kitchenette and refrigerator, a round table with chairs nearby. Another large TV, mounted in the right corner, appeared to be on the fritz, the display a stream of static.

The gym was deserted, the equipment abused. A strange, stale scent – familiar – wafted from the rubbery floor mats. Satisfied that she'd taken a long enough look, Frank moved along.

After going down a level to L2, he showed her the meeting room, down a hall to the left, passing several closed doors with keypad panels mounted next to them. Returning to the main corridor from the elevator, they visited the MedBay where she met another man – a gangly fellow, shorter than Frank but taller than her, with a scruffy chin and teeth too big for his mouth.

"Spencer Hersch, OMR. Ah, onsite medical rep," he said.

"Nice to meet you." She extended a hand, and he shook it, his palm damp. She resisted the urge to use her trousers as a towel.

"What do you think of the place so far?" Hersch asked. "Did you see the game room? We have Street Fighter."

"I saw. It's a lot roomier in here than I thought it would be."

"Yeah, cool, cool," he said. "Ah, I guess we'll be meeting soon. I'll be there. I have answers if you have questions… I'm sure you will…"

Frank stepped between Olivia and Hersch. "Ah, yeah, Spencer, I'm sure she has questions. I'll be back down after we finish up the tour. Do you have the presentation saved on the laptop?"

"I do, yeah."

"Good. I'll check it out then. Let's move along, Ms. Nelson."

Frank returned to the elevator with Olivia in tow. He pressed the button for L4 and stood tall with his hands clasped behind his back. Next to him, she glanced at the numbers as they lit up above the twin, metal doors.

"What about L1?" she asked.

"Off limits, sorry. At least for this tour."

"What's there? Something to do with the minerals?"

"It's the processing plant and the lab. RME's main shop is down there. They've got a shack up top too."

"And further down? I've heard about the part of the facility built into the sea floor."

"S1 access is off-limits for everyone here right now. Trust me, you're not missing anything. If you saw the news special, you saw it all."

"I did see that special."

"There you go then. Feel free to explore the common areas, of course," he said. "I mean, you're here for a week."

"Thank you for showing me around." She nodded, head aching along the scar. Olivia rolled her shoulders as the lights flickered and the compartment hummed.

The call with Leblanc was impossible to maintain as the signal continuously dropped. They managed to get a few words in before she gave up and sighed, rubbing her forehead. She tried to send a text, but that too failed. Frustrated, she slid her phone into her pocket and made her way to the mess hall.

With the men gone, she had free reign over the kitchen and wandered around, opening the cabinets and pantry. She studied the stacks of little plastic cereal bowls and boxes of instant mac'n cheese wedged between the canned goods, chips, and biscuits. In the fridge, she found cans of soda, milk, eggs, and the makings for sandwiches – huge packs of cheese and three different sealed containers of deli meat. The freezer was stuffed with unlabeled bags.

Olivia made herself a turkey and cheese sandwich, grabbed a can of cola, and traveled back to her cabin. It was tricky to push the button on the elevator, but she managed, and rode in silence. Along the way, she saw no one else.

After a light meal, she reclined on the bottom bunk, a pillow rolled up for support, to read. Fifteen minutes later, her phone alarm sounded, startling her out of a particularly good scene. Olivia shut the book and laid it on the bed.

She opened her luggage, rifled through the folded clothing, and pulled out her blouse, skirt, and pantyhose. Her nose crinkled as her eyes moved over the fancy set of pumps with a one-inch heel. Imagining herself tripping and slipping on the grated walkways, she glanced at the sneakers on the floor beside the bed.

Olivia, dressed in her classy blouse, skirt, and pantyhose, stood contentedly in her sneakers as the elevator descended. The doors opened onto L2. She hung to the left after exiting and passed several closed doors on the way to the meeting room. She hadn't noticed them during the tour, and they hadn't been pointed out. A young, handsome fellow wearing glasses slipped out of a closed area filled with humming servers, offered a weak wave, and rushed off without a word. It was then that she saw the plaque on the door – 'IT'.

Mr. Wert, Site Lead, met her at the meeting room door. It was easy to find, the hall labeled. He shook her hand, showed her to the table, and pulled out an office chair for her. She took a seat and crossed her ankles. Large windows along the entire left side of the room let in warm sunlight, inadvertently baking the occupants in the process. The climate control thrummed to life to cool the room.

"How was the tour?"

"Nice, but…" Olivia frowned. "…it seems a little deserted. Where is everyone?"

Wert smiled. "We've got it down to a science here, Ms.

Nelson. Only have a team of thirty roughnecks workin' the rig at one time and most of 'em were sent back to shore due to the investigation, what with the drill being shut down."

"Why? I needed to interview them."

"Company orders. You can interview the crew here now. They were all here. We were all here," Wert said.

"Mr. Wert, I had to talk to them. Why would the company do that? They're impeding an investigation."

"I 'spose they have their reasons. Sorry I don't have a better answer for you," he said. "Maybe the fewer the witnesses there are to interview, the quicker this'll go and we can get back to business."

"That's not how this works."

"Can't do much 'bout it now, can we? I'm sure it'll be a big point in the report." Wert cleared his throat, gestured toward the small kitchenette. "Coffee?"

Defeated, she forced a curt smile and nodded. "Ah, sure. I live on the stuff."

"Need a constant supply, eh?"

"I'd bleed coffee if cut."

"Hah, you'll fit right in, Ms. Nelson. Sorry you're here under these circumstances." Pushing himself out of his swivel chair, Wert made his way to the kitchenette, the counter cluttered with paper cups and sugar packets.

"So am I."

He poured her a steaming cup. "Cream, sugar?"

"Black. Please."

"Yeah, you'll fit in just fine."

"I didn't think the drills ever stopped running in places like this," Olivia said, watching him turn back toward her. Cool air from the vent directly above chilled her, sent a wave of shivers through her body. "Every second it's off, you're losing money. The company is losing money."

He shook his head, approached the wooden table. "We

aren't your typical offshore drilling rig, Ms. Nelson. As you know, we're not after oil. We dig up rare minerals, buried deep in the rock under the ocean. Big Tooth can afford to take a nap from time to time. Keeps her from overheating."

"Big Tooth?"

"The drill. We named her that."

"Ah." When he handed her the cup, she clutched it tightly in her fingers, enjoying the warmth it provided. "Where's Mr. Wilcox? I imagined he'd be here before me."

"Mr. Wilcox said he'd call me when he was ready, like the scheduled time didn't matter a lick to him, but…" With a smirk, Wert held up his cellphone. "…seems like we don't have service at the moment. Happens sometimes."

"We should wait for him."

"I figured we would. Not that he's here to listen to me. They already received all of the reports. No, he's here for you." Wert pointed at Olivia as he took a seat.

"Is he?"

"You're the one writing the determination."

"Lucky me."

"I'll be forthcoming during the investigation."

"As you should be…"

Wert chuckled dryly, the sound lacking mirth. "Did you happen to check out our salaries?"

"Hm?"

"Pays well, this line of work. Has to. This far out in the middle of the ocean, exposed to the elements. Heavy equipment. Isolation. It's dangerous. Not for the faint of heart, I'll tell you that. I was two days from the end of my three-month assignment when it happened. I'm staying a little longer for the investigation, obviously. I'll get three months off, then back I come. The other Site Lead gets to wait it out offshore. It's a good job, Ms. Nelson," he told her. "I'm not looking to lose it."

"Are you afraid you might?"

"No, just making you aware that I'm here to assist."

Tilting her head slightly, Olivia considered her next words. They never left her lips. Frank and Hersch entered the meeting room, Hersch getting to work setting up the laptop and connecting it to the projector.

Petry, the small man from the mess hall, showed up next and took a seat next to Wert, the two chatting quietly. Timmons, the pale haired fellow, came in and sat across from her.

Finally, Wilcox strode in. He carried his briefcase, his black jacket closed, his silk tie red. Once he'd assessed the room, he chose the chair directly beside Olivia and flashed her that cold, charming smile. "Billion-dollar facility, no reception. Figures, doesn't it?"

She nodded tightly, civilly. "Hm."

"There's some weather heading our way, rounding us from the west," Petry said. "That's probably the issue. We always lose the satellite link when it gets choppy."

"Where's your tech support?" Wilcox asked.

"Our man Vazquez is on it," Wert replied. "Can't say he can do much to combat nature though. Only so much you can do when a storm hits."

Olivia sat up. "A storm? The forecast didn't mention that."

Petry eyed her. "Weather can turn on a dime out here. With the satellite out, it's near impossible to track on the radar, so we just wait and see in situations like these. Not sure if it'll change course and hit us head-on. If it does, we're equipped to handle it. We've withstood hurricanes."

"That's good to hear, I guess," she said.

"Are we ready?" Wilcox opened his briefcase on the table.

"Yeah, ah, here we go. Hersch, you got that file ready?"

Frank took a seat next to the OMR.

"I do," Hersch replied.

"I'll present," said Wert, catching Frank's surprised expression. "I've had to read the dang thing how many times now? Once more won't kill me."

Chapter 2

"At 22:30, Joe Timmons, RME Lead, was called down to take a look at a busted fuel line between Decks 1 and 2 after the drill hit something, ran hot, shut off. Timmons got David Tremont on the horn since he's – he was – the pro on the rope. Called him *Spiderman*. Mark Mitchell was called in to assist him. Bradley Norris was tasked to operate the hoist on Deck 4, off of L4. He knew that machine like his own hands. There's enough visibility, even at night, so the boys don't have to use flares to signal between the decks. That's what the walkies are for. They've all got walkies," Wert said. The image projected onto the huge, white screen was that of the fuel line – fixed in the picture. The next image was the winch and cable roll, then the operator compartment. "You can see the walkie there, in the charger."

"I see it," Olivia said. "Are they left on?"

"At all times."

"Right. Is Mr. Norris here to question?"

"No, he wasn't doing so well after. Got sent to the shore."

"Oh."

Wert continued. "At 22:40, Tremont stood on this platform on Deck 1, Level 1. Here's a shot of that. Mitchell passed the cable down through the mousehole on Deck 2 – that's this here, basically just a hole in the platform – and Tremont connected it to the harness, latched in. Anyone who services between decks is trained in fall protection, Ms. Nelson. Most of the techs are, actually. Comes with the job. The harness was recently inspected, passed."

"Alright."

"At 22:45, Norris engages the winch, pulls Tremont up,

and Tremont services the fuel line. At 23:30, Tremont waves up at Mitchell, who gets on the horn and tells Norris the work is done." Pausing to take an extended sip of his coffee, Wert cleared his throat. "At 23:35, Mitchell finds Tremont dead, partially pulled up through the mousehole by his harness on Deck 2, Level 2."

The next slide appeared.

Olivia did not wince. Graphic as it was, she fought to maintain her composure, having seen similar scenarios with equally gory results. The sight of that much blood, bone, and viscera was easier to handle in picture form – and she'd seen plenty of pictures over the years. Up close and personal, she'd nearly lost her lunch… the first time. There was a certain cognitive dissonance she could rely on to kick in, a subtle voice whispering that it wasn't a person. It couldn't be a person. Then why were there shreds of flannel cloth in that mess? Bile rose in the back of her throat.

"He was snapped in half. That's… part of his torso. Frank and Hersch were called immediately, of course… Not that they could do much."

She blinked. "All of this, save for the pictures, was detailed in my briefing. What I'm missing is the 'how', Mr. Wert. Between 23:30 and 23:35, what happened?"

Wilcox pulled a tablet from his briefcase, appearing ready to take notes. "What happened between 23:30 and 23:35, Wert?"

"Tremont got pulled up through the mousehole. It's only eight inches in diameter. There's no way he'd survive that," Wert replied.

"How far did he have to travel to reach the mousehole from where he was hanging?" she asked.

"About ten feet."

"How fast?"

"The winch is… slow."

"How didn't anyone notice?" she asked.

Wilcox looked up from his tablet, expression stern. "How *didn't* anyone notice?"

Wert eyed the man oddly. "We don't know."

"Is there an emergency shut off mechanism outside of the hoist control compartment?" she asked, glancing sharply at Wilcox. Rather than echo her, he regarded her coolly. It felt somehow worse, and Olivia looked away.

"No, there is not," Wert replied.

She continued, brows knitting. "Why was he being lifted and not lowered if the work was done?"

"I don't know."

"Were there any other witnesses?"

"No."

Wilcox cut in. "There are a lot of questions and not enough answers. All of the safeguards were in place. The training is there. The methods of communication. Everything was provided – Samos-Barnes makes sure of that. However, it is on the RME Lead to supervise risky jobs like this, yes? You were there, right, Timmons?"

"I… was not. No."

"Oh, why?" Wilcox blinked mechanically.

"It was routine maintenance, not risky at all – not like you're thinking. These men were all experienced. Tremont knew what he was doing. So did Norris and Mitchell. I didn't see a need to observe." Timmons tensed, grimaced.

The junior partner sighed, shook his head. "And we see the outcome of that decision. No one has a straight story."

Timmons shook his head. "Something went wrong."

"The machinery was assessed and deemed to be in good condition. You said so yourself. Were you wrong?" Wilcox asked.

"Well, no…"

"So, it wasn't the hoist. It was the crew. Someone wasn't

paying attention. Norris, probably. Flipped the wrong switch and turned away, didn't hear Mitchell calling him. If I saw what Mitchell saw, I'd be in shock too. I'd blank out and forget the details," Wilcox said. "Either that, or Mitchell wasn't paying attention, didn't notice Tremont was in danger – or wasn't in a state to understand the danger."

"I don't think that's what happened exactly, Mr. Wilcox," Timmons stated, bristling.

Wilcox prepared to take a note on his tablet. "When's the last time you drug tested your techs, Mr. Timmons?"

"Y'know, Mitchell's down in the shop if you want to talk to him, ask him some of these questions to his face." Timmons glared at Wilcox, his cheeks splotchy. "I'm sure he wouldn't mind coming up. I could call him."

Petry coughed. "I wouldn't, Joe. I wouldn't."

"A man is dead," Wilcox said. "With the possibility of it being a mechanical failure eliminated, we are left with one unfortunate conclusion… Human error. No, don't call Mitchell up. I won't blame him. It could have been either man. We'll never know now, will we?"

"Something had to have distracted them," Olivia said.

Wert shook his head. "We just don't know, I'm sorry."

"How is that possible?" She tilted her head, top lip lifting.

"We all lost five minutes, right then." Hersch looked up from the laptop, shrinking under Petry's dark gaze. "I mean, ask around. We all lost five minutes. Everyone I talked to, at least."

Olivia eyed him. "What was that?"

"You were confused, Spencer," Wert said. "I'm sure that radio call gave you the fright of your life. It gave everyone the fright of their life."

"No, I distinctly remember playing one of the arcade games. I couldn't sleep. I was winning and then suddenly, I was in the elevator, going down. I don't know how I got there. Smith, Sok, and Vazquez were with me. Smith isn't here, but the other two, they are, and they'll tell you. It was the freakiest thing." Hersch's forehead glistened with beads of sweat, his hands dropping to his lap, under the table. "We all lost time."

Frank exhaled, rubbed the bridge of his long nose. "Spencer…"

Olivia studied the younger man's face, watched as he licked the front of his prominent teeth. "You believe that the accident happened because of this loss of time, Mr. Hersch?"

"I do," he replied.

"Oh, come on…" Wilcox rolled his eyes.

Frank held up a hand, frowned. "Spencer, we'll have a talk after the meeting. Ms. Nelson, Mr. Wilcox, please disregard those comments from our young OMR. The stress at the time was beyond measure, and I'm sure many of us walked away with immense PTSD."

"You're trained to handle medical emergencies, aren't you?" Wilcox asked.

"Well, of course, but…"

"It was a tragedy, yes," Wert said hastily, preventing Wilcox from interjecting. "Preventable? Also, yes. Someone messed up. A man died. I wish I had more to offer."

"I saw cameras outside. Was there footage?" Olivia asked.

Wert cleared his throat, looked down. "Yes and no."

She blinked, confused. "What do you mean?"

"I mean that there's footage. The camera angle isn't the greatest, though that's not the main issue." He placed his hands on the table and shrugged. Wert's gaze settled on Hersch, his eyes narrowing. "The problem is that the tape – the digital tape – is too distorted to make anything out."

26

"Is there a problem with the cameras?" Olivia asked.

Wert nodded. "There was at the time of the accident. All of them, actually. A systemwide glitch affecting all of the equipment, the servers... It took IT an hour to get us back online to contact the authorities. We've been having connectivity issues ever since. More than usual, I mean. There's a lot of problems with the computers here."

"Nothing is wrong with the equipment," Wilcox stated. "Was anyone from IT monitoring the servers or satellite hub at the time? You have two techs staffed for coverage, don't you? Nightshift and dayshift?"

"Yes, Dennis Sok was in the server room," Wert replied.

"Maybe we should bring him in," Wilcox said. "Ask him why he allowed the link to drop."

Wert frowned, shook his head. "He'd be sleeping. We can ask Austin Vazquez since he's our dayshift tech. He'll know enough to answer your questions, whatever they are."

Olivia listened to the men talk, her skull aching along her scar again. She touched the side of her head, winced. A strange reverberation, like an electric chill in her bones, wriggled its way through her body. The lights flickered. For a moment, she didn't even realize that the room had gone silent. Looking around, she caught each man in some state of dreamy staring, their eyes lost, fixed on nothing, lips parted.

Then, Wilcox continued speaking. "No need. The servers going down had nothing to do with the accident."

"No, not at all," Wert stated.

"It is, however, an unsettling trend, don't you think? The link, the cameras?"

His expression turned steely and Wert squared his shoulders. "Sok was at his station, I assure you. Never have I met a more dedicated employee in my entire career — at any company."

"He's right, sir," Petry chimed in.

"And yet the system went down…"

"Mr. Wilcox, these things happen," Wert said.

"I'm done with this line of questioning. What's next?" Wilcox's nose crinkled; his tablet raised.

"Do you want to see the machine, Ms. Nelson?" Timmons asked.

"The hoist?" Her voice sounded small to her ears.

"Yeah, did you want to see it?" He tilted his head.

"Yes, I would."

The hoist compartment smelled like cigarettes, but she saw no ashtray. Flecks of ash on the floor gave it away, however. She said nothing, noting it in her mind for later.

"Someone has been smoking in here. That is definitely prohibited." Wilcox pressed in close behind her as she leaned into the compartment, their bodies nearly touching. "Stinks, doesn't it?"

"Ah…"

"That *is* cigarette, right? Or does it smell like something else to you?"

"No, just cigarette," she replied.

Wilcox seemed dissatisfied with the answer and backed off, giving her air. "Oh."

Olivia dug around and found a few adult magazines stuffed under the seat. Face warm, she shoved them back under. "I don't see the manual anywhere. It's supposed to be in the compartment." No response, only the low, roaring song of the wind and ocean. Peering over her shoulder, she saw empty space outside of the compartment and exited onto the platform. Three yards away, Timmons debated quietly with Wert, Petry, and Wilcox while Frank hovered nervously nearby. Dark clouds broiled above.

"I'm ready to move along now," Olivia said, approaching

them. "Are we done up here? Hello?"

Wert shook his head, teeth bared. "Right, yeah. Moving along."

They went down to Deck 2, Level 2. Timmons smoked a cigarette in the open air, standing with Wert at the bridge, his face red and crumpled as he whispered. Frank kept a distance, watching silently. Hersch had left the party, presumably returning to his office in the MedBay. Petry, Wilcox, and Olivia strolled toward the center of the platform.

From horizon to horizon, the dark blue sea surrounded the rig, and she felt tiny, insignificant. A strong gust of salty wind threatened to pull her off her feet. She gathered herself, not wanting to appear frazzled. *Don't let it get yah down, Livvie, don't let it get yah down.*

She was glad to see that the blood had been cleaned away. All that remained was the mousehole, an eight-inch wide, two-foot-long cylinder hole in the middle of the platform. She approached it and looked down, stared into it, and saw the deck below. That was clean as well. Her imagination replayed the scene, the torrent of blood that would have rained on that lower platform bright red and thick. Next, his gray shiny guts would have splatted on the-

A gull cried out close by, startling her. She stood up straight, caught her breath, and looked up at the sky to see the large bird floating awkwardly in the air currents. A Western gull, like the ones at the dock. White headed with gray wings, it called again in a shrill voice and then drifted below the platform and out of sight.

"Ms. Nelson?" Petry said.

She turned to him. "Yes?"

"You alright?"

"I'm good."

"Anything else you want to see?"

The breeze picked up and her bangs brushed along her forehead. "No, not right now."

Petry nodded. "We'll go back in then."

After reconvening in the meeting room, Olivia listened to the men discuss the details. Once or twice, she raised her hand and attempted to interject. Ultimately, they were arguing too fervently to allow her a word in edgewise and she chose instead to jot down anything she found to be noteworthy.

She wrote that the training manuals for all onsite equipment were down on L1, with RME. She would find the lock out procedure for the hoist there as well. Wilcox repeated several questions that she had asked earlier. Olivia could tell from Wert's face that he was growing weary of the assault.

"Should we pick back up tomorrow?" she asked.

Wert brightened slightly. "That would be good."

"We're scheduled until 1900," Wilcox said.

"Most of the day was spent traveling, and I'm exhausted. I hope you all can forgive me for wanting to call it a day early." Olivia shrugged. "We can start fresh tomorrow at 8, as planned."

"Yes, please," Wert insisted.

Wilcox smirked, shrugging as well. "I guess 8 it is."

The elevator hummed as it began to rise. Wilcox stood too close to her, briefcase at his side. "Good job today, Ms. Nelson."

"Thank you."

"You're very knowledgeable."

"I've been doing this for a few years now."

"I can see why Leblanc chose you. I would have too."

She'd been watching the numbers light up on the panel. Her gaze lifted to his face. That plastic, pantomime smile greeted her, the right corner of his top lip tugged up to bare his brilliantly white, straight teeth. The uncanny perfection of his features was unsettling. Her stomach clenched. "Ah, thank you again, Mr. Wilcox. That's kind of you to say."

The elevator doors opened, and she walked out.

Olivia stopped in the hall outside of her room, turning to see Wilcox on her heels. He stopped as well, expression oddly expectant. While she wanted to snap at him, her tone came out softer than she'd have liked. "Can I help you?"

"I think we should discuss what we've learned today."

"Should we?"

"Before you write anything down in ink, I mean."

"I've got to sit and think about it, Mr. Wilcox. By myself."

"Dinner then?" he said. "There's no harm in it. We don't have to talk about the investigation. Just a bit of socializing to pass the time. Why, in my cabin, I've got-"

"I don't think so, Mr. Wilcox." She slipped her room key from her pocket and clutched it between her fingers for him to see.

"We got off on the wrong foot. I was very rude, and I'm sorry. I was expecting George Leblanc. We go way back, for all the wrong reasons. I shouldn't have… been a dick to you, Ms. Nelson. Olivia… May I call you Olivia?"

"I'd rather you didn't. Look, I've got a lot to process here. I'm going to sit down in my cabin, write down my takeaways. The email cited a pretty strict agenda for the week, so you'll get to hear my thoughts soon enough. We have to run an RCA board by Friday. You'll want to have your side plotted out, I'm sure. So… goodbye." Spinning on her heel, she unlocked her door, felt his shadow fall over her back, and glanced at him over her shoulder. "Mr.

Wilcox."

"I understand and I apologize," he said, his smile evaporating. Wilcox cleared his throat and eyed her up. His gaze lingered for a few long seconds on her clenched fist and the manner in which she held her keys. He took a step back, nodding. "So, right. Goodbye."

With that, he turned and stalked away.

She shuddered and entered her room, locking the door as soon as it shut.

Chapter 3

Opening the door – a few inches, merely a crack – she peered out into the cool light of the hallway. Empty. A cloth satchel slung over her shoulder, she left her room and locked the door before making her way to the showers.

A plaque mounted on the corridor wall at the next junction pointed the way. On the left, 'WOMEN', with a little pictograph of a simple, skirted character. On the right, 'MEN', with the stereotypical pants-wearing figure. She entered on the left and studied the row of stalls, noting the dry, sterile scent in the air. The women's showers were pristine, the tile floor white. With a small smirk on her face, she considered why they were so immaculate, so untouched, so clean. She sat on a long bench, observed the lockers on one side, the stalls on the other. Quickly, she disrobed, wrapped herself in a large towel. Sweeping a stall curtain open, she stepped inside and turned on the water.

Her cell was useless, and the cabin phone wouldn't connect to an outside line, so Olivia pressed 0, and waited while the tone sounded. A male voice greeted her. "IT, how can I help you?"

"This is Olivia Nelson, room 7, on L4. We still don't have reception, do we?"

"No, sorry, Ms. Nelson. Probably the storm."

"Oh, it's alright. Sorry to bother you."

"No worries," he said. "If the storm turns away, we'll be back online in the morning. If it turns toward us, well… sorry, hate to be the bearer of bad news, but you won't be able to play your mobile games for a day or so."

She laughed. "Oh no, I see. Thank you anyway."

"No problem. Anything else I can help you with?"

"I don't think so. This is Austin Vazquez, right?"

"Righteo."

"Ah," she said, phone pressed to her ear. "I'm curious, and, well, sorry for how random this is… I wonder, were you asked any questions during the initial investigation?"

"When the suits were out? Or the police?"

"Either."

"Well, sure."

"Did they ask about the footage?"

"They did. Why?"

"Ah, can you tell me what happened?"

"It was just static."

"I mean, can you tell me what happened that night?"

"Yeah. It was a normal shift 'til then. Dennis Sok was in the server room, doing routine checks. I was on my computer, mucking about and falling into way too many rabbit holes online. I'm a bit of an insomniac. Then, it happened out of nowhere. Please tell me Spencer told you about the elevator thing."

"Yes, that you woke up there together."

"'Woke up' isn't exactly the phrase I'd use. 'Became aware again' is more accurate. How much did the other guys tell you? And I don't mean Bill or Joe, because they swear we're all crazy. You talk to Casey Lee in RME yet? Mark Mitchell? Yuri Ursov, the drill operator? You should go ask them what happened. That'll rattle your brains."

"What did he mean when he said you lost time?"

"Exactly what it sounds like. I was doing a thing, and then I was suddenly in the elevator going down with three other people who also had no clue how they got there. Weird shit, right?" Vazquez paused. "Hey, you want to talk to the guys right now?"

"Ah…"

"Dennis'll be asleep, but Ursov, Lee, Mitchell… they'll

be up. Might be having a beer or shooting some pool. I can call them to the server room if you want to come down and talk."

She swallowed. "I am pretty curious."

"Yeah, come on down. I'll call 'em. This is going to blow your mind. I have a theory, but you'll have to wait to hear it."

"Alright."

"See you soon!"

"Sure," she said. He hung up on her. She placed the phone back into its nest on the cabin wall and then took a seat on the edge of her cabin bed. Olivia blinked, looked down at herself and ran her hands over her striped pajama pants, her oversized tee-shirt with the print of a kitten holding onto a tree branch billowing around her. She would need to change clothes first, obviously. In a moment, she was digging through her open luggage.

Austin Vazquez turned out to be the handsome man with glasses she'd seen earlier in the day leaving the server room. He had a few inches on her and they might've been the same age – in their late twenties. He had a close shaven beard and messily combed hair, his eyebrows thick and expressive. His grin was wide and infectious.

As soon as she shook his hand and made eye contact, Olivia found herself smiling as well.

The server room was cramped and smelled of something slightly astringent that burned her nostrils. She rested her hip against one of the walls, arms crossed. She'd thrown on a pair of jeans and a nice top – both of which she'd packed 'just in case'.

Casey Lee, RME tech, was a shorter, stouter young man with almond shaped eyes and a pleasant smile. He yawned loudly, shook his head, sipped his coffee. "No Spencer?"

"No, when he tells the story, he gets all worked up. Better if it's just us," Vazquez said. "Mark, I'm glad you came, man."

Mark Mitchell, RME tech, shrugged, looked up at the other man with deep set and bruised eyes, the color of which might have been dark brown or even black. He rolled his shoulders, nodded weakly. "Yeah, no problem. They didn't call me in, so this is probably the only chance I'll get to talk to OcSaf." He ran his grubby fingers through his thinning black hair, the grays very noticeable.

Ursov, a titan of a man when standing, gazed at the flashing lights in the server room. "I was not called in either."

"I told Ms. Nelson we'd talk about the black out," Vazquez said. "Who wants to go first?"

"There isn't much to tell." Mitchell eyed her, shrugged again. "Dave gave me the thumbs up from ten feet down through the hole, and I lifted the walkie, brought it right to my mouth. Felt a little woozy for a second. And then I heard that hissing and popping, that whistling scream that the line makes when it's snagged, caught on something. I looked down and…"

Olivia remembered the picture and flinched. "Oh."

"Not much else to say, sorry," Mitchell said. "We all got to talking afterward, and other people had blacked out too. Everyone on Decimus had felt it at the same time."

"Big Tooth, she hit something hard, snapped fuel line, locked up," Ursov said. "Called up top to let them know she'd jammed. Waited for an hour, maybe. I decided to go back up, didn't know how long it would take to fix. Got halfway to the access terminal and then I was back in the control room, hand on the toggle, about to engage Big Tooth. I stopped. I don't know how I got there."

Vazquez leaned toward Olivia. "Freaky, right?"

"Yeah."

"Next!" Vazquez gestured toward Lee.

"I was in the shop, working on the bridge canopy for outside. It gets slippery on the scaffolds when it rains. Anyway, I was welding…" Lee cleared his throat and raised his hand, showing off a bandage. "I came to in the access terminal, in the lab. I guess I burned my hand bad. They offered to let me leave the site, but I said no. Spence treated me, and I stayed behind. I wasn't going to let them send me away."

"Samos-Barnes gave you the option?" Olivia asked.

"Not really. I just stood my ground."

"I see." She turned to Vazquez. "So, what's your theory?"

His hand lifted to his face, adjusted his glasses. "Almost there. I forgot to mention one thing from my story."

"Yes?"

"A minute after I came to in the elevator, I had a seizure," he said, holding up a hand in response to her shocked reaction. "I was fine. Dennis and Spencer caught me. I've been on meds for years, haven't had one in just as long. The thing is, something had to have triggered that seizure. Something that also caused us all to lose time, lose our memories."

"Mm?"

"My theory is that Big Tooth hit something huge, metallic, magnetic, something that resonated with such a strong field that it literally scrambled our brains when it hit us, twenty minutes after we set it off. Us in the lower levels, closer to the source, we wanted to go check it out. The guys up top just spaced out, froze to the spot. Then, it wore off, leaving us with no memories. Problem is, some of us were, uh, occupied at the time." He grew solemn. "Hence, the accident."

"That is some theory. How many people were onsite when it happened?" she asked.

"All thirty-five," Vazquez replied.

"And everyone was affected?"

"A few might deny it now, but yeah. At the time, everyone was confused. Everyone was scattered. Then we saw what happened and it turned into pure chaos. Not until later did we all start asking questions, digging deeper."

"And the drill hasn't been run since?"

"No – strict orders. Big Tooth sleeps," Ursov muttered.

"And the cameras?" she asked.

"I can show you the footage, if you want to see it, but it's all just fuzz and static for five minutes straight. Everything digital skitzed out. Climate control reset. Satellite link disconnected. Sok and I were sweating bullets trying to get us back online to get the call out."

She hesitated. "Did any of you feel anything earlier today?"

Vazquez's face twisted up. "Not like before. I've had a headache off and on for hours. Did you experience something?"

"I don't know," she replied. "Is there any way we could go down there and see what Big Tooth hit?"

Mitchell shook his head. "Not a chance in hell."

"Why?"

"That area's restricted."

"Oh."

"You'd hate it, I promise," Vazquez said. "It's not like you can just take an elevator down. There's a pressure chamber inside of the access terminal and a system of cables set up to drag you down the tube to S1 – or, as we like to call it, the Pit. It's not fun and your ears pop like crazy. Thanks to advances in the tech however, it's a mercifully short trip. Still, when you're down there, you always sort of feel like you're choking, being crushed."

"I do not feel that way," Ursov stated.

"That's because you're made of cinderblocks," Lee said and took a sip of his coffee.

"Ursov, you were down there when the drill got stuck, right? Did you see anything?"

He regarded her with his steely gray eyes. "The sensors, they were recalibrating. Camera on Big Tooth was offline, resetting. I did not stay long enough to see what she found and link to control room terminal has yet to be reestablished."

"Ah yeah, we have to go down there and reconnect manually if we want to see the view from the camera mounted on Big Tooth," Vazquez said. "That's assuming the camera isn't damaged or malfunctioning."

"And you haven't been told to do that yet?" Olivia's brows knit.

Vazquez shook his head. "No, not yet. After you're done here and we get back to business, they'll absolutely send Sok and me down to fix it. Going to hazard a guess that they don't want to complicate things during the investigation."

"I'm surprised that they didn't want to see it immediately…"

"Trust me, I know these people. They'll want you gone before they start asking us to poke around in the Pit. If it was operational, there's a chance you'd want to go take a look and you'd have every right to go down and see it. No, they're waiting for you to leave." With a tight grin, Vazquez shrugged. At the sound of muted beeps coming from the closed server room door, he twisted to face the entrance.

The door opened and a tall, thin man entered, closing the door behind him. Young, eyes dark and sharp, his hair black and his glasses low on his elegant nose, he studied each face carefully. "Oh, hello!"

"Dennis, hey, this is Olivia Nelson, from OcSaf," Vazquez said.

"Hello!" Dennis Sok exclaimed, quickly approaching her with his slender hand extended. After an amicable and enthusiastic shake, he took a step back and nodded, leaning forward ever so slightly to avoid looming over her. "Didn't expect to find everyone in here! What's going on?"

"They were telling me about the black out," Olivia said.

"Oh, yes, that. Wow, um, did you get your answers? I'm sorry I wasn't here earlier. I'm the night watchman; I was sleeping."

She found it hard not to smile at his polite head bobbing. "Is your story the same as theirs?"

"Ah, it is, I'm sure. I was here, actually. Monitoring the system, checking for updates. Then I was in the elevator headed to L1 with Jacob, Spencer, and Austin. So, yes, it's the same story." Sok perked up, hands folded. "What do you think of Austin's theory?"

"How'd you know I told her that?" Vazquez asked.

"Oh, I just figured you did…"

"You've been telling everyone who'll listen," Lee said. "Dennis is just too nice to say you're predictable, that's all."

Sok cringed slightly, shrugging.

"Well, it's a good theory, right?" Vazquez fixed his glasses.

Olivia cleared her throat. "It's a possibility. Outside of my area of expertise, that's for sure."

"I said it could have been a gas leak," Lee said.

Vazquez crossed his arms and sat on the desktop closest to himself, a thick brow raised. "Doesn't explain the electronics bugging out."

"I'll need to figure it out before I leave Decimus," Olivia told them, chewing on her bottom lip for a few seconds while she considered her next words. "I don't think OcSaf is going to accept 'magnetic resonance' or 'gas leak' as a root cause. Tell me, is there any chance that it was human error? Any chance at all?"

Mitchell coughed, rubbed at his face. "Fuck…"

She tensed. "Oh, I didn't mean-"

"We all experienced something that night," Vazquez said quickly, cutting her off. "That something caused us to lose time, knocked us offline, disrupted the camera feeds. Whatever it was, that's what killed David Tremont."

"No one here's a rookie." Mitchell swallowed thickly, arms crossed, and chin lifted. He stared at the drop ceiling, the lines in his chiseled face deepening. "Dave died because we were all in some kind of trance or something. Just praying to God he was in the same trance and didn't feel it…" He spun, hand on his mouth, and jogged to the door. "I can't do this right now. I'm gonna grab a beer. Goodbye."

Mitchell left, the door closing behind him.

Olivia's jaw worked loosely. "I didn't mean to offend, I was just…"

"He was the first person to see it. To see Dave after the accident. I can't blame him for walking out." Lee eyed her. "Thing is, he wanted to stay, just like I wanted to stay, to tell the true story to you, or whoever came to ask questions, so the company didn't just bury it."

"You think Samos-Barnes would do that?" she asked.

"I sure do," Lee replied. "They love to blame the workers and not their shitty installations. You think this is the first facility of theirs I've maintained? Yeah, I'm not an old fart like Wert or Yuri, but I've been around."

"I have worked in worse places," Ursov said.

"Is this a shitty installation? Vazquez, you said it was high tech."

"It's high tech, yeah." He shrugged. "But Dennis can tell

you, same as I can, how many corners they cut. It means we have to work twice as hard to keep things running. That's how you lose connectivity to the camera on Big Tooth – she's got a direct feed to the control room down in S1 and from there, it diverts up to the lab on L1. If the control room goes down, it's in the dark until we go down and reset the router. Positively medieval."

"Ah, yes, it's, ah, not very efficient and I've suggested a direct feed. A dual feed if you will. But the company doesn't want to nudge the budget. It is quite inconvenient to have to go down there every time there's an issue with the router," Sok said.

Ursov managed a small, stiff smile. "I tell you before – you call me, and I fix it because I am there."

"Hitting it isn't fixing it, Yuri," Vazquez muttered.

"And yet it worked, yes?"

"Once." Turning his attention back to Olivia, Vazquez sighed. "Anyway, now you know the truth, Ms. Nelson, despite what Wert says. I don't know what you can do with the information, but you've got it."

Her eyes closed. "Why do you think you were trying to go down? I mean, you and the others in the elevator?"

Vazquez tilted his chin up. "Hm? We were the closest to the source, so we were probably going to go check it out."

"Then why did Ursov come to with his hand on the controls?" She opened her eyes and looked at their faces, one at a time. "Why would he want to reengage the drill as soon as they'd fixed the fuel line?"

"Maybe I think it best to get back to work," Ursov replied.

"You wouldn't have thought to see what the drill hit first? To see why it got stuck and blew a line?" Olivia studied him.

Ursov rubbed his square, jagged chin. "Hmm, I would

have checked, yes."

"But you didn't, because you couldn't…"

"Right, I could not. Camera feed offline."

"So why would you engage the drill?"

His eyes narrowed, his nose scrunched. Ursov grimaced. "I do not know. Maybe I was not myself."

"Gas leak," Lee said.

Vazquez heaved a sigh. "Casey…"

"I don't know what happened, but I'm pretty sure that it wasn't a gas leak, Mr. Lee. I'm sorry." Olivia shook her head. She pushed herself to her feet and took a step toward the door.

"Can't write this in your report, can you?" Vazquez asked.

"No, I can't."

Sok blinked. "What if there is no answer, Ms. Nelson?"

"I can't leave without a determination. The Samos-Barnes rep, Wilcox, he'd love that because he could blame Mitchell or Norris. After hearing everything you've told me, I believe there might be something to the drill theory – ah, that it… hit something unusual." She lowered her head, eyes on the linoleum floor. "Of course, to collect the data, I'll need to go down to S1."

"We told you – it's off limits," Lee said.

Olivia pivoted on her heel and stared at him. "I'm the OcSaf inspector. If I say we're going to look at something, we go look at it."

Lee lifted his brows. "You can tell that to Wert then."

"I will."

"He'll tell you no."

"He's not allowed to tell me no."

"A 'lotta power in your position, eh?" Lee asked.

"Authority, Mr. Lee."

"I would be happy to show Ms. Nelson the dig site."

With a thunderous clap of his hands, Ursov stood at his full height, towering over the rest of them. "If Wert agrees, I will give the tour personally. Big Tooth, she is mine after all, yes? She and I, we have long history. Five years I run the drill. I sleep when she sleeps. She is mine alone."

"No one else runs the drill? Just you?" Olivia asked.

"Just me. Four hours on, four hours off, day and night during the week and partial shifts during the weekend."

"I see…"

"Wilcox might veto your petition to visit the Pit if he thinks the drill had anything to do with the accident," Vazquez said.

"Again, I will tell him we're going tomorrow." She exhaled. "He doesn't get a choice in the matter. I call the shots."

Lee smiled tightly. "Good luck with that."

"Ah, I need to get to work so… if you guys are finished in here…" Anxiously, Sok tapped his fingers together and glanced at one computer in particular.

"Okay, Dennis, we're out," Vazquez said. "Let me know if you need anything."

Olivia left the room, hovering outside in the corridor with Vazquez, Lee, and Ursov until, after a round of quiet, hurried goodbyes, she found her way to the elevator and returned to her room.

Chapter 4

The next morning, Olivia woke in the small bunk bed, the blanket wrapped around her legs, and checked her cell. Still no reception. She wondered at the number of emails she'd find waiting for her when they fixed the satellite and winced at the thought of having to wade through that mess.

She dressed quickly.

As she adjusted her blouse in the mirror, Olivia tilted her head and trained her ear toward the soft pitter-patter of rain striking her cabin window. She wandered over to look at the pale gray sky and dark blue water on the other side of the foggy, rain-streaked glass. Serene, really. If she didn't have the meeting, it would be a great morning to sleep in.

With her tablet and notepad in hand, she locked up her room and made her way to the elevator.

Patiently, she waited for the elevator to arrive on her floor and for the doors to open, holding her things tight against her stomach. She glanced to the left, noting the stairwell.

The heavy stairwell door opened smoothly, and she stepped inside to stand on the cement landing. Immediately, she frowned. This area was not well lit, only one bulb located in the top corner of the landing. A faint glow from above and below indicated another bulb on another landing in both directions. She jotted that fact down on her notepad, shaking her head in disapproval.

While the first order of business was pouring and distributing coffee, there was also the task of setting up the laptop to the projector. Frank struggled as Hersch hovered over his shoulder.

"If you'd let me, sir…"

"No, I've got this. I saw you do it yesterday."

Hersch fidgeted, nodded. "Okay."

Wert had brought a box of assorted breakfast foods – all from the pantry, none freshly baked – and spilled them across the middle of the large meeting room table.

Olivia took a small pouch of blueberry mini-muffins with her coffee and found her seat, choosing the same spot from the previous day and setting up camp.

"Do you want me to call Vazquez?" Wert asked.

"No, I've got it. Ah… there we go." Frank glanced up at the projector as it connected, displaying the scenic mountainsides of the laptop background. "Ready."

"Just in time. It's eight on the dot," Wert stated.

Timmons smirked. "I've got time to burn one, right?"

"Maybe two." Petry sipped his coffee.

A thoughtless chuckle escaped Olivia and she cleared her throat to mask the sound. She looked around the meeting room, the morning sun filtering in through slanted blinds. Once again, Wilcox was nowhere to be seen.

When he did show up, ten minutes later, he sat at his previous place at the table, and casually opened his briefcase. He had his tablet in front of him, expression cold.

"Mr. Wilcox, good morning," Wert said. "Coffee?"

"No. Let's get started."

The discussion on the hoist and pulley system had dragged on for nearly an hour before Olivia leaned forward. "I want to go down to S1 and see the dig site, Mr. Wert."

"We can't go down there," he replied. "Company orders."

"I was told I'd be allowed to see everything."

"Well, ah…"

Wilcox slid in, tapping his stylus loudly on the tablet screen. "Everything relevant to the investigation, Ms.

Nelson."

"And the drill isn't?"

He regarded her with his cool blue eyes, shook his head. "No, it had nothing to do with the accident."

"Even if it hit something and that led to the fuel line breaking? That's the cause of all this, isn't it?" she asked.

"I still fail to see the relevance."

"Indulge me. I have the authority to demand a full tour and if I am denied, it will reflect poorly in my determination. I'm sure you'd prefer not having to explain that to Brett Chambers," Olivia said, face warm and prickly. Her insides knotted up as she clenched her fists under the tabletop and smiled politely. "Am I correct, Mr. Wilcox?"

A flash of contempt in his eyes, then a chill. He smiled right back at her, nodded his head. Charming again, he rubbed his chin. "If it's mandatory, then how can I refuse? Though, if I could, I'd suggest making the trip down tomorrow – to give me time to prep. I've got the blueprints for S1 back in my room and I'd rather be ready to answer questions. Would you be amenable to those conditions, Ms. Nelson?"

"Yes, I would be." Pride swelled in her chest, her heart fluttering. She turned away to hide the flush in her cheeks. Victoriously, she popped a mini-muffin into her mouth and chewed. It wasn't lost on her that his gaze turned contemptuous for one, fleeting second. That too, felt good. She sipped her coffee. A cuppa had never tasted so delicious.

He squared his shoulders, turned to the Site Lead. "Wert, make sure that's on the itinerary tomorrow, first thing."

Wert nodded. "Yessir. Eight sharp?"

"Yes," Wilcox replied.

"Should we wait for you then?" Timmons asked.

"Excuse me?"

47

"Oh uh, just askin', Mr. Wilcox… if we should wait for everyone or, ah, just have a few of us go down," Timmons said, grin subdued. "The carriage holds five."

"No need for a field trip. Wert will escort Ms. Nelson and me down to the drill site. She can take a good, long look at anything she pleases, at her leisure."

Timmons sipped his coffee. "Ah hah, okay."

Their discussion moved on, and Olivia exhaled shakily. She began to take notes again, her pulse slowing.

They took a break around noon for lunch, and she stood, listening as Timmons and Petry exchanged quiet banter in the doorway. Each glanced back at her before walking out of the room, their hushed conversation continuing out of earshot.

If they were talking about her, she didn't know. The brief but heavy gazes of men were not unfamiliar to her in the environment in which she worked. Warehousing, construction, the labor industry in general, trended male. Not that she didn't encounter other women at all; it just tended to be a rarity. Olivia always smiled, always paid attention. She knew that she was usually the tiniest person in the room. That had been the way of it for most of her life if she were honest.

She'd stopped growing at age fourteen and remained the same height and weight for most of her young adult life. Short and slim. Sometimes, it was a sore subject – one would get teased for being so slight. Other times, friends were envious of her ability to eat liberally without consequence. She'd yet to, of her own volition, spend more than an hour in a gym. Finding flattering, professional clothing was a nightmare. At her stature, she'd adopted the habit of lifting her chin when in direct, face-to-face conversations. She'd adopted a serious veneer to offset her youthful femininity.

More than once, eyes had rolled and – men and women alike – had exchanged snide glances while she spoke. It didn't help that she had a naturally high-pitched voice. She actively spoke in a lower timbre when she remembered to do so.

She flexed her shoulders and shook off the dust. Whatever they were talking about, it didn't matter. Even if they were talking about her, Olivia had a job to do. Let them gossip and complain. In a few days, she'd never see them again.

Wert and Frank drank coffee, Hersch had left the room entirely. Wilcox closed his briefcase and watched her. It wasn't subtle. He commanded her attention with a nod. Olivia smiled tightly, like a reflex, turning her back to him. She glided toward the door.

"Ms. Nelson?" Wilcox called after her.

She paused, pivoted. "Hm?"

"Can we talk for a moment?"

Wert and Frank had zeroed in, leaning on the counter next to the large meeting room table. She saw their intrigue flare.

"Ah, sure."

Wilcox's gaze flitted over the others in the room before returning to her. "That was good. Earlier, the line about Brett Chambers. I could see that scribbled on a flashcard in your pocket – in George Leblanc's handwriting. It was good."

Her throat felt dry. "I'm sure I don't know what you're talking about, Mr. Wilcox. Flashcards?"

"He told you the magic words. What a guy, that Leblanc."

"He didn't tell me anything."

"Oh, so that was all you? Clever."

She frowned. "I wouldn't say it's clever. It's just business."

"Ugh, humility is so unbecoming. Accept the compliment." He rolled his eyes and stood.

Her brows knit. "What?"

"Never mind. Back at one?" He turned to Wert.

"Yes, Mr. Wilcox. One."

Wilcox strode toward the door and paused when he reached Olivia. After a deliberate glance down at her sneakers, he slipped past her and left the meeting room, his wake cool and dry. She peered back at the two men in the room and found Wert shaking his head.

"I don't know if I can sit in this room for another three and a half days with that one," Wert muttered. "Sorry, Ms. Nelson, not very professional of me to say that around you. I'd hate to get fired if that ends up in the report."

"I won't put that in the report."

"Are you sure? You can attribute the quote to me," Frank said. "I've, ah, heard the severance pay is nothing to scoff at."

"Frank…"

"I'm serious… Ah, I'm joking, sorry…"

Olivia smiled. "That comment is between us."

"Thank you," Wert said.

"You'll have three months off after this, won't you?" she asked, hand on the doorframe.

"Three months, yeah," Wert replied. "Just need to make it another week. Not too long."

"Ah, well, I'll be back at one and then we can get back to it, right? Have a good lunch." She nodded, waited for them to nod back, and then left.

The mess hall was occupied when Olivia arrived. She went into the kitchen, made herself a sandwich, and grabbed a can of soda from the refrigerator. There was an open box of chips on the counter out front, where the empty buffet stand sat in front of the long, kitchen serving window. She grabbed a small bag and sat down at one of the long tables.

Not five seconds later, the occupants of the other tables sat down at hers, in front of and beside her. Soon, Timmons, Petry, and Ursov had joined her, fencing her in.

"I wanted to fuckin' salute you back there," Timmons said, leaning forward. "Sorry, that was inappropriate, wasn't it? Shit, sorry. That was funny as hell though. You see his face?"

"Ah…"

"That's what you wanted to say to her, Joe? You idiot." Petry gripped the bridge of his own nose, lowered his head. "I'm so sorry, Ms. Nelson. When he said he wanted to tell you something, I had no idea it would be… that."

"What did she say to him?" Ursov asked. He had brought his own lunch over, along with a plastic cup of what was obviously beer, the foam thin and the smell recognizable.

"She threatened to tell Brett Chambers on 'im unless we took her down to see the drill," Timmons replied, grinning as he lifted his own cup of beer to his lips. "Mr. Peacock's feathers got ruffled *real* quick. Looks like they're dropping down the tube tomorrow mornin', bright and early."

Olivia coughed. "What are you drinking, Mr. Timmons?"

He sniffed. "Ginger ale. It's just a lil' fermented."

Petry covered his face with his hand. "Dammit, Joe."

She smiled. "Got another one?"

Ursov let out a laugh.

Her eyes on the clock, Olivia twisted around in her seat, her plate empty and a beer in her hand. "Ten-minute countdown, guys. Don't worry, none of this is going in the report."

"Is this considered fraternizing?" Timmons asked. "Or does that require a few more beers?"

"It was a nice lunch. Besides, I was advised to talk to the team here on Decimus. I'm your advocate after all," she said. "I want you to feel comfortable sharing your experiences with me."

"Ooh, sharing." His eyes lit up.

Petry sighed. "Sometimes the less you know, the better. Especially with Joe Timmons here. Don't encourage him."

"I prefer an open dialogue." Olivia finished her beer.

"Ah hah." Timmons eyed her up. He raised his left hand and wiggled the fingers. "I'd like to draw your attention to the lack of a wedding ring. I see you don't have one either. How is that possible? I mean, I've got this ugly mug... but you?"

"Inappropriate, Joe," Petry muttered.

Ursov folded his arms over his massive chest and listened, brows lifted incredulously at his crewmate.

She shrugged, picked up her soda. "My standards are too high. That's all I'll say about that."

Timmons smirked. "Got any kids?"

"No."

"None?"

"No."

"Want any?"

"No."

His eyes widened. "Really? Man, I got four back on dry land. Best things to ever happen to me. Each one's a blessing. A really fuckin' expensive blessing, but a blessing. You sure? You're young yet, aint'cha? What are yah, like twenty or so?"

"Or so. And, I'm sure."

"Oh, you're so young... you can't know that yet."

"Oh, but I do, Mr. Timmons."

He chuckled. "I said the same thing at your age. You just wait. It'll happen when the time's right. A blessing, each one of 'em. Their mothers on the other hand..."

"We need to head back in a few minutes," Petry said. "Maybe you should have a mint, hide the smell of that beer. Same for you, Ms. Nelson. Wilcox is going to have a fit if he smells alcohol in the meeting room."

"Dude'll throw a fit anyway – ain't that right? What a priss. You know he had his own personal menu shipped here, don't you? Last week, it came on the supply ship. Requested a fridge and a toaster oven in his cabin. Do you wanna know what this guy eats? Au natural organic fru-fru premade meals. A case of bottled water – glass bottles. Probably melted glaciers or something, or Brett Chambers' bath water."

Ursov chuckled.

Petry scowled. "Probably the latter."

"Do you know," Timmons began, his grin wide and seditious as he bent over the table toward Olivia, "that Astor Wilcox won't even use the men's showers on L5? He wanted his own private one in his cabin, but boohoo, we don't have any with those. So, you know what he does? You wanna know?" He waited for her to nod. "He uses the women's."

"Wow. I mean, no one else is using it, so..."

"You think that's something, huh?" Petry sighed, his top lip curling slightly. "Last night, I received a call asking about laundry services. He expected someone here to handle it for him and wanted to know how it worked. I explained that it's self-serve and he short circuited, hung up on me."

"That's sort of sad, isn't it?" When the men looked to her with twisted up faces, Olivia continued. "He's got no idea how to survive on his own and he's out here all by himself. Wasn't even prepared. That's sad to me."

"I don't feel sorry for men like him," Ursov stated. "Heartless men with more money than brains. Men with no soul. They feed on the rest of us, give nothing back. Only take."

"Just makes me mad," Timmons said. "Man, I might just crack open another beer and bring it in with me. Let's see what he says about that, huh?"

Petry shot him a look. "Let's not push our luck, Joe."

"So, don't light up in the room either?"

Ursov let out a loud belly laugh and clapped his hands over his tray, throwing back his head.

Olivia chuckled as well. "Absolutely no smoking in the facility at all, Mr. Timmons. Outside only."

"Damn," he said.

With a few minutes to spare, she took a seat in the meeting room. The laptop's projection onto the big screen showed an internet connection and she jumped at the opportunity. She got a cursory glance at the mass of emails clogging her inbox. She cringed, scrolling quickly with her thumb to search for important messages. There were more than a few from Leblanc.

Wilcox sauntered in, took a seat, saw her on her cell and put it together. Immediately, he had his out as well and attempted to access his email and texts, his entire being focused on this one task. That cool composure dropped.

Olivia looked up and saw Wert watching, his expression amused. She laughed softly. "Ah, internet's back…"

"I gathered," he said.

Frank leaned on the counter, arms crossed. He smiled too, chuckling. "You old enough to remember dial-up?"

"Rob, I'm sure they're not that young…"

"Hmm, don't know."

"I've heard of dial-up," Hersch said.

Olivia's heart sank when the bars on her cell disappeared and her message program froze, alerted her to the lack of internet connection. She'd been in the middle of a reply to Leblanc's status request. With a sigh, she locked her screen. "It was nice while it lasted. How do you guys deal with this?"

"We know it's a possibility during inclement weather and we just hunker down and wait it out," Wert replied. "In the event of an emergency, we're prepared to handle it ourselves for as long as we need to. We've had to before."

Frank coughed. "We got lucky the last time. Whatever knocked out the satellite, ah, IT took care of quick."

Wilcox dropped his cell on the table and grunted, expression tight, contained. "This is impossible."

"Sorry, it's just the nature of the beast. The company knows that comms are sketchy here on Decimus. You were briefed on it; I saw the emails and was in on the calls. They'll understand radio silence."

"Mr. Wert, I realize that your staff is more than halved presently, but don't you think it would be prudent to have them fix the systems we pay them to maintain?"

"Sir, they can't change the weather."

"Samos-Barnes has invested billions into this facility…"

Wert tensed, kept his cool. "IT is always on duty. They can't help that the tech is outda-"

"It's cutting edge. Don't you say it's anything but."

"There is room for improvement."

"The facility is fine," Wilcox stated.

"Should we, ummm, get back to it?" Frank asked.

Olivia, enraptured by the intensity of their debate, blinked suddenly. "Yes, please."

The presentation appeared on the screen.

Dinner was in the mess hall, and she happily took a seat with Ursov and Timmons, politely declining the offer of another beer to celebrate the end of the day.

"To be honest, I don't really drink that often," she said. "I'm a lightweight. Yeah, I know that's hard to believe…"

Timmons eyed her, raised his brows. "This cup's like ten percent your body weight, ain't it?"

"Ah…"

"Do you play pool?" Ursov asked.

"Not really, no."

"Darts?"

"Ah hah, I mean, I have…" She pushed an errant strand of hair away from her eyes and tucked it behind her ear. "Are you inviting me to play some games?"

"Perhaps."

"Now that might be fraternizin'," Timmons stated.

Lee and Vazquez walked into the mess hall, Hersch not far behind. Each paused, offered a wave.

While Lee and Hersch went into the kitchen, Vazquez waltzed to Olivia's side and kneeled on the seat, resting leisurely against the table. He smiled. "This looks like a mutinous little gathering. What are we discussing, comrades?"

Ursov snorted. "Dobryy vecher, tovarishch Vazquez."

"Mind the language, we're not a union, boys," Timmons said.

Vazquez scoffed. "Yet."

Olivia smirked. "I'm keeping my mouth shut."

"Smart move. I shouldn't even think about that word with an SB suit on prem." With a nod, Timmons sniffed, leaned away from the table. "Y'know he'duv dropped down from the ceiling, SWAT style, if he'd heard me."

Vazquez perked. "I'd like to see that actually."

"I wouldn't. Shit, I'd have to fix the damage. No thanks."

"Nothing a little duct tape couldn't handle."

"Duct tape won't do shit to fix broken ceiling panels."

"I meant for the suit."

"Pfft, get outta here…"

Olivia couldn't help but laugh.

Ursov grinned widely, showing off a gold tooth. "I was just inviting our advocate to shoot some pool, maybe throw some darts. What do you think?"

"It's not Friday, but I wouldn't mind a game night," Vazquez said. "Let me just grab some grub and I'll meet you guys in the rec room if you're down. I know Case and Spence would dig it. What say you, Ms. OcSaf? You want to aggressively hurl sharp metal darts at a wall in a small, enclosed area?"

"I just might," she replied.

Music played from the speakers in the corners of the room, Vazquez's laptop plugged into the sound system. His choice of tunes was easy on the ears, for the most part. Some of it was a little eclectic, comprised of bands she'd never heard of before that he felt compelled to explain in painful detail while she waited her turn to take her shot at the pool table.

He slurred, currently on his fifth beer, and gave her the in-depth background of a band with an unpronounceable name. His shoulder touched hers. "You want, ah, you want the vinyl for them. Vinyl sounds the best. The imperfections make it, you know? Pops and crackles. That's where it's at. You have a record player? No? You need a record player. Get a record player."

"I'll look into that," she assured him, grinning.

Darts was next.

Timmons, Ursov, Vazquez, Lee, and Hersch crowded around her as she aimed, threw the dart, and wailed as it bounced off the board and skittered across the floor.

"Good try, good try!" Ursov hollered.

Her opponent, Lee, landed every shot in the grids closest to the dead center and raised his hands victoriously.

She clapped for him, smiling, nodding. "I can't compete with that. Someone please tag me out before I embarrass myself any further. Please!"

Timmons jumped in, picked the darts off the floor. "Get ready to go back to school, son. The champion has arrived."

Despite herself, she did have another beer, and Olivia leaned against the wall, watching them play their games and joke around. Ursov had commandeered the laptop, fumbling with the music program, and lightly argued with a visibly intoxicated Vazquez over the selection.

At some point, hours later — she'd lost track of the time — fatigue tugged at her eyelids, and begging their forgiveness, excused herself. They taunted her only briefly before wishing her a good night.

Chapter 5

The blare of a car horn sent her reeling and she nearly toppled out of the bottom bunk, her eyes wide and blind in the darkness. Olivia cried out, clutched the rough blanket, and, panting, remembered where she was. She thought of the little cabin and bunk beds. She thought of the boat trip out and the crane that carried the container to the platform. Her racing heart – the pounding so intense that she felt it in her throat – led to a dizziness that yanked on her guts and pulled up bile.

It took many minutes to catch her breath and settle her stomach. The beat of her heart slowed to normal as she panted.

The dizziness remained, an ache forming in her skull along the suture above her right ear. She touched it, the skin smooth and hairless around the scar. Mouth dry, she reached for her cellphone next to her pillow, unplugging it from the charger in the process.

Still no bars. The time read 0220, the digital display going fuzzy as she squinted at it. Eyes still tired and unfocused, she rubbed at her face and stared at the display again, watching it crinkle, turn black, come back fuzzy and distorted. Olivia frowned.

A crash sounded from outside her room.

Throwing on her robe over her pajamas, Olivia tied her hair back and turned on the little light in her cabin. She went to the door and opened it to peer at the dimly lit hall. She thought she saw shadows moving out there and heard the shuffling of feet on the linoleum flooring. Grabbing her key, she slipped out of her room and locked the door. She walked down the corridor, socks muting her steps.

Turning the corner, she was surprised to see Casey Lee

at the elevator tapping the panel repeatedly. Jogging over to him, she frowned. "Mr. Lee, did you hear that crash?"

He did not reply; he only hummed.

Olivia stared at his face, saw that his eyes were dreamy and distant. Once again, he tapped on the call button and swayed in place, humming softly under his breath. She gave him a little shake and stepped away when he didn't respond. Looking down, she noted his bare feet.

A thumping came from the stairwell directly to the left and she scurried over and opened the door. Petry was shambling down the steps in what had to be his sleep clothes, his pajama pants dark blue.

"Mr. Petry?" she asked.

He too, had tired, dreamy eyes. The man continued down to the landing beside her, hung a left and took the next flight down toward L3. She blinked, confused.

Olivia ran down the steps, passing him, descending the flights until she reached L1. At the base of the stairs, she found two more men skulking at the bottom landing, the first of them pushing the door open and humming loudly. One of them was Larry Wert himself, dressed in sweatpants and a jacket, still in his sneakers as he limped. He smelled like the rubber mats from the gym.

The other man was Austin Vazquez, and he was stark naked. She might've cried out in shock, but in the moment, Olivia wasn't sure what sound came out of her.

Taking off her robe, she swept it over him, tied it around his waist while he tried to hobble his way down yet another hallway, mindlessly following after Wert. She saw more of him than she'd bargained for in the process of covering him up. He had a full-color tattoo of a retro game system on his chest and a musical note on his lower belly, near his hip.

"Mr. Vazquez? Austin? Can you hear me? Mr. Wert? Hello? Hello?" She tried to shake Vazquez and then hurried forward, grabbing Wert's arm. "What's going on?"

Still a little dizzy, she paused to get her bearings, arm on the wall as she watched them turn left and open another set of doors marked 'LAB1'. With a huff, she went after them. The elevator doors opened behind her, and she spun at the sound. Out came Astor Wilcox, wearing a pair of nice silk boxers and nothing else, showing off a smooth, hard-earned home-gym body. Aesthetics indeed.

Robin Frank, the Safety Manager, fully dressed for bed, in a robe and everything, teetered out behind him and both men passed her without even an acknowledgment.

Her face twisted. "What the hell?"

She beat them to the lab and went in. They had passed the lab itself and were heading down a corridor labeled 'ACCESS TERMINAL'. Olivia saw the lab on her left as she ran down the hall and made a right. And there, through a broken set of doors, she saw Dennis Sok pawing at a panel impatiently.

"Mr. Sok?" she asked, approaching.

Sok, night-shifter, dressed for work and looking professional, feebly attempted to type in an access code over and over. The glass doors refused to open, buzzing in error.

Olivia stepped closer and realized that she was looking at a massive, enclosed glass tube. She glanced at the signage and saw 'S1' on the wall beside the door. Another sign read, 'CAUTION: PRESSURAZATION – 5 MINUTE DELAY'.

Whatever was supposed to be in that glass tube, whatever Sok was trying to access, just wasn't there. She narrowed her eyes and turned around to see the others making their way in, each in turn pawing at the glass and humming, moaning, whining.

"Guys, please," she implored. "Someone, wake the fuck

up."

The men assembled in the lab, eyes dreamy, swayed around the empty tube like worshippers to some glass idol, pawing, humming, moaning.

She screamed, "Wake the fuck up!"

A roar.

A rumble.

The floor shook beneath her feet and her skull nearly split in half. Both hands went to her face, Olivia bowing, falling over, stumbling from the blinding, searing agony that sizzled along the right side of her head. A soft, distant scream deafened her. Then, silence. The throbbing of her brains waned, her breathing loud in her ears.

"What?" Wilcox was the first to speak. "What am I... what?"

"Oh shit, it happened again!" Vazquez exclaimed. "What am I wearing? Holy shit, am I naked under this? I'm naked under this!"

Olivia stumbled to feet, wiping at her wet eyes. "You were all in a weird trance. Wouldn't respond."

"Why am I here? Where are my pants?" Wilcox stumbled backward, eyes accusatory. "What is this?"

"Oh dear," Sok said. "So, we were trying to go down to S1."

Wert and Petry arguing behind her, Olivia rushed to Vazquez and Sok. "I felt it too. It didn't affect me like it affected you, but I felt it. My head, it was on fire." She reached up and touched her temple.

"Are you okay?" Vazquez asked.

She rubbed her scar. "I think so, just-"

"Is this some sort of fucked up prank?" Wilcox hollered. "Someone fucking answer me right now!"

Frank slipped in close. "No, Mr. Wilcox. This is the phenomenon that occurred the night of the accident. The thing young Hersch was referring to. The thing we said, ah, didn't happen."

Wilcox snarled. "I need to make a call right now! Where's the phone? Give me it! Come on!"

Sok raised his hand, a finger in the air. "Sorry, um, the satellite is still… we're not connected, I mean… and the storm…"

"Fuck you people!" Wilcox groaned.

Somewhere in the distance, Timmons began to shout curses.

"Is everyone okay? That's what matters right now," Olivia said, walking up to each man and looking them over. Vazquez clung to the pink robe, his awkward little smile once again inspiring her to smile right back. She nodded to him. "You, uh, can borrow that."

"I'd prefer to keep it. It's comfortable." He grinned widely and then his eyelids dropped, his focus blurring. Vazquez collapsed. He would have hit the floor if Frank hadn't dived in and caught him, rolling him onto his side.

"Oh my God," Olivia breathed.

"He's seizing," Frank stated.

Vazquez convulsed on the floor, lips parted, foamy spit dripping from his mouth as Frank gestured toward the others. Sok moved quickly, pushing a nearby chair to a safe distance.

Wert gave Olivia his jacket and she knelt beside Vazquez, making it into a pillow to support his head as Frank nodded in appreciation.

"He said he had a seizure the last time," she said.

Timmons came in, shaking himself off. He was dressed in a pair of boxers and a v-neck. "Jeeee-sus. Holy jamolie, am-I-right? You like that, Mr. Wilcox? That was a hoot, yeah?" He lit a cigarette and sauntered into the middle of the room before noticing Vazquez. The cigarette fell to the floor, and he straightened. "Oh, shit, Austin."

She ignored the others, stared at Vazquez. For the next few minutes, the world around her faded to a buzz of background noise as she watched him and held his shoulder.

Vazquez calmed, his eyelids fluttering, and he reached out to grab her arm. His fingers felt hot. "Ahh..."

She leaned down, brushed his damp hair away from his forehead. "Austin?"

"An angel. Hi." His eyes attempted to focus on her.

"Ah, no, it's Olivia." Wetting her lips, she offered a comforting smile. "You're safe, okay? You're alright."

He replied softly, "Oh, okay."

Olivia looked up and saw Frank smiling weakly at her. She dropped her gaze back onto Vazquez. "We should check on everyone else. I don't see them all here."

A shadow appeared at the door. It was Hersch. At the sight of Vazquez on the floor, he came sprinting over and checked on him, his mouth hanging open.

"He's okay," Frank said.

"Mitchell's hurt," Hersch said. "Not bad. He just kinda twisted his ankle. Guess he fell down the steps."

"Where's Lee?" Timmons asked.

"I saw him at the elevator," Olivia said.

"He's with Mitchell now. They were gonna stop at the mess hall to grab a drink or two. Jeez, I really wanted to join 'em but I knew I had to come down here and see for myself."

Petry stepped up. "See what, Spencer?"

"See if you all were here. I told you. I told you it really happened. And now it's happened again. I told you." He heaved slightly, large teeth exposed.

"Yeah, you were right." Wert nodded. "I'm sorry, Mr. Wilcox, but you see why we kept it quiet, right? This is madness."

"Nyuh…" Wilcox took a step toward the door. "I don't know what it is."

"Where's the carriage?" Sok asked.

"Hmm?" Wert turned to him.

"The carriage down to S1. The pressure chamber."

Wert frowned. "Huh, it appears to be down there."

"Who the fuck is missing?" Timmons asked.

"I heard something," Olivia said. "Something rumbled. It was loud. The whole place shook. And then you woke up."

"The whole place shook?" Petry asked, paling. "That sounds like the drill hitting something again."

"Re…so…nance," Vazquez whispered.

"But it shook after you all gathered down here," she said, growing intense. "Which means whatever had you guys, whatever trance you were in, wasn't caused by the drill hitting something."

A sudden crackling noise caused all of them to jump. From a desk to the right, an interface popped up, a single line appearing, dancing on the screen as a thick accent spoke. "Hello? Is anyone up there? Can you hear me?"

"It's Ursov!" Petry exclaimed, then ran over to the computer. He opened a receiving line. "Ursov, it's Petry. Where the hell are you?"

"Down in the Pit. You need to see this."

"Need to see what? Ursov, what do you mean, you're in the Pit? Why are you down there?" Petry asked.

"Don't know how I got here, but here I am. Turned on the drill. Don't know why I did it, but I did. Hit something. Broke something. You need to see what came out."

"What came out? What are talking about?"

"Found something interesting. Something I have never seen before. There are so many of them…"

"So many of what?"

"…Things."

Wilcox transported himself beside Petry, nearly knocking him aside. "What sort of things? Minerals? Rare minerals?"

"They appear to be rare, alright."

"We'll be down then," Wilcox said. "Give us twenty minutes."

"Ah, good. That is exactly how long the carriage will take to get back up to you," Ursov replied. "I will meet you at the access door on S1."

"Are you sure it's safe to go down there?" Olivia asked. "I mean, right after what just happened. Maybe you should wait."

"I want to go see what we've found." Wilcox offered her a plastic smile and stepped away. "So, if you'll excuse me, I'm going to go put on some fucking clothes." He left, the doors closing behind him.

She looked to the others. "Who's going down?"

"I will," said Petry.

"Eh, me too, I guess," Timmons added. "I want to see what the knucklehead found down there. Bet it's good."

Wert frowned. "I'll leave you boys to it. I need to stay up here, keep an eye on things."

"I'm going down there too," Olivia said.

Timmons balked. "Oh, no way. No way, José."

She scowled. "I insist. I need to see it."

"Don't… don't go down there…" Vazquez stirred, moving to sit up. He leaned on his elbow. "The resonance will… fry your brain."

"I'll be fine, trust me. I need to see what's down there. I need to know what caused this." Olivia patted his shoulder and stood, folding her arms across her chest, puffing up. She realized that she was the smallest person in the room. She was the smallest and also wearing an oversized nightshirt with a cartoon panda eating bamboo on the front. Her brows knit, her chin lifting. "I'm going with you."

"Okay, you're going," Timmons said. "Hey, I'm gonna get dressed too. It's a little drafty in here, don't you think?" Timmons stepped away, hands up. "Back here in twenty minutes, right?"

Petry nodded. "Right."

Olivia nodded as well. "Right."

Hersch had taken Vazquez up to the MedBay with Frank to meet Mitchell and Lee. She, along with a dismissive Wilcox, had been prepped on the pressurization chamber and what to expect.

Olivia had taken long, gentle breaths as the chamber thrummed around them, her hands on the straps of her body belt. She sat loosely on the soft seat that ran a ring around the carriage. Her head tilted back while she hid the discomfort each time her ears popped, and her stomach did a somersault. Wilcox grimaced, turning green.

She was sure she caught Timmons and Petry – pale but composed – sharing concerned glances and nodding toward Wilcox as he struggled to stifle a gag.

The trip down in the carriage was indeed unpleasant, just as Vazquez had warned her. Her ears popped several more times and she began to feel the sides of her head throb. The lower they went, the louder the carriage thrummed, the heavier her body felt.

Fifteen minutes in, Olivia swallowed to relieve the pressure in her ears and spoke, breaking the crush of silence that had dragged on for too long to bear one moment more. "I wish there were windows. I'd love to see what's out there."

"It's just black. No light reaches down this far. Water's too deep," Timmons replied. "Nothing to see."

"Oh."

"You good, Mr. Wilcox?" Petry asked.

The junior partner nodded, eyes shut tight.

At the bottom, the carriage came to a turbulent stop and Wilcox groaned loudly, pitifully, before clenching his jaw. He whispered to himself, his voice ragged. "Mind over matter. Mind over matter. Mind over matter."

Again, Petry and Timmons exchanged worried looks.

The chamber roared for the next few minutes, the air growing lighter. As it finished whatever cycle it had run, she began to feel more alert, less sick to the stomach. In five minutes, she was able to take in a deep breath and stretch. A life-sapping weight she hadn't noticed stealing her energy away, piece by piece, had sloughed off her shoulders, the world returning to a near normal state. She inhaled deeply.

Soon, they were all up and Petry opened the carriage door. A platform led to another set of doors, these the glass doors of the tube. Ursov waited on the other side, in a landing area next to a sweeping desk covered in flashing lights.

The glass doors opened and stale, cool air rushed in, tousling her hair. Olivia stepped out with the others.

"Welcome to the Pit," Ursov said.

Petry sighed. "Don't call it the Pit, please. It's S1, Yuri."

"Where is it? Where's your find?" Wilcox asked, walking forward on unsteady legs. He braced himself against the desk to regain his balance, his eyes rolling in his skull. "Ah…"

"Sir, just relax for a moment." Petry offered a hand and lowered it when it was waved away. "It can take a few minutes to adjust."

"I'm fine. I want to see what he found."

Petry turned to her. "Ms. Nelson, how are you feeling?"

"I can definitely feel the pressure, but I'm good."

"We've got barf bags if anyone needs 'em,'" Timmons stated. "Yuri, you know where they're at, right? I'd keep one on hand for, uh, y'know..."

"I don't need a..." Wilcox stopped himself, wiping at his mouth with the back of his hand. "I'm fine, thank you. Please, can we get on with it? Where is the tunnel?"

Ursov shrugged and turned on his heel, gesturing toward the big, metal doors at the end of the room. "Come then, follow me."

S1's construction materials and floor design were different from those up on the rig. The facility on the ocean floor was claustrophobic, cramped, with riveted metal paneling along every wall. Ducting and air vents lined the ceilings, pipes running the length of the halls as they traveled together. There were no elevators here, only grated metal stairwells that took them further down until they reached a massive portal, an open bulkhead.

Ursov gestured toward it. "Third bulkhead should be kept closed at all times. I keep it open to bring you down. I will accept the write-up."

"No, it's good, man," Timmons said, then eyed Olivia. "I mean, unless OcSaf has a problem with it... in which case, uh, you're in hot water, Yuri. Might gotta let yah go."

"This wasn't in the special," Olivia said.

"The special? Oh, that news thing with footage taken down here? Ah, yeah, you wouldn't have seen this part of the installation on TV. No way." Timmons smirked and walked through the portal into a long round tunnel. "Every seal is a failsafe, in case the tunnels flood."

"What are the chances of that?" she asked.

"Hasn't happened yet, but with Yuri at the helm..."

"I dig down, not up," Ursov muttered, leading the way.

The tunnel in which they walked had been carved into

the rock and then smoothed mechanically, the floor covered in long, rubber mats. Lighting fixtures ran the length of the tunnel, directly above them. A junction approached and Ursov hung a right, leading them to another bulkhead.

"Where's the control room?" Olivia asked.

"We passed it. I'm taking you right to Big Tooth."

Chapter 6

There were several other tunnels to traverse, the trajectory of their path gradually angling downward. The floor mats grew less plentiful until they were walking on rough, striated rock. Even the lighting became more erratic, the corridors dimming as intermittent hanging lamps replaced the tubes.

Olivia smelled old earth, salt, and gasoline. Another smell, like sickly, burning rubber, turned her stomach. Up ahead, the last chamber seemed positively sunny compared to the tunnel they had to walk through to reach it.

A twenty-by-forty cavern with a stony ceiling met her eyes as she stepped through the last bulkhead. No ceiling lights here, only lamps on tripods. And there, to the left, was Big Tooth. It was a giant metal beast, the digging end shaped more like a sharp pinecone than a drill. That biting tooth was ten feet long and four feet thick at the base, jutting out the front of the hull of a mammoth-sized vehicle, the spiked, heavy treaded wheels reminding her of those she'd seen on a tank. Olivia was unsure of what she was looking at for a moment, blinking at the machine incredulously. Behind it, she noted another bulkhead, this one gigantic and closed, a red light flashing slowly in the center.

"This is Big Tooth," said Ursov.

Olivia gazed up at it. "How do you get in?"

"I don't. I run her from the control room."

"Oh…"

"Where is it?" Wilcox rushed in, began to search the cavern floor. He too paused to stare at Big Tooth then shook himself out of the daze, stalking into the area to search it.

"Come see." Ursov strolled over to the cavern wall in

front of the machine, a few yards from where the tip of the drill hung in the air. He nodded up and then down.

Olivia walked over and gasped softly, breath caught in her throat. A hole, ragged and shallow, had been punched into the cavern wall, spilling out hundreds of small, black balls. Inky. Dull. Their sheen in the light betrayed an imperfect surface – round but not perfectly round. Smooth, but not perfectly smooth. The size of golf balls, they sat in piles or alone many yards from the gaping wound they'd burst from in the rock.

"What am I looking at?" Wilcox screwed his face, standing beside Olivia, intruding into her personal space with little more than a sideways glance when she stepped away from him defensively.

"Some kinda pellets?" Timmons asked. "Are they metal?"

Ursov replied, "I do not know. I did not touch."

Her eyes moved up and away from the black balls and back to that shallow, jagged tear in the rock. Olivia was struck by the eerie way the edges of that hole were formed, her head hurting again as she studied the protrusions, rib-like and black. A viscous yellow dew beaded on those growths, the light from the tripod subtly illuminating the inside of the cavity, the striations asymmetrical with intricate branching veins. Segments. Her guts ached.

"We should have brought equipment," Petry moaned. "Jesus Christ, those could be radioactive and here we are without any protection. Ursov, what were you thinking?"

"No radiation. Geiger counter quiet."

"You called us to come down to look, why?"

"Camera feed's not sending. Thought you'd want to see. This is what wanted to be found, I think. This is what called to us that night."

Timmons grimaced. "You think these things called to

us?"

Ursov shrugged. "That is what it seems. When it let me go, I waited so I could check the feed when it rebooted. And I see these."

"I doubt that's what happened," Petry said. "It's coincidental at best. Whatever the case, it's something new I've never seen before, and I have no idea what it is."

"What do you think they're made of?" Timmons asked. "Man, we shouldn't have sent Benzi home. Could really use a geologist right about now, or any of the boys in the lab. That was their job, you know – analyzing the minerals we dug up."

Ursov shrugged. "Take a sample for later."

"I don't want anyone touching them," Petry stated, shaking his head. "Even if they aren't radioactive, we don't know if they're toxic to handle. I've learned that if I don't understand a thing, I don't touch it, and it's served me well throughout my life. We should head back up. They'll get a sample when operations start again."

"That's good with me," Timmons agreed.

Petry stalked off toward the bulkhead and stepped into the tunnel. "Ursov, join me in the control room. I want to see what the data sensors pulled when they broke through that wall."

"Of course," the other man said, and began to follow.

Timmons hung back, smirked. "The discovery of the century, eh? I'm sure the boys in the lab will figure out what they're made of in a jiffy, as soon as we're up and running."

"Huh, well, they'd better be worth something." His lips pulled back and Wilcox gave one of the balls a little kick with his shoe, sending it into a brief, rolling tumble. It came to a stop less than two feet from him and he lifted a brow.

Olivia tilted her head. "That didn't sound like metal to me."

"No?"

"No. It didn't sound like stone either," she added.

Wilcox dropped to one knee. "Hmm."

A fast frown appeared on Timmons' face. "Hey now, Mr. Wilcox, you better not touch that thing."

"If they're neither stone nor metal, what are they?" Wilcox asked, staring at the ball he'd kicked. Tentatively, he ran his fingertips over the surface and smiled, pushing it to-and-fro. "It feels cool, like stone. Smooth."

"Jesus man, stop that!"

Wilcox picked the ball up and stood, letting it roll around in the palm of his hand. "Interesting. It's got some heft to it. Not heavy like metal or stone though. Huh, I think you might be on to something, Ms. Nelson."

She flinched. "Ah, well..."

"What a strange texture! I'm not sure what it is, honestly. Maybe you'll know since you're so perceptive. Have a feel." He tossed the black ball at her, smirking.

Despite her aversion and the pit in her stomach as she saw the ball fly toward her, she instinctively sent out both hands and caught it. Heavier than a golf ball, it felt smooth and faux-fleshy like silicon, cool like glass. It felt wrong, sickly, disgusting, the inky surface both dull and shiny at the same time. She cupped the little ball, felt the warmth drain from her skin. At once, vibrant colors began to appear under her fingertips, turned red and orange then blue, mesmerizing her. That surface squirmed unnaturally, a weighted motion rocking the ball from within.

A sharp pinprick on her right palm startled her. Two needle sharp prongs had burst out, cracking the surface, and gouged her skin, drawing blood. With a shocked cry, she threw the wriggling ball right back at Wilcox.

He caught it, dark amusement etched into his handsome face. Then, the ball tore itself apart and something black, something fast, came out, scurried like quicksilver up his arm, and slipped under his shirt. He let out a bloodcurdling scream, beginning to dance in place before bolting out of the tunnel, nearly knocking Timmons over.

Shrieking, Wilcox wrenched himself out of his jacket and bloodied silk shirt, tearing buttons off in the process until he thrashed about topless in the corridor. One hand flew to the center of his back, the other to the nape of his neck. His fingers dug into the skin, prying at something dark and dull. It took Timmons and Ursov working together to restrain him, forcing him to stop tearing at his own flesh.

Petry jumped to the side, eyes bulging and palms out, barking orders, commanding the others to 'hold him'. Wilcox kicked, flailed, screaming his head off in the men's grip.

Timmons had him by the crook of his arm and kept him still, turning him around to take a peek at his shoulder. "What in the fuck is on him?!" He released Wilcox, face twisted in revulsion.

Olivia unlocked her feet from the floor and raced over, head swimming in the sea of frantic shouts. She too wanted to see what Wilcox clawed at with such dreadful fervor.

Ursov grappled with Wilcox, snagged both of his arms in one fluid motion, and held him fast against his wide chest, the other man's cheek flattened as he howled. He too got a look at the man's back and scowled. "What is that?!"

Olivia froze at the sight of it, lips parted, lungs emptying.

A black thing had attached itself to Wilcox's upper back. This thing had long, tendril-like appendages stemming from the bulk of its mass between his shoulders, the shape of it asymmetrical, organic, and yet so closely resembling a chitinous insect carapace that, for a moment, she thought some large bug had fastened itself to him. A hand's length in size, the creature nestled into his skin, those appendages drawing blood where they'd pierced him.

"Holy shit," she breathed.

"Help me!" Wilcox cried out, struggling in Ursov's grip. "For fuck's sake, help me! Oh my God, it's digging into me!"

Wild, desperate instinct drove her into action and Olivia jumped in, attempted to wedge her fingers under the black thing. The shell was hard and, on closer inspection, intricately detailed like the inner workings of a machine in some complicated CAD drawing. Organic. Thick. Mechanical. Its black exterior shifted color under her fingertips, leaving bright red and blue echoes of her touch as she felt for a gap between it and his skin. Slippery hot blood stained her fingers, his wails frenetic as his powerful back muscles tensed and released with his undulations.

She could find no gaps, her probing fingers shaking. It had rooted itself deep into him. Before she had the chance to speak, to apologize to him for her failure, he passed out in Ursov's arms, his body going slack and heavy.

Olivia glanced frantically at the others, eyes wide. "We've got to get him up to MedBay!"

"First thing's first – what the fuck is that thing on him?!" Timmons cried, pointing at Wilcox.

"I don't know!" she replied.

Timmons shrunk back. "It came outta that black ball – I saw it! Ran right up his sleeve! Jesus, what is it?"

"Whatever it is, it's on him good," Petry said, nearing cautiously. He licked his lips. "Maybe we can remove it up there. We'll have the tools in MedBay."

"Oh no, I don't want to ride in the carriage with him, with that thing on him," Timmons stated, shaking his head.

She winced. "We don't have a choice."

"We do have a choice. We can leave him down here. I don't want to bring that thing back up with us. Don't want to be trapped in the carriage with it. Don't want it on the rig either." Lips pulling back to bare his teeth, Timmons again shook his head, this time more emphatically. "No way, José, no-no way."

"We can't leave him here," Olivia said.

Petry looked to her, then to Timmons. "She's right."

Timmons sneered, sweat standing on his brow despite the chill in the tunnel. "Then you guys take the long trip back up with him and I'll wait here, how's that?"

"You want to stay down here? With the open chamber? With those things that came out of the rock?" Ursov asked.

Timmons clenched his jaw, turned away. "Fuck!"

"Please, let's just get him up there," Olivia pleaded. "The thing, the bug – whatever it is – doesn't seem to be moving. It's stuck on him. It's really in deep. I don't think it's going to come after us. Please, help him."

Ursov shrugged, adjusting Wilcox's weight in his arms, his gaze locked on the dark, bug shaped thing latched onto the man's back. "I would also rather just leave him here. But I will not. Ms. Nelson is right."

"Come on, Joe," Petry whispered, gesturing toward him.

Timmons cursed under his breath again and forged ahead suddenly, making his way back down the tunnel toward the lobby. The others followed after, Ursov grunting softly as he lugged Wilcox along like dead weight.

Chapter 7

Wilcox shifted limply as Ursov laid him belly down on the exam table and stepped away. Arms hanging like dead weight, his legs splayed oddly, he breathed slowly, deeply, mouth open and lined with specks of thick foam. That black thing on his back quivered, the tendrils ever so slightly thicker than Olivia remembered them being in the tunnel.

"What is it?" Petry asked.

"I don't know," Frank replied, examining Wilcox closely, but not too closely. He kept one foot behind him as if ready to spring back.

"It kind of looks like a silverfish. You know, those things you get on your apartment walls? Kind of looks like one of those," Timmons said. "But bigger and uglier."

Petry grimaced. "Do you mean a cockroach?"

"No, a silverfish. They're more, uh, triangular?" Timmons drew the shape in the air with his hands. "Quick fuckers."

"So, it's a bug?" Petry asked.

Olivia's brows lowered. "It's got to be some kind of insect or crustacean, I think. I don't know, it's just… the shell and the number of legs, if you can call those legs. Damn, I've never seen anything like this before."

"It came out of that little black ball," Timmons said. "Shit, there's hundreds more down there. They filled the cavern when the drill broke through. Hundreds of those black things."

Ursov tilted his head. "Eggs."

"Eggs! Jeee-sus! It's an alien, isn't it?" Timmons asked.

"Under the sea?" Petry eyed him. "More like some kind of animal we've never encountered before. It's been down here for fuck-knows-how-long, buried in that cavern, until

78

we broke through that wall."

"It called to us," Ursov stated. "Sang the song that kept us drilling until we found it. It wanted us to break through."

"Song?" Olivia looked up from the black thing on Wilcox's back and shimmied away from Frank as he tentatively touched the thing with a cylindrical metal instrument. "What do you mean by a song? What did you hear?"

"I heard nothing. I saw nothing. Only knew I had to keep digging. That is what it wanted. I don't remember any of it, but here we are," he said, shaking his head.

She stiffened. "The missing time. You're saying it was… those eggs calling to you?"

"He's not saying anything," Timmons cut in. "Look, we're all pretty fucking freaked out, Ms. Nelson. Some weird undersea bug just attached itself to Astor Fucking Wilcox and it's probably digesting him as we speak. There's hundreds more down there, spilled all over the place. Who knows when they'll hatch and hunt us down."

"The… egg… it reacted. I saw it change color, before it..." Olivia blinked, removed one of her gloves.

"Ms. Nelson, I wouldn't touch it," Frank hissed.

"I did before when I tried to remove it. It's already on him. Let me just show you something, please…"

"I advise against it."

"Duly noted, but watch..." Despite her better judgement, she touched the smooth, hard flesh of the dark creature imbedded in Wilcox's skin. Round, bright red fingerprints appeared immediately – fading to orange, yellow, green blue when she lifted her hand. It shivered, the tendrils swelling, pulsing. "It changed color! Like that… just like that."

Wilcox made a sound in the back of his throat.

"It reacts to warmth?" Frank drew closer and frowned.

"Specifically, body heat, I think," she said. "Something

living, warm-blooded maybe. The only egg that… activated was the one Wilcox picked up and held in his hand."

"Huh…" Frank's brows knit. He too removed one glove and lightly traced his right forefinger along the angular, reticulated flank of the creature. The colors did not shift from the dull, flat black. He eyed Olivia suspiciously, lips tight over his teeth.

She shrank. "Maybe my hands are warmer."

Petry neared. "It attacked him because he handled it?"

"I believe so." Her head lowered.

"You handled it too," Timmons said.

"For a second. Not even."

"Did you?" Petry asked.

"Well…"

Timmons paled. "Wilcox picked one up. He tossed it at her. She freaked out and tossed it back at him. Then, it… that creature, came out and attacked him. So, yeah, she touched it too. She touched it and it didn't attack her. Who's to say they only hatch when handled? We don't know shit about these things."

She glanced down at the bruised abrasion on her right palm and clenched her fist to hide it. "Right. Is there a way to seal that cavern? Can you lock down the drill wing?"

"Lock it down?" Ursov lifted his chin. "Yes, we can."

"Can we also do something to keep the pressure door sealed? Ropes? Chains? Can we weld it shut?" she asked.

Timmons balked. "You think we'd want to go back there?"

Olivia pulled her glove back on. "You all collectively blacked out two weeks ago and then, just now, against orders, you continued drilling. You were all… dreaming on your feet. I saw you."

"Trust me, none of us want to go in there. Look at it on him… It's killing him. Jesus, it's killing him."

"We have to get it off him," Petry said, staring intently at the creature attached to Wilcox's back. His gaze moved to Frank.

Frank turned to him. "Oh, I don't think that's a good idea. We don't know what removing it would do to him. We don't know what it'd do to us if we removed it."

"I don't care. Get it off."

"I think… I think it's connected itself to his spine," Frank said, brows knit as he traced the shape of the root-like tail imbedded in the unconscious man's flesh.

"Then you'll have to surgically remove it. Where are the scalpels?" He stalked toward the corner of the room. Opening the top drawer in a thigh-high mobile cabinet parked there, Petry searched around with shaking hands.

Frank recoiled. "What?"

"You'll have to remove it."

"I'm not that kind of doctor, Bill."

"I know. I don't care. Just do it."

"I refuse."

"Then get the fuck out of MedBay."

"Happy to oblige." Frank blanched and, after a stiff nod, stalked to the door, threw it open, and disappeared into the hall.

Petry turned his attention to Olivia, his expression severe. His small eyes looked even smaller when he squinted them so harshly. "Are you medically trained, Ms. Nelson?"

"Just basic first aid."

He grew red in the face. "So, you can't help either?"

"No."

"Then I'll fucking remove it myself." Petry found a slender pair of forceps in the top drawer and set them on top of the mobile cabinet. He gloved up quickly, picked up the forceps, and scurried over to where Wilcox lay on the exam table.

"I think it's a bad idea…" Olivia said.

"I'm going to save this man's life," Petry muttered. He reached for one of the tendrils and grabbed for it, the shell too smooth to grip at first. As he dug in, tinier offshoots, like burrs, slid out of its leglike growths and jabbed into Wilcox's flesh.

The executive woke, cried out, and almost toppled off the table. Ursov dove in, held him by his arms, his large, meaty palms clamping Wilcox down solid.

Olivia covered her ears, shielding herself against the screams that broke from Wilcox as Petry pried and peeled at the hard, gnarled spokes jutting out of that carapace. Frustrated, Petry abandoned the forceps and dove his gloved hand back into the drawer until he produced a capped scalpel. With this, he dug in under the root system, right where the creature's knobby, twisted bulk swelled at the junction of Wilcox's shoulder blades.

A dark blur, sharp, whiplike, erupted from that insect-like creature, right along the curve of Wilcox's spine, near the nape of his neck and suddenly Petry was staggering back, silent in the torrent of shrieks, the scalpel dropped as he covered his face to hold back a bright, red splatter.

Petry fell back, his hands soaked in blood, and exposed a wicked slash across his cheek and eye, the flesh flayed. "Ah! Son of a bitch!" He stumbled to the sink, yanked a towel out from underneath, and pressed it to his face. "Fucking shit!"

A taillike protrusion whipped back and forth on Wilcox's upper back, threatening Ursov, who had the sense to lean away.

Wilcox calmed, his shrieks halting abruptly, and he gulped, twisting feebly on the table until that thing, that black, reticulated tail-whip, settled and slowly slid into the rest of its mass along his spine, as if into a hollow sheath.

As it found its place, the creature quivering, Wilcox groaned softly.

Petry gagged, hunched over the sink with the towel over the left side of his face. "My eye… my fucking eye! I can't see out of it. Fuckin' thing blinded me!"

Timmons hurried to help Petry to the bathroom, opening the heavy door for him as the injured man stumbled toward the room. "Come on, man, let's get a look at that."

"Wait, I'll go get Frank," Olivia said.

"I don't want his help!" Petry snapped, and the two men disappeared into the bathroom, the door clacking shut behind them.

She reluctantly made her way to the exam table just as Ursov released Wilcox and stepped away. The bedraggled man swallowed thickly, rolled his shoulders. If he were in pain, he didn't show it. Crusted blood flaked around the root systems growing out of that thing where it had latched onto him, sank into his flesh. It swelled and shrank with his breaths.

Olivia found gauze pads in a drawer under the sink and dampened one with a saline bottle from an open first aid kit on the counter beside her. Not wanting to summon that black whip, Olivia timidly dabbed at the fresh blood pooling where Petry had cut into Wilcox's flesh, along the parasite's intricate black roots. When she lightly wiped at the tendrils themselves, they quivered and constricted, going taut.

Wilcox woke suddenly, violently, his cry startling her. She jumped away, hands up to defend herself. A low moan tore from his throat, and he relaxed, sagged on the exam table.

"Mr. Wilcox?"

He stretched, back muscles flexing. "What's going on? What happened? Is it… is it still on me?"

"It's still on you," Olivia answered.

"Oh God, get it off…"

"It's attached. We can't. We tried to, and… I'm sorry."

"Oh God… Oh God…"

"Does it hurt?"

Wilcox licked his lips, eyelids fluttering. He'd broken out in a sweat. "No, but… I feel it now. It's in me. It's… in me." Beginning to writhe, he sent a hand up, over his shoulder to probe at the black growth. "Oh God!"

"Lie still, please. I know you're scared but try not to move."

"Do you want me to hold him down again?" Ursov asked.

"Please don't… don't…" Wilcox whimpered.

"How do you feel, Mr. Wilcox?" Olivia moved his hand aside to continue cleaning away the dried blood. Remembering the parasite's reaction, she avoided direct contact and kept to his skin.

"I'm going to be sick."

"Is there a bucket? The trash bin… the small one in the corner. Ursov, could you grab that for me qu-"

Wilcox retched, vomiting up stinking bile that splattered on the tile floor. He let out a wet sob, gripping the sides of the table. "Oh God!"

At that exact moment, Timmons left the bathroom and stopped at the sight before him. His top lip curled as he shook himself off and rushed to the corner to rifle through the drawers of the mobile cabinet, gathering several bagged items into his arms before returning to assist Petry. He kept silent the entire time, face flushed. The door clicked shut behind him.

Despite the smell of it – she'd dealt with worse – Olivia grabbed paper towels from the dispenser above the sink and went to work cleaning up the mess. She placed the trash bin on the floor next to the table. "As soon as the radio is back online, we'll get a call out, request emergency assistance. Whatever is on you, Mr. Wilcox, they'll remove it. Might be… a parasite or something, but if you aren't in pain, if you don't feel weak…"

"Get the radio working!"

"The guys are trying. As soon as they do, they'll let us know," she said.

"Call them and tell them to hurry!"

Ursov grunted. "They're working as fast as they can."

"I've got a… a thing, a parasite attached to my fucking back! I want you to call them and tell them to get the radio on right the fuck now!" Wilcox gulped on the air, pushed himself up and sat on the exam table. The blood returned to his face, turning his cheeks splotchy red. Shaking from the exertion, he spoke again, more calmly. "Could you at least try to remove it?"

Olivia took a step back. "Petry did and it attacked him. We don't have the equipment to remove it here. I'm sure they'll be able to take care of it at the hospital when-"

"And if I'm dead by then? Then what?" He reached over his shoulder and pawed at the hard black mass taping into a point at the nape of his neck. "Where's a mirror?"

"There's a mirror in the bathroom, but Petry and Timmons are in-"

"Do you have a phone? Take a picture of it and show me."

Ursov bristled. "Do not bark orders at her."

"And don't talk back to me!"

She relented. "I have a phone. Just a moment."

Ursov grunted again, arms crossed as he leaned on the wall. "It's an ugly black bug. Seeing it won't change a thing."

"I want to see it!"

Olivia pulled her gloves off and tossed them in the bin

before taking out her cellphone from her pocket. Frowning at the lack of reception, she walked a half-circle around Wilcox to snap a picture of his back. She came around front and offered him the phone to show him. She let out a stifled gasp when he snatched it from her hand. "Hey!"

His eyes bulged, sweat beading on his forehead. "My God, it *is* ugly." Twisting at the waist, he contorted oddly on the table. He handed her the phone and rubbed at the black shell again. "Ah, it feels so weird. Is it attached to my spine? I heard someone say that it is."

"Frank did say that, but you… you weren't awake."

"I guess I heard somehow."

"Or you faked being unconscious," Ursov said.

"I didn't fake anything!" Wilcox whirled where he sat, staring icy daggers at the massive bald man.

Petry and Timmons exited the bathroom, Petry's left eye patched with wads of pink stained gauze, the tape pulling at the skin of his face. He waved off Wilcox and marched over to the table.

"How is it?" Olivia asked.

"It's not so great and that's all you need to know about that. Right now, we're going to go down there, seal off the drill chamber, and lock down S1 – the whole wing. Need to update the other guys, tell 'em what happened down there. I'm sure Frank's already told 'em half the story. They need to know everything. What we found. What we saw," Petry said. "I think it would be best to keep Mr. Wilcox confined to the MedBay for the time being, seeing as how he's infected."

Wilcox scowled. "Excuse me? What?"

Petry scowled, directing his weighted attention to the horror-stricken man. "Infected, Mr. Wilcox. You're infected with some kind of aggressive parasite, and I don't want it slipping off you and attacking anyone else. You're in quarantine until the authorities show up."

"You can't do that!" Wilcox spat.

"Oh, but I can, sir."

"Do you know who I am?"

"I know and I don't care."

Ursov snickered. "I'll get the padlock for the door."

"You can't lock me in here. It's the MedBay, for God's sake. What if… what if someone's injured?" Wilcox forced a desperate, skeptical smirk, the sweat on his brow shiny. "What if someone gets a nasty cut and needs stitches?"

Petry smiled stiffly. "There's ten of us on this rig right now. Ten hardy, stout boys who can avoid major injuries for however long it takes to get a rescue ship out here with a nice little crate crane to evac us with. I doubt we'll need access to the MedBay and, just to be safe, I'll be taking the mobile cart with me when I leave."

"Who put you in charge?" Wilcox asked.

"I'm the planner, so I'm planning. I'll run it by Wert and I'm sure he'll be on board – especially when he hears the intimate details about our new guest."

Wilcox looked at Ursov, Timmons, and Petry one at a time, brows heavily furrowed. "You were all exposed."

"Last I checked, I don't have a… whatever that is… on me," Timmons stated, shaking his head. "I didn't touch shit either, unlike you. You picked it up, didn't you? Right after I told yah not to. Started fucking around with those things."

"Eggs," Ursov grunted.

"How would I have known?" Wilcox clenched his jaw, sent his dark glare around the room again, and settled on Olivia. "And she touched it too! She had it in her hands!"

"No bug on her. She doesn't have to stay in here with you," Ursov said, rolling his thick shoulders to push himself off the wall.

Wilcox shivered, wrapping his arms around himself. He

glared at each face in the room. "So that's it then?"

"Sorry, Mr. Wilcox," Timmons said, his expression and tone wholly unapologetic.

Wilcox muttered under his breath, grabbed a long segment of medical exam paper on the table, and threw it over himself like a cloak. As he clutched it, his top lip curled into a snarl.

Petry stepped toward the MedBay door. "Okay, I'll head up, talk to Wert. Ursov, you take care of closing off S1, right? Timmons, I want you to have your boys help IT in any way they can. We need to get a call out asap."

"Can do." Timmons saluted Petry, clucking his tongue at the same time, and moved to follow him.

"What can I do?" Olivia asked.

"You can wait in your cabin. We'll call your room when we get the comms up," Petry said sternly. "Thank you."

"Oh."

Wilcox sat up. "Wait, are you leaving me in here alone?"

"That's the point of quarantine, Mr. Wilcox," Petry replied.

"No!" Wilcox slid from the table to teeter on shaky legs, gripping the exam paper tight against his chest. "Shouldn't... shouldn't I be under observation? I need to be monitored! What if I need help! What if..."

"We'll check on you as frequently as we can," Petry said.

"I'm sure you will!"

Olivia cleared her throat. "I can help with that."

"Ms. Nelson, there's a phone in the MedBay. If he needs something, he can patch through to the comms room, line one." Petry's tone had softened, his single visible eye narrowed. "There's a camera anyway." He indicated toward the top corner of the room, to the right of the exit door.

"I don't want to be alone." Wilcox took a seat again, his knees giving out from under him. "I don't... I don't feel so well. Weak… dizzy…"

"Lie down then," Petry said. "There's not much else we can offer. Not until help comes."

"My stomach… I think I'm…" He clutched himself, eyes unfocused. Olivia backed up expectantly along with the others, concern etched into their expressions. A low sickly gurgle escaped his guts, rumbling loudly toward the end of the extended complaint. Wilcox swallowed, coughed softly. "I'm hungry."

Timmons balked. "I don't know how you could eat right now…"

"Maybe I've got a fucking parasite on me!"

"You won't starve to death, I promise. Ursov wasn't kidding about grabbing a padlock, but we won't leave you in here to die. So, calm down," Petry said, standing beside the door.

"Calm down…" Wilcox muttered again, head low.

"I'll bring him something to eat," Olivia said. "Is that alright, Mr. Petry?"

Petry nodded tersely. "Sure, if you really want to. Joe, can you watch the door? Keep him from getting out? I'll deal with Mitchell and Lee, give 'em the rundown."

"Eh, yeah, whatever…"

They dispersed soon after, leaving Wilcox by himself.

Chapter 8

Wilcox glared at the food on the tray, revulsion apparent on his face. He took it with trembling hands and studied what she had brought him. "You… made me a sandwich."

"It's turkey and cheese. It's not much but…"

"White bread?"

"Yes, that's white bread." Olivia watched his brows knit. He looked physically ill, pale, and sweaty.

"Oh…"

"If you don't want it, Mr. Wilcox…" She reached out.

He shrank back protectively, shielding the plate. "No, it's… it's fine. Thank you."

"You're welcome."

Then, he ate greedily, messily, eyes flitting back and forth between his food and Olivia with equal intensity. When he was done, he held the tray on his lap. "I'll need a bed."

"I can ask if they have any spare cots."

"I'd rather have the cabin, filthy as it is…"

"I'm sorry."

"Nyuh, I'm sure. Ah, it feels strange to lie down on my back. The shape of the …thing is uncomfortable on a firm surface." His eyelids drooped. "Do you think I'll die?"

She searched for words. "A parasite wouldn't kill its host that quickly, I'm sure."

"How do you know?"

"I've read a lot of books."

He squinted at her suspiciously. "Books about organisms like this one?"

"Not exactly like it, but… close enough."

"Does it come up that frequently in your line of work?"

"No, I read those books before I got this job."

"So, it wasn't your area of study…"

"It was, but it wasn't… I didn't pursue it, no."

"You decided to go the OcSaf route instead."

She bristled. "Right."

"Is that what you wanted to do?"

"What sort of question is that?"

"I'm asking what you proclaimed your dream job was when adults gathered around you at your eighth birthday party and posed that age old question of… what you 'wanted to be when you grew up'?" He sniffed. "Did you tell them it was a health and safety inspector?"

She paused to consider her answer. "No, actually, I told them I wanted to be a veterinarian. I wanted to work with animals, take care of them, heal them."

Wilcox snorted. "It all makes sense now."

"Thanks."

"So why aren't you doing that?"

"Turns out it costs a lot of money to go to school, Mr. Wilcox."

"There's ways to make it happen if you try."

"I did try. I couldn't work full-time and go to college. I had other obligations, bills to pay. We weren't wealthy."

"Do you think that I have an easy life?"

"I don't think anything about you, Mr. Wilcox. Are you finished? May I take your tray?" She held her hand out.

"In a moment. Do me a favor, would you?"

"Yes?"

"Look around my ribs, along my spine. Tell me if you see it there. I think it's spreading but I don't want to look in the mirror. I'm too afraid. Can you? Would you do that for me?"

"Sure."

He turned and looked back over his shoulder at her as she stood beside the exam table. His brows flattened, lips parted. "Is it bad?"

Olivia studied his back, saw how the black thing had grown again. It was longer than a hand now, coiled, and thick between his shoulders. A row of little, toothlike protrusions stuck up from the center of its mass like pointed sawblades – teeny at the nape of his neck, growing larger, then tiny, to nonexistent toward the small of his back. Those insect legs and roots had spun out, spread. She could see them, black and veiny, under his skin.

"Is it bad?" His voice wavered this time.

"It's… bigger."

"God, I don't know what to do."

"I'm sorry, I really am. I need to go though. Timmons is waiting outside and you want a cot…"

"You could stay a bit longer."

"I don't think so."

"If it's because of the things I said, I'm sorry. I won't do it again if you stay. We could talk about other things…"

"No, I have to go."

Twisting around to stare at her with big, icy blue eyes that shone wetly in the bright lights, his body at once began to shudder, shake, and his lips pulled back. He tried to stand, lost his balance, and flopped meatily to the floor to push himself toward the wall. A racking gag escaped his throat, his hands flying to cover his mouth, to stifle the wretched cries before they could slip from him again. Something broke. He began to sob, waving her away.

"Mr. Wilcox?"

He tensed, quieting, then began to murmur a familiar mantra. "Mind over matter. Mind over matter."

"I…" Her stomach ached, her heart thudding softly in her chest. Finding herself unable to find the right words, her mind a blank, she swallowed, took a step back. "I'm going to go find a cot and some blankets for you. You need to rest."

"I need to rest… yes." The man slumped against the wall.

She left the MedBay and faced Timmons. He leaned against the wall outside, casually smoking a stinking cigarette. A small, mirthless smile appeared on his lips when he saw her, his expression ever so slightly combative as they made eye contact.

I dare you, she imagined him thinking, *I fucking double-dog dare you to say one gottamn thing about this gottamn cigarette.*

"Lock 'im up," Timmons said.

"He needs a bed. Do you have folding cots?"

"Are you kidding me?"

"You can't expect him to sleep on the floor."

"He can sleep on the exam table. Spence does it all the freakin' time when no one's lookin'. Come on now."

"Please, Mr. Timmons."

"You're a bleeding heart, you know that?"

"Please."

He shrugged and led her down the corridor, shaking his head as he exhaled smoke. "Fine, yeah."

Olivia carried the folded cot and blanket down the hall toward the MedBay, Timmons behind her, hands in his pocket. They stopped when Ursov blocked their path. She blinked up at him, greeted him silently. He nodded in response.

"IT having any luck with the radio?" she asked.

"No, no luck. Not in this storm."

"Damn."

"Why are you his nursemaid?" he asked, gesturing toward the cot. "He is a rude man. Disrespectful."

"I'm trying to show him a little human kindness. I can't imagine how afraid he's got to be, what with… you know."

"We are all afraid."

"I know, Mr. Ursov."

"Yuri. My name is Yuri."

"Yuri."

"You came here with far different intentions than that man. He came to defend the company, to discredit you. He does not care about us – any of us. You owe him nothing."

Timmons lit another cigarette. "Preach, brother."

She glanced away. "How's Petry?"

"He will lose the eye," Ursov replied matter-of-factly.

"Oh no... I'll be up to see you guys after I drop this off."

"We would prefer you return to your cabin. It's safer."

Olivia's gaze moved to his chiseled face. "Did you seal off the chamber?"

"Sealed, yes. And S1 is locked down."

"Didn't take long."

"Don't need to go down there to bulkheads. Can do it from the IT room, on computers. The IT room and S1 control share access."

"Oh, great. Glad it was easy. It's done then."

"They sang a song, called us to them. They might do it again. You should stock up in mess hall, stay in your cabin, wait. I would feel better if you did, and I am sure the others, they feel the same." Ursov nodded solemnly, studying her face in the flickering tube lights.

"I never heard a song, Yuri."

"And yet a song there was. Why is it that you were unaffected?"

Her free hand cupped the right side of her scalp, near the hairline. Eyes closing, she furrowed her brow. "I have a metal plate in my head from an accident a few years back. Maybe that's why?"

"Maybe. Take the company bastard his bed and stock up with bottled water and food from the dry storage.

Hopefully, help arrives before they sing to us again."

"I should stock the MedBay too."

"We will take care of that. Not your responsibility."

She nodded. "Alright. Thank you. He is… a bastard, for sure. But he doesn't deserve to suffer. He might even learn a little humility from this experience… if he survives." Her laugh was sharp, insecure.

"Don't count on that. He will play it up when rescued. And then, he will take credit for the discovery. We both know this." Ursov smirked, exposing his gold tooth. "Hurry now and go, please."

"Sure, yeah, on it." She smiled weakly and went on her way, Timmons at her heels.

She dropped the cot and blanket off in front of a despondent and unresponsive Wilcox who had yet to move from the floor. He whispered to himself, breaths shallow and eyes unfocused.

"Mr. Wilcox, do you need help setting up the cot?" Unable to discern any meaning from the garbled madness streaming out of his mouth, Olivia backed away and left the room, shutting the doors behind her. Timmons locked the chains together, puffed smoke in her direction.

"I hope you feel better. This entire endeavor cost me at least an hour of work."

"It was the right thing to do," she said.

"Whatever you say, Florence Nightingale."

They parted ways, Olivia's face hot.

While reading in bed, her room phone startled her when it broke into a metallic, warbling wail. She jumped up, answered on the third ring. "Hello?"

"Ms. Nelson, it's Wert."

"Oh, hello. Any updates?"

"Thought you should know that the skies are getting darker up here. That storm we were hoping would miss us? Yeah, it's coming this way. A direct hit, in fact"

"Is it going to be a big problem? The storm?"

"She'll weather it. Just wanted to let you know that the comms won't be back up anytime soon."

"It's just going from bad to worse."

"Look on the bright side – in five days, your boat home will show up regardless. Even if we got a call out right now, it'd take the same amount of time to get someone out here."

"At least they'd be prepared."

"It is what it is. Just hoping that thing doesn't get too big that it kills him, pops off and starts coming after us."

"And the eggs?"

"Not as worried about them with S1 closed off."

"Any of you could go back down there."

He cleared his throat. "You have a better plan?"

"Lock the lab doors and give me the key. I wasn't affected."

"That ain't such a bad idea, miss."

"I wanted to suggest it earlier. Just… didn't get a chance."

"I'll put Petry on it immediately."

"Thank you."

"No, thank you," he said. "That's smart. Real smart."

"Hm, yeah…"

"I'll have him drop off the key with you before too late. If anything changes – anything – I'll give you a call, Ms. Nelson. Just be patient. Help is on the way."

"Sure, yes. Thank you."

"Talk soon."

"'Night." She hung up after waiting to hear the click from his end, her eyes suddenly very tired. A low rumble shook her room, and, for a moment, she imagined Big

Tooth digging into the broken rock wall, digging into that gaping hole with the black, rib-like appendages bowing out like fingers spreading to grab at her. That yellow oil dripped, beaded on the floor where the eggs had spilled and piled together. Deeper, Big Tooth plunged, spraying dried viscera and bits of desiccated flesh into the air instead of rock dust. Another rumble followed, the howl of the wind across the rig growing louder.

The phone rang, startling her. She picked up. "Hello? Wert?" A second later, a click sounded. Olivia tensed.

From her cabin, what began as a low hiss became a deafening cacophony of rhythmic, monotone sound as rain pelted the hull in violent, powerful sheets. The lights flickered. Her eyes moved to the one, small window in her cabin and her heart sank at the sight of the blind gray turmoil.

The storm continued to rage into the next morning when she awoke, sinuses stuffed and head achy. It wasn't her scar, at least. Olivia fixed her appearance in the mirror after dressing and left her room. Finding the elevator panel dark, she took the stairs instead.

She saw Vazquez just as she stepped into the mess hall.

His eyes widened as he approached her. "Whoa, hey, what are you doing out? Aren't you supposed to be in your cabin?"

"I wanted to make a proper breakfast in the kitchen."

"You don't follow orders very well, do you?"

"I wasn't aware that I was under orders, Mr. Vazquez. It was advice, as far as I was concerned."

"I see. You should cook your breakfast quick then."

"Why's that?"

"Because I was here first to do the exact same thing."

Olivia managed a smile. "Well, why don't you join me

then? There's two stovetops. We can share the kitchen."

With a sigh, he nodded. "Sure, yeah."

She fried an omelet on the stove, and he made toast that he buttered haphazardly. They stood in the kitchen as they ate, the coffee brewing on the counter next to the industrial steel refrigerator.

"How are you feeling?"

Vazquez made a face. "Good, yeah. Not bad. I was back up again in an hour. Which was great timing because you guys dragged the suit and his pet bug into MedBay right after I left."

"Has anyone checked in on him?" she asked.

Vazquez chewed on his toast pensively. He swallowed. "Sure, they have. Spence and Frank went in and took a look at him this morning. Brought Wert with to see. I heard he was not happy."

"Wert?"

"Wilcox. He blew up at them."

"Blew up at them how?"

"He's pissed, being locked up in the MedBay. Heard he had an absolute meltdown, cried like a baby. Spence said he broke some stuff too."

"His condition?"

"Frank said it's spreading, getting bigger, whatever it is. I don't want to see it. Timmons described it well enough for me."

"That's what Wert was worried about." She sipped her coffee. "The thing getting bigger, I mean."

"Frank said he eats like he's feeding it. Petry suggested they cut his portions down to see if it slows the growth."

"Cruel."

"Might be necessary."

"It makes sense, I guess. That's how it goes in nature.

Parasite feeds off the host, grows bigger. Host gets weaker and weaker until…"

"Until what?"

"Well, the parasite usually kills the host before it drops off to continue the next step in its lifecycle…"

He cringed. "Eh! Yeah? What's that?"

"I mean, I've never seen a thing like it, so I have no idea. It could cocoon itself up, metamorphize into something else entirely, or ah, I don't know… lay eggs? Start the cycle all over again? There's no telling."

"Comforting thought."

Olivia picked up her plate and fork, took a bite of her cheese omelet and chewed slowly. Appetite waning, she set the plate down on the long, kitchen island they stood beside. The wind outside howled, the hanging pots and pans shivering, clanging softly. "Must be some storm out there."

"They always are."

"I still can't believe this is real," she said.

Vazquez shrugged. "Yeah, same."

"It's like some bad B-movie on late night TV."

"I was thinking the same thing."

She perked. "Yeah?"

"Yeah. That's why I didn't say anything. The first person to say something is usually the first one to die, you know. The guy – or gal – the well-meaning idiot who raises their hand, they get it first. So, I was going to keep my mouth shut. I know how these movies play out. I've watched enough of 'em." He smiled.

"It's good that this isn't a movie then. That this is real life."

"That might be worse, honestly," he said. "There's no formula to follow. No rules. It's a free-for-all. None of us would be safe."

"Lovely breakfast conversation."

"You opened that box, Pandora."

"Florence Nightingale... now I'm Pandora..."

"Hm?"

Olivia puffed out air, ruffling her bangs. "Nothing."

"Huh. Nothing, eh?"

"Timmons called me Florence Nightingale because I wanted to make sure Mr. Wilcox had a bed to sleep on. And now, you just called me Pandora because I opened my mouth."

"I didn't mean to insult you or anything."

"It's okay," she said. "I'm just collecting nick-names at this point."

"Hey, can I call you Olivia?"

Sipping her coffee first, she nodded. "Sure."

"Cool. And you can call me Austin, okay? I can't stand the 'mister' thing from anyone. Fuck formalities, I say."

"I can get behind that."

They exchanged pleasant smiles and finished their meals.

She took a collection of dry food back with her to her cabin, Vazquez at her side in the stairwell helping to carry her bounty. They continued to talk, and she laughed a little before reaching the closed door to her room.

"My cabin's literally four down from yours, by the way," he said, nodding down the corridor. "So, maybe later, y'know..."

Her brows lifted. "What?"

"We could..."

"I'm not that kind of woman."

Adjusting the boxes in his arms, he balked. "You can come and visit after five or six if you're bored. We could hang out. Watch a movie or something. I wasn't suggesting... I mean, darn, I know you saw me naked, but we literally just met. What do you take me for?"

"My mistake. What's your room number?"

"Eleven. Call me first. You just punch in 4, then 11."

"Four-one-one. That's funny."

"I thought so too." That wide smile spread across his lips.

Juggling the items in her arms, she unlocked her door, and they went in together. She knelt, placing her haul in the far right corner while he set his down next to her open luggage, the clean clothes inside folded and ready. Her laundry bag was stuffed under the little writing desk. Vazquez stood, wiped his hands on his jeans, and looked around her room.

She noted his amused expression. "Thank you for your help."

"Yeah, no problem. Looks like you're settling in nicely."

"Hah, sure."

"Not even going to unpack?"

"What's the point? Just have to pack again."

"Valid. However, you are kinda stuck in here…"

"Don't remind me. I wish I could do more."

"Eh, don't worry about it. Not much any of us can do right now, other than just keep trying to get a call out. At least by you being here, we'll have one clear head if we all go into a funky trance again if those egg things call to us. That's what Yuri theorized, you know. That they called to us looking for hosts." Pausing to fix his glasses, Vazquez frowned. "No saying how long they were down there waiting to be heard, trapped in the rock."

"I think there's time before they call again," she said. "The first incident was two weeks ago. Whatever hold they had on you, they lost it. You didn't find them. Then, this last time, it stopped again, right when Yuri opened the rock wall. If they'd kept calling, he'd have been infected first. Every one of you would have crammed into the chamber when it returned to L1. You would have gone down there… would have all wound up hosts to those things. But you didn't. Because it stopped."

"Why do you think that is?"

"I think it's because they need to rest, that it takes effort to exert that much energy into whatever method they use to call you. It's obviously some kind of frequency, like your resonance theory…"

"Huh, I could've been partially right."

"My first day on Decimus, I felt something. It was over so quickly; I didn't think anything of it at the time. I guess they were trying again and just couldn't do it yet."

"You didn't turn into a zombie," he said.

"I believe I'm immune." At his quizzical reaction, Olivia shrugged. "I was in an accident years ago and have a metal plate in my head. I bet it blocked whatever frequency those things were sending out. They won't do it again any time soon."

"I hope you're right. I don't want to end up like Wilcox."

"In any case, you won't be able to get down there." She smiled a little, chin low. "If they call again, you'll be safe. I do, ah, want to make one suggestion though. For you, specifically."

"Yeah?"

"Don't sleep in the buff anymore, Austin."

He laughed. "I make no promises."

Opening the door, he stepped out, waving at her as he left. The door closed behind him, and she exhaled loudly, eyes suddenly focusing on the pastel blue bra she'd hung to dry from the top bunk.

After eating a light dinner, she grabbed her towel and walked down to the showers. The lights flickered as the barrage of rain and wind rattled the rig. Lightning cracked.

Thunder rolled.

As she stood in the hot stream of water, Olivia tilted her head, hair wet and clinging to her skin. A gust from the air vents caused the white stall curtain to shiver, sway. From the corner of her eye, she caught the movement and turned, a cool finger traipsing up her back, tickling her spine all the way to her skull. She swallowed, frozen, waiting.

From the locker room came the soft echo of clicking, low and grating, like the cogs of an old machine hitching up.

Her towel hung on the rack just beyond the water's reach. Tentatively, she extended her hand toward it, her other arm braced against her breasts to shield them from view.

Towel wrapped around her body, she pushed the curtain aside and saw the bathroom was empty. The air vents sputtered again. Olivia sighed. A keening moan from inside the walls gave her a jump, the water pressure of her own shower dropping noticeably. Then, two male voices, muffled, echoing, started back and forth.

She finished her shower, dressed, and returned to her room.

Chapter 9

A soft female voice, familiar, sung to her:

Beautiful Dreamer, wake unto me,
Starlight and dewdrops are waiting for thee;
Sounds of the rude world heard in the day,
Lull'd by the moonlight have all passed away!

Her eyes opened, wet with tears. Darkness greeted her. Wiping at her face, she gulped on air and sat up in the bottom bunk, careful not to hit her head on the top beam. Her skull still smarted from the last time she'd done it.

Sniffling, wiping her nose with her arm, she picked up her cell and unlocked it, went to the camera. Swiping through the photos, she stopped on a picture of herself and an older woman with eyes just like Olivia's laughing, sitting together at a restaurant table. The screen turned off after ten seconds.

In the black void that swallowed her up, Olivia's breath hitched. Her lungs ached, her eyes hot. Rolling her shoulders, she exhaled slowly, purposefully. A sharp inhalation.

"Don't let it get yah down, Livvie," she whispered, putting her cell back down on the bed, next to her pillow. "Stand back up. Don't let it get yah down."

The cabin phone rang.

She woke her cell again and looked at the time. Midnight. Still no reception either. The cabin phone rang a second time. Her eyes narrowed in the stark shadows. Setting her cell back on the bed, she got up, letting the cabin phone ring a third time before answering it.

"Hello?" Her voice sounded small to her. Strange,

choppy breathing met her ear. "Hello? Who is this? I'll hang up."

"Ms. Nelson…"

"Mr. Wilcox? It's midnight. Why are you calling me?"

"Ah, could you come to the MedBay? Please?"

"Why?"

"Just come, please."

Her brows knit. "Mr. Wilcox, I can't help you."

"Yes, you can."

"I'll call comms, get Frank."

"No, just you."

"If you're trying to trick me, it won't work."

He grunted. "I'm not trying to trick you. Ms. Nelson, I am begging you to come to the MedBay. I'm scared. The others, they don't care about me. You do. I know you do."

She fiddled with the phone cord and bit her bottom lip. "Well…"

"Please… please… please."

"Alright, Mr. Wilcox, I'll be down in ten minutes." Olivia closed her eyes, listened as he thanked her over and over. She hung up.

Her hands trembled as she removed the padlock and caught the chains before they could fall noisily to the linoleum floor. She closed the door behind her and walked into the MedBay, the lights sterile and bright. There was no sign of him. At first, she was confused until she spotted a shadow on the other side of the exam table in the treatment room. Cautiously, she made her way over and turned.

When she saw him, she came to a halt, frozen to the spot. Wilcox sat shirtless on the cot. That thing had expanded across his back, grown in both size and complexity. The serrated row of spikes lay flat against his spine as if at rest. A sort of segmented armor wove into his shoulders, down his arms. Paler now, the tan had drained from his skin.

He wrung his hands and peered up at her with large wet eyes. Both pupils had burst into huge pools of blotted ink, swallowing up the blue of his irises. Thin black root systems ran along his jawline, through his messy hair, branched from his temples to his forehead. He scratched at them, drew blood, and stopped. "Thank you for coming."

"Oh God," she breathed.

"It feels a lot worse than it looks, I assure you."

"Are you in pain?"

"Yes? No? I can feel it moving under my skin, inside of me... inside of my body." He felt at his stomach. "I don't know."

"How did you get my phone code?"

Chin low, he cleared grit from his throat. "I remembered your cabin number."

"Right." She took a step closer. "What do you want?"

"Look at me." He leaned back on the cot, posing almost suggestively for her scrutiny. Thicker black roots like the ones on his face branched and thinned like veins, trailed across his chest, disappearing into his pecs. Wilcox cleared his throat, bared his teeth.

"It's spread," Olivia said.

"Yes, obviously," he replied, tone acidic. His demeanor shifted, humbled as a strange, guilty look appeared on his face. "I need your help."

"I'm not a doctor, Mr. Wilcox."

"I know. I didn't call you here for your opinion."

"Then why did you call me?" She shied away when he leaned forward. The small MedBay felt even tinier, felt like a trap, as Wilcox sat at attention on the cot before her.

"I was so hungry earlier," he mused. "I've emptied the fridge. Look at the bin over there."

She glanced at the trash bin in the corner, noting the cans and thin cardboard boxes spilling out from within. "You want me to bring you more to eat, is that it?"

"No, now I'm …lonely."

Olivia blinked. "Ah, okay. There are other people to talk to, you know. Not just me."

"You're the only one I wanted to see."

"Why? It's not like we hit it off, Mr. Wilcox."

He licked his lips, face flushed. Catching his bottom lip between his teeth, he studied her face. His fingers tugged at the fabric of his trousers. "We still could though."

Her eyes dropped by accident, attracted to the motion. His intent strained, bulging the zipper of his fly outward. Face burning hot, Olivia turned to the side, looking away. "I don't think so."

"Why not?"

"I just don't."

"I'm frightened. Please sit and talk to me."

"What about?"

"I don't know. Anything. What's your favorite book? Where did your family vacation when you were young? Where did you grow up, go to school? I don't know. Anything. Just talk to me."

"Why don't you tell me about yourself first?"

"I… I don't know what to say. I'm just so afraid." His dark eyes searched her face and his nose scrunched. Then, Wilcox shuddered and let out a wet sob. He wrapped his arms around himself. "I don't want to die here. I don't want to be killed by this thing on me. They're going to leave me all alone in this room. They're going to let me die."

"You're not going to die."

"How can you know that?"

"I just do. When help arrives, they'll get that thing off you, Mr. Wilcox."

"Please call me Astor."

"Astor."

"I'm not the easiest person to get along with, I know that." He licked his lips, a tremor audible in his voice when he continued. "Even if you don't like me very much, I don't see hatred in your eyes. Maybe there's a chance we could… connect. What do you think? Could we try?"

Olivia sucked on her teeth before replying. "Maybe."

"We could be friends…"

She might've smirked. "Friends? That'd take some time."

"Might not have much of that…"

"Oh." Her expression sobered. "We didn't meet under the, ah, best circumstances, that's for sure. Whatever I wrote about the investigation won't matter anymore, will it? Whatever you came here to do won't matter either. We're not adversaries anymore, Astor. Not sure what we could be instead. We don't have that much in common, do we?"

Teeth gently chattering, he stared up at her with his large, black stained eyes and gathered himself. "We're both alive."

"That we are, Astor."

"Although, I feel like I'm dying…"

"I know, but you're going to be okay. I promise."

"I… I believe you."

Olivia managed a small smile. "Good."

His shaking hand reached for her. "Please, lie with me?"

"What's that?"

"Sex."

She stiffened in shock. "No!"

"Please?"

"Astor…"

"Nyuh." He laid back on his cot, swallowed thickly, his Adam's apple bobbing. Biting his bottom lip, Wilcox slid his hand down along his flat stomach, stopping at his belt. "Five-thousand."

"Excuse me?"

"Five-thousand dollars. What would you do for five-thousand dollars?" His heavy-lidded gaze passed over her face.

"I'd leave this room right now."

"Ten-thousand then."

"Astor, stop it. If you meant it, meant what you said about being my friend if- when we get out of here, you can't say that kind of shit to me."

"I'm sorry. I'm frightened and saying stupid things."

"I'm going to go for now," she said, pivoting on her heel. "But I'll check in on you, alright? Tomorrow."

"Thank you."

"Just… please, don't talk to me like that again."

He tilted his head, watching her inch away from him. His inky eyes grew sad and weary. "I'm engaged, you know."

"I'm sure she's a lucky lady, Astor." As she sidestepped closer to the door, she kept him in sight, careful not to expose her back.

"Actually, she's a vapid, chattering mannequin."

"Cancel the wedding."

A bitter laugh escaped him. "Oh, if only."

Her hand rested on the right door handle. Unable to continue looking at him, she turned to stare at the frosted glass, the metal frame dull. "You have more power over your life than you know, Astor. You don't have to do anything if you don't want to."

"Again…" A wet gag burst from him. "If… if only."

"You can live whatever life you choose." She cringed when she heard a thick phlegmy whine behind her.

"My life has been decided for me. I was… ech… never in… never in control."

"Then take back control," she said.

"Olivia?"

Her eyes closed. She heard flesh slap against tile, the sound unsettling. His joints must have popped out of place when he moved. Her stomach lurched. "Yes, Astor?"

"Why is it that I feel this way for you?"

"I don't know. Maybe you have a fever. Maybe you're scared and not thinking straight."

"I feel like we're already one."

"Okay, goodnight. Please rest." She opened the door.

"Wait, please…"

She paused. "Yes?"

"Your blood is in my veins. It's on my tongue. Why is that, Olivia? Why do I know how you taste?" His voice cracked.

She turned back to look at him and froze. Practically crawling across the floor toward, her, his body twisting and angling in unnatural, frightening ways, Wilcox stared up at her with wide, ink blotted eyes. His blackening fingers curled like talons, his bones crunching and popping. A sawblade jutted from the mass of the creature along his spine, freshly shredded skin draped like a veil over the cutting edges of the sharp protrusion.

He extended a hand toward her, fingers spread. Intense, hopeful desperation screwed his features before he shrank back down and whimpered, tensing as if in pain.

Her stomach churning, she slipped out and closed the door, locking the chain to the padlock. Olivia tripped over her feet as she scurried off, afraid to look back.

Chapter 10

Olivia's imagination held on tight to that awful image of him crawling, animal-like, across the floor, his body contorting painfully as he came closer to her. She lay awake and fretted, contemplating the usefulness of a cry for help – for him. He had a phone in that room, and obviously knew how to use it, if he could. He could call for help if he needed. If he were dying on the floor, what good would it do him anyway? If he were dying on the floor, with that parasite ready to detach and find a new host, what good would it do any of them to rush to his aid? He would die alone on the cold floor, and she'd sleep in her warm bed.

Chest tight, she leapt from the bunk and unplugged the phone in her cabin. He'd have to call someone else if he had the strength to try. She curled up under her covers and stared into the darkness, her eyes adjusted. Thunder rolled.

Olivia barely slept and when she did, her dreams were unpleasant and haunted her well past waking.

She checked the time on her cell and sighed. At 7AM on the dot, she left her room, glancing back and forth in the corridor. Olivia took the elevator down to L3, then marched to the mess hall.

This time, Vazquez wasn't alone in the room. Petry and Timmons were with him, sitting at one of the long tables eating breakfast, having coffee. Their eyes locked onto her as soon as she entered.

"No coffee maker in my room," she stated, waving at them, and pushed open the door to the kitchen. She poured herself a cup of coffee and the door opened.

"You could have called and one of us would've brought you up a coffee, Ms. Nelson," Petry said, his patched eye wrapped much better than the previous day.

She studied his polite yet taut little smile, the sentiment obviously feigned for her benefit alone. "Oh, maybe next time. I'm already here, Mr. Petry."

"Make it quick then."

"I'll just chug it, right? Just chug the scalding hot coffee."

"Wait, Ms. Nelson, I…"

"No, I'll make it quick." Lifting the cup to her lips, she blew the steam and prepared to gulp it down.

A voice, frantic, blared across the speaker system. "Get down here! Get down to MedBay now! Hurry!"

"That was Frank!" Petry shouted, stumbling backward.

Olivia dropped her coffee, the mug smashing on the kitchen floor. She staggered, pulse racing. "What? What's going on?"

Petry flew out of the kitchen, ran into the mess hall with Olivia close behind him, her mouth hanging open. Timmons and Vazquez were already on their feet. He pointed at them. "Down to the MedBay! Now!

"Fuck! Let me grab a weapon. If that bug's loose, I'll smash it good!" Timmons cried. He ran to the wall, pulled off a fire extinguisher. "Like a fuckin' cock-a-roach."

"Come on!" Petry ran out of the room.

Vazquez shot Olivia a glance before he and Timmons went jogging out into the corridor. She ran after them, heart pounding in her chest, and found that they'd already reached the stairwell at the end of the hall.

Frank called out again over the speakers, "For gods'sake, get down here! Hurry!"

She broke out from the bottom of the stairwell and spun to run toward the MedBay, her breath caught in her throat. Ahead of her, gathered in the corridor, Timmons and Petry spoke to a frazzled, bloodied Frank.

"He grabbed him! He grabbed him and… and just…"

"Who? What happened?" Petry asked.

"Wilcox. We brought him something to eat. He lost his mind, went berserk, grabbed Spencer, and he … he went down to L1." The tall, gangly man grimaced, shook his head. "I wasn't going to go down there alone!"

Timmons brandished his fire extinguisher, looked back and forth in the hallway. "How'd he get there? The stairwell?"

"No, he…" Frank pointed down the hall.

Olivia froze up as she realized he was pointing at her. No, he was pointing past her. She slowly stepped to the side and turned around to see the elevator doors had been pried open two feet, dark within.

"How do you know he went down?"

Frank shuddered. "I heard Spencer screaming – below."

"Fuck, he's lost it," Timmons muttered.

"Frank, do you have anything that'd knock him out? I do, but it's all the way on L5." Petry eyed the other man.

"I have… sedatives. Strong sedatives."

"Get one ready to dose him up."

"I don't think it'll work on him, Bill. If you'd seen him…"

"Just get it ready." His lips pulled back and Petry looked between Timmons and Vazquez. "Looks like it's just us for now. Ms. Nelson, you can assist Mr. Frank and let the other guys know what's going on when they show up here, any second now. We're going down to L1."

Timmons cursed. "Fuck my life."

In the dark MedBay, broken glass under her feet, Olivia assisted Frank in preparing a syringe of the sedative he'd spoken of only minutes before. They both eyed it warily when he'd finished, and he exhaled shakily. She attempted to follow him when he stalked out of the room. He stopped at the stairwell, glaring at her with dark, narrowed eyes.

"What do you think you're doing?"

"I'm going with you," she said.

"No, you should go back up and wait." Frank opened the stairwell door, stopped again. "I mean it. You have no idea what he's become."

"I can handle myself, I promise. Please, Mr. Frank, let me come with you," Olivia pleaded.

He frowned, nodded stiffly. "Fine."

They descended the steps together and came out on L1, the level dimly lit with sputtering, flashing lights. The tube lamps along the ceiling had been smashed, the drop paneling knocked to the floor. Cries erupted from the lab up ahead and Olivia broke out into a sprint, Frank outpacing her and reaching the doors well before she got halfway down the corridor.

The thick glass doors had been pulled off their hinges, the one hanging loosely like a broken jaw. What was left of the chain had been tossed aside, the links pulled apart at the broken ends. Shards of glass sparkled on the linoleum floor.

"Holy shit," Frank hissed.

Olivia rushed to join him, stepping through the wreckage to enter the lab. Ceiling lights had been shattered, knocked out, destroyed, rending half the room dark, shrouded in churning shadows. Toward the back, the massive glass tunnel with the chamber resting inside gleamed. The chains remained, the padlock intact. To the right, in the squirming void, something moved into the light. Her heart skipped a beat at the sight of it.

It was Wilcox… but it wasn't.

While there were patches of skin visible on his face and chest, most of his body was covered in that *thing* – that black, intricate, segmented, mechanical and organic thing.

Not an insect, not a machine. Sawblades had erupted from his arms. Sharp protrusions along his calves had torn his pantlegs to shreds. He crouched, showed off metallic teeth, and opened his gaping black mouth, jaw dislocating as he shrieked. He'd dragged something with him into the light and now loomed over it – something limp and red and white. A human shape, still and lifeless.

That shape on the floor was familiar. Horror washed over her, stunned her into silence. She recognized that overbite, that wild hair. It was Spencer Hersch, his stomach ripped open to expose loops of gray intestines, his head turned the wrong way, off kilter. The dark, deep bruising around his neck suggested an ugly break.

The Wilcox-thing hunched down, contorted his shoulders, and focused those unsettling, shiny black eyes on her. Those eyes were still his, even if they were the color of wet ink. He made a clicking sound, a low whine following – a whimper in his own voice, choking.

"Fuck!" Timmons jumped in while the creature appeared distracted and swung the fire extinguisher. It struck the Wilcox-thing dead in the temple with a loud theatrical THONK, knocking him over onto the floor. The cry that came out of Wilcox was pitifully human, and he wailed as Timmons began to pummel his body. In that wailing, she heard the words 'please' and 'stop'.

Frank shoved Olivia back out into the hall. She forced her way back into the room, face hot. She wanted to tell him off but couldn't speak. Instead, she stared at Timmons as he shouted angrily, words slurred, and attacked Wilcox. There was hardly a struggle at all. Wilcox had completely frozen up, curled into a fetal position on the floor as Timmons slammed the fire extinguisher against his back, his side, his head.

A horrendous, agonized sob broke from Wilcox's throat,

his clawed fingers digging at the sides of his rutted, sinewy face. Bits of the parasite came out of his flesh, the blood less red and more amber, like thick tree sap. Oilier. Yellowing like sun baked resin.

Vazquez dove in, hooked Hersch by his underarms, and dragged him a few feet, clear of the fray. Petry and Frank ran forward, dropped down to check on Hersch. A few seconds after he pressed his fingers against the young man's purple throat, Frank blubbered, shook his head violently.

"You fucking! Piece! Of shit!" Timmons hollered, sharp face red and sweaty as he bludgeoned Wilcox. On the last blow, something cracked, the snap of bones muffled, waterlogged.

"Stop it!" Frank appeared beside Timmons, pushed him aside. He fell to one knee next to Wilcox, shoving the syringe into an exposed patch of skin along his neck, close to the jugular. Tears in his eyes, his jaw working madly, Frank held out a hand to shield the creature on the floor. "Joe, stop it! Stop! He's down!"

"I'll make sure he damn well stays down!"

"What happened?" Olivia cried, watching as Frank checked on Wilcox. She approached until Petry stopped her. "Hersch, he's… he's dead, isn't he?"

"He got through the lab doors, got in here," Petry said, breaths heaving. "We found him in here, having some sort of… meltdown. He killed Hersch. Tossed him around like a doll. He fucking killed him."

Vazquez wiped at his own face, glasses in his hand. "Dammit. Spencer, man…"

Stepping around Petry, Olivia made her way over to where Frank crouched over the creature. In better lighting, she could see it was Wilcox's placid face, his eyes closed. That parasite had grown deeper into him, an elaborate shell made from thousands of smaller, working parts. Some portions were symmetrical and others not so much. Spiraling designs ran across his new, harder skin where it had assimilated the original, pale flesh. He kicked feebly and went limp, eyelashes fluttering.

"It worked," Petry whispered.

"Great." Timmons raised the fire extinguisher.

"I said stop!" Frank cried. "Dammit Joe, this man is sick. You can't just smash his head in! That's murder!"

Timmons snarled. "He murdered Spencer. Fuck, he's not even a man anymore, Frank. Look at him! He's… he's a bug too! The thing on his back is still there, it's bigger, and now he's the same thing. He's a fuckin' alien bug. And he's dangerous."

Wert, Ursov, Lee, and Mitchell spilled into the lab, their eyes wide and their expressions lost. They each reacted at the same time, Wert loping forward to kneel stiffly beside Hersch.

"Oh no. No no… What happened? Spencer?"

"Wilcox killed him, Larry," Timmons hissed. "He's a fuckin' monster. Look at him. Just look."

Mitchell turned away without a word, covered his face. He walked back out the door, head low.

"We should kill him," Ursov said.

"We can't," Wert muttered, shaking his head. As he struggled to stand, he met Timmons' accusatory glare with one of his own. "We can't kill him, Joe. We've got to lock him back up again. Chain him up."

"He tore the chains apart, Larry. Like fuckin' silly string."

"Yeah, we saw it ourselves," Petry said. "Larry, if you'd seen it too, you'd get it. We have to kill him. Consider it a mercy. Look at the son'uva'bitch, man. He's sick."

Timmons licked his lips, slumped forward. "And he killed Spencer. He killed Spencer."

"I know you want to kill him, and I know why! But we

can't. We… we can't because he's…" Wert stopped himself.

"'Cause he's a company man, right?! 'Cause he's Brett Chamber's lapdog?! Is that it?!" Timmons shouted. "Are you fucking kidding me?!"

"No, it's because he's sick, not in his right mind! Killin' begets killin' unless we stop it right here! We make it so he can't hurt anyone else while we wait for help!" Wert hollered, his face red. "I don't give two shits about who he is!"

Timmons forced a loud, sharp laugh. "Oh, I bet!"

"No more killin'!"

"He's right!" Frank said. "He's right, Joe. No more killing."

"We'll lock him in the RME cage," Wert stated.

"No way, you can't put him there!" Timmons shot back, clutching tight to the fire extinguisher.

"Then the MedBay again. But we chain him up – heavy duty. Barricade the doors. Bolt them down. We do that. We leave him in there until help comes, and we let them figure out what to do."

Olivia stepped forward. "That would kill him too, Mr. Wert."

"Yeah, maybe," he said, turning to her. "I'd rather that than just smash his brains in. I can't risk having him out. I can't kill him either. We'll wait until help comes. They'll know what to do."

Before she could speak again, Vazquez took her shoulder and gave it a squeeze. She peered back at him, and he shook his head, pulled her away and toward the door.

Olivia went with him quietly.

Spencer Hersch was wrapped up and placed in the deep freezer, much to Frank's displeasure. The tall man fretted, paced the corridor outside of the mess hall, and rambled to himself. Olivia watched, standing alone many yards away, her mind a blank and her tongue numb.

"It's for his family," Petry said, placing a hand on his friend's arm. "Rob, he looks bad enough. Imagine if we left him out, man."

Timmons called over from where he stood near the stairwell doors. "Gonna need you in MedBay in a few minutes, Frank. Need your head on, brother. Come on."

Olivia walked with Wert, Timmons, Mitchell, and Lee back down to L1. She assisted where she could as they dragged the welding equipment over from the RME cage.

Back up they went, hauling the heavy tools up the steps.

A disheveled Frank met them at MedBay and opened the door, peeked in at the darkness first. On went the flashlight in his shaking hand. He went in, leading the way, and knelt awkwardly over Wilcox's lifeless body. Another dose of sedative was administered.

Timmons glared down at the unconscious man-creature on the floor, seemingly lost in a trance as he shone his own flashlight over the body. He lifted the wireless drill clutched in his other hand and pulled the trigger, letting it whir loudly.

"Sir?" Lee eyed him.

"Use every foot of the 80-grade that we got on this asshole," Timmons said.

"We used a lot of it the first time around – need to save some for the door. I think twenty-five foot'll do for this shit-head."

Thunder rolled. Olivia pointed a flashlight directly at Wilcox, tracing the spotlight along his form. Her gaze moved over the reticulated network of dark, dull segments that ran across, covered up, and delved into his body, his face. They ran through his hair, to his temples, down his jaw. His teeth were the color and texture of polished pewter. Those patterns and designs decorated every inch of the creature's shell – interwoven machine parts connecting the organic carapace of some unworldly mechanical insect. It was assimilating him. Swallowing him up. Growing and building on his flesh, into his flesh. The way he laid on his back with his hands above his head, breathing with jutting, accentuated ribs, revealed a set of symmetrical, knobby tumors under his armpits. Each growth sported a tiny claw. She could see it clearly now. He wasn't just wearing it; he was becoming it.

"Do it," Wert said. "Then secure this room. Lock it down tight."

An hour had passed, and she attempted to eat, lightheaded and scattered as she was. Olivia picked at her food in the mess hall, listened to the sound of the men as they shouted back and forth, their voices echoing in the stairwell. She heard them working one level below, the power tools whirring and thrumming.

Vazquez entered and took a seat beside her, his hair uncombed. Folding his arms, he leaned forward on them. "Hey, Olivia, can we talk?"

She set her fork down on her plate. "Yeah."

"Not here."

Olivia frowned. "What's going on?"

"I want to talk to you in private. In the IT room."

"Why?"

"Just 'cause. Come on."

Sok anxiously tapped his fingers on the desk as he saw her walk through the door. He stood, bowed slightly, and cleared his throat. Behind the shine of his glasses, his dark eyes blinked frenetically, the lids red and fatigued. "Oh, that was fast. Hello again, Ms. Nelson."

"Mr. Sok, you're still awake?"

"Haven't been to bed yet."

"Just call her Olivia, Dennis. Same for you, Olivia. That's Dennis. I can't stand this mister-miss-missus crap."

"Ah hah," Sok began. "He means it!"

"So, why am I here?" she asked.

"Dennis, why don't you tell her?"

"Me? Oh, well, alright. Ah…" Sok sat down again and gestured toward his computer. "Well, as you know, I have access to all of the cameras."

"Did you get the cams on Big Tooth up and running?" Olivia asked, taking a seat as well. "Did you see something down there?"

"Ah, no."

"That's not what we're here to talk about," Vazquez stated.

"What are we here to talk about?"

Sok hesitated. "You."

"Me?"

Vazquez pulled up a chair beside her and spun it around, eyes missing their typical, jovial warmth. His smile had completely evaporated. "Olivia, you visited Wilcox."

Her face flushed. "You saw it on the camera."

"Dennis did."

"I found it while going through the footage from last night before the attack. You went in a little after midnight and left when he, um, began acting erratically," Sok stated.

"I did, yes."

"You didn't tell anyone, Olivia?" Vazquez asked, face twisting. "You didn't think to tell any of us about his behavior? About the way he was changing? Why?"

"It… it was late and…"

"One call, Olivia. One call was all it would have taken. We would have known, been warned. Spence would still be-

"

"You're blaming me for his death?"

Vazquez's lips moved silently. He looked away, jaw clenched. "His death might have been prevented if we'd known and taken precautions. Take that however you want."

"I'm sorry. I was scared," she said. "He wasn't violent last night – just feverish, sick, saying strange things."

"He turned violent today." He wiped his eyes under his glasses. "Dammit."

Olivia's face crumpled, the first tear sliding down her cheek. She rubbed at her face. "When he called me to MedBay, he said he was scared and alone. He didn't think anyone else cared but me because I was nice to him. I thought whatever was happening to him was killing him, not making him stronger. I didn't say anything because he didn't seem dangerous. I didn't say anything because I thought he was dying. Honestly, when Frank first called, I thought he'd found Wilcox dead."

"I see…"

"I didn't think…" She pressed her hand to her mouth.

"You should've said something. Anything. Even if they'd thought he was sick, at least they'd have gone in on high alert, you know? Seeing the way he moved on camera scared the shit out of me. I would have called Frank." Vazquez clenched his fists, swallowing thickly. "I would have called anyone."

"I'm sorry."

He lowered his chin. "My friend is dead and you're sorry."

"I can't go back and change it!" Olivia cried.

"I know!" Hands shaking, Vazquez took off his glasses and cleaned them with the edge of his shirt. A slow breath left his lips. "I… I know you can't change it. I know. I just wish you'd done …anything."

"So do I," she whispered.

He squeezed the bridge of his nose. "Dammit…"

Sok watched quietly from his chair, hands folded, and looked back and forth between Vazquez and Olivia. "Ms. Nelson is not the only one to blame for what happened to Spencer. While she was visiting Wilcox, I was working on getting the connection up and running again. I wasn't watching the cameras."

"You're not a machine, Dennis," Vazquez said, frowning at the other man. "You can't do it all at the same time. You didn't know."

"Fixing the satellite link right now, during a storm, was such a useless waste of my time. I should have been monitoring the MedBay." Sok licked his lips, his jaw tight. "If you're going to blame her, blame me too."

Vazquez sighed. "Shit, I'm not going to blame anyone."

"I'll tell them," she whispered. "They deserve to know the truth. That it's my fault. I'll tell them, Austin."

"No, don't." His hand went to her shoulder. "It won't change anything now, them knowing. Just, keep it between us – us three. Okay, Dennis? Dennis, can you keep this between us three? All of it. Everything we said in this room."

Sok swallowed, nodding. "I can, yes."

"I don't know if I feel right keeping that secret."

"We all make mistakes, Olivia," Vazquez said.

She wiped at her eyes, chin lifted. "My mistake cost someone their life. You said it yourself."

"I didn't bring you here to yell at you. I just wanted to know the truth. Spencer was our friend." Vazquez offered her a box of tissues. He took one after she did and blew his nose. "You thought the suit was dying, I get it."

She sniffled. "What did he do after I left?"

Sok leaned over to meet her eyes. "He... convulsed violently and lay still. Like he had died. After ten minutes, he started to... twitch and jerk around. He got up and went to the desk and did some writing like nothing had happened. Then he lied down on the cot. He tosses and turns the rest of the night until they bring him his breakfast. Then, well, you know..."

Her bleary eyes narrowed. "What did he write?"

"Ah, the cameras aren't that good..." Sok shrank.

"It was on the desk?" she asked.

Sok shook his head. "Ah, probably on the floor now."

"And there to stay," Vazquez said. "It was probably nothing, Olivia. Maybe a goodbye letter to his family. A long apology for being a douchebag even. Who knows."

"I'm sorry."

"I said I didn't bring you here to yell at you..."

Her brows knit. "And they haven't called to us."

"Hmm?"

"What made him lose his mind, go berserk? And why did he just lie down and let Timmons wail on him back there, after tearing apart chains and busting down locked doors?" Olivia lifted her head, her eyes shining.

"I don't know."

"They haven't called to us yet because they're too weak, but he's got one of them on his back, Austin. They haven't called to us, but maybe they're calling to him, to the creature on him. He was trying to take Spencer down to S1. That's why he was down in the lab." She sat up straight, face growing stern. "And when Timmons hit him in the head, they lost their hold on him."

"Those eggs are controlling Wilcox?" Vazquez blinked.

Olivia nodded. "We need to hold a meeting ...now."

Chapter 11

They gathered in the mess hall, sitting at the long tables. Olivia couldn't blame them for not wanting to use the meeting room down on L2, seeing as how the MedBay was currently occupied by something they wanted to keep at more than an arm's length away. Even the unflappable Ursov glanced anxiously at the open doors leading into the corridor, his heavy brows furrowed.

Sok, obviously exhausted, slouched in his seat.

"We're all here. So, what is it, Ms. Nelson?" Wert asked.

She sucked on her teeth, collecting herself. "I want to talk about those eggs down there in the drill chamber."

"They're locked behind a bulkhead. I told you we closed down the entire wing. You can't even access the pressure chamber without that key in your pocket," he replied.

"But they're still there," she said. "I hypothesized that they were too weak to call to you again, or else they would have kept calling until you reached them. And there hasn't been another trance incident involving any of you in this room."

"Any of us in this room…" Vazquez echoed.

Petry took a hard swig of his coffee. "Your point, Ms. Nelson?"

"My point," she continued, "is that they might be too weak to call to you, but maybe they're able to communicate with that creature on Wilcox. It's the same species, right? They called to it, and it triggered him, sent him on a mission to bring them another host."

"Jeeee-sus christy," Timmons mused.

Ursov grew pensive. "They called to their sibling on him to get to us? They controlled his body?"

"Yes, that's what I believe happened," Olivia said.

"Well, let them try again," Petry said, his one visible eye narrowed to a thin, angry slit. "He's wrapped in twenty-five feet of chain behind reinforced walls. And that door is not opening without bringing in some heavy machinery to cut it apart."

"I saw what he did to that type of chain, Mr. Petry," she said. "You did too. You all saw. If he wants to get out, he'll get out."

Timmons snorted. "And ya'll shot me down when I had the chance to bash his brains in. Hope you're happy with yourselves, y'damn softies."

"There's still a man in there, Joe," Frank said. "I saw it in his eyes when you had him on the floor. He was terrified. Just as confused as we were. Confused and in pain."

Olivia nodded. "Exactly. He's still in there. I saw it too. We have to do something now, while he's incapacitated."

"What are you suggesting, Ms. Nelson?" Wert asked.

Petry muttered to himself. "Mercy kill…"

"Boy-o boy. Now we're talkin', Bill…"

"We'll need to cut the rebar we just welded…"

"Hah, we need that hotworks permit signed?"

"Stop it! I'm not suggesting that we kill him. I think what we need to do is go down there and destroy those eggs before they call to him again. Or, God forbid, help arrives, and they find them and end up parasitized." Crossing her arms, she eyed each man at the table.

"You want to destroy the eggs?" Ursov asked. "How? They survived in deep rock, deep cold, for years and years. How do you destroy something like that?"

"Fire, as a general rule, kills most things, Yuri," she replied.

"You want to go set S1 on fire?" Lee's face screwed.

"The drill chamber, yes."

"This is a multi-billion-dollar installation, Ms. Nelson,"

Petry said, his one eye widening in disbelief. "Do you have any idea what Samos-Barnes would do to us, as the leadership team, if we allowed such a ludicrous thing to happen?"

"The alternative is waiting until he breaks out again and kills all of us, Mr. Petry. Or being responsible for the rescue team being attacked by the creatures. Personally, neither of those options appeal to my conscience. How about yours?"

"Huh…"

"We have enough gas to do it," Mitchell said quietly.

Lee nodded. "I'd sleep easier knowing they were gone."

"Sure, go light 'em up. Sounds like a blast. You can roast some marshmallows while you're at it. Oh, but, um, jeez…" Timmons shook his head, lit a cigarette at the table. "Who's gonna go down there? Because it sure as hell won't be me."

"I'm not up to it either," Petry admitted. "I haven't been feeling too well since… this." He gestured toward his patched eye.

"I will go," Ursov said. "I am the one who broke them free."

"It wasn't you, Yuri; it was those eggs controlling you," Olivia said, her face warm. She swallowed. "But I'm going."

"Huh? No, you can't do that," Vazquez exclaimed.

"I have to."

"Olivia, you… you don't have to, okay? Trust me. You don't have to." He implored to her with his deep brown eyes.

"I want to."

"Better you than me," Timmons said.

Wert lowered his head. "I guess I should go too."

"I wouldn't, Larry," Petry said. "Not with your bum leg. If anything goes wrong, you wouldn't be able to run away."

Lee sighed loudly, dramatically. "I'll go."

"Dammit, Casey," Vazquez groaned.

"What? They'll need help lugging the cans. Besides, I know a thing or two about controlled fires. You think I haven't started a few in my day?" Lee forced a smile.

"Then I'm coming too."

"Hell no, Austin. You're sittin' your butt in the IT room with Dennis and closing the bulkheads remotely. Can't do it from the control room if we're starting a fire, can we?" His smirk brightened his face somehow and Lee winked at his friend. "Just need you to close the doors behind us, guy."

"Uff, sure, Case."

"One more set of hands wouldn't hurt though. Mitchell, you up for it, man?" Lee asked.

"No, I'm sorry, Lee. I'm not up for it. I can't do it."

"Right, sure, it's all good."

Frank exhaled. "I'm glad we pulled the medical cabinet. I'll get the burn kit ready."

"Give me a little more credit than that, Frank," Lee said.

"When are you doing this?" Petry asked.

"As soon as feasibly possible," Olivia replied.

Lee stood, stretched. "That sounds like longhand for *right now* if you ask me. I'm going up to the shack to grab some cans of gas. If you guys could prep the chamber, that'd be swell."

Ursov also moved to his feet. "I will join you, friend."

Outside, thunder rolled.

Olivia clenched her jaw, soaked to the bone despite her raincoat as she helped carry one of the cumbersome gas cans from the shack to the metal stairwell leading back down from the roof. The rain pelted her, the wind shoving her from side to side. Out in the elements, exposed to the wrath of the storm assaulting the rig, she shuddered in anticipation. It wasn't the thunder that terrified her. It wasn't even the biting wind that threatened to send her flying out into the tumultuous waves crashing all around them, the mist thick and salty in the smothering air. No, it was the coming task that filled her with dread. The cleansing fire needed to reach those eggs. She had to help bring it there. Legs already weak, she fumbled, rushed forward.

Ursov carried two cans, one in each hand, and hadn't bothered to wear any protective gear. Rain streamed down the sides of his face, down his back and arms. He turned to her, offered his elbow to brace her as she nearly slipped on the grated steps.

"Careful, Olivia, the steps are slippery," he said, his voice low and nearly inaudible under the roar of the storm.

She spit rainwater. "Thank you!"

It was an arduous journey down to L1, each flight of steps taking a little more energy out of her. The dread remained, a tightness in her chest and stomach. She thought of those black eggs and shivered. Her imagination reminded her of Wilcox's black eyes and dislocated jaw. Had she seen concentric rows of those gunmetal gray teeth in that mouth of his — shark teeth growing in from above the mottled gumline — or had her fear addled mind been playing tricks on her in the dark? She shook herself off.

The chamber was ready when they arrived.

Down the tunnel to the Pit, they went. Her ears popped and her stomach clenched. The entire way down, Olivia stared upward at the chamber lights circling the ceiling and was thankful that there were no windows to the black sea surrounding them.

The bulkheads had been opened for them. Carrying her can of gas, she followed Lee and Ursov through the ocean floor facility, past the finished sections and down into the tunnels.

A few times, she nearly slipped on the floor mats.

It felt like a longer walk this time until they reached the drill chamber and the gaping hole in the wall. The air felt colder now. Stifling. She could see her breath.

In the tripod lights, she saw the piles of black eggs. They hadn't stirred or moved as far as she could tell. They simply lay there, waiting. Waiting to be picked up and handled by something warm. Something living. Her insides flopped, bile rising in the back of her throat.

At once, Lee and Ursov began dumping the gas onto the eggs, careful to avoid stepping on the things as they circled the immediate area. The smell was sickening.

"Sorry, girl. I am so sorry," Ursov said, glancing sadly at the drill. He continued to pour the gas, shaking his head.

Olivia opened her can, let the cap swing free, and hefted it to the side to pour its contents over the eggs as well. She neared the break in the rock wall and stared at the source. They'd spilled out of that shallow hole. That shallow hole with the protruding, accentuated rib-like growths with those striated inner walls like…

Like the inside of something that had once been alive. A hollowed shell of a larger version of those creatures. A being that had ribs, a spine. She could see it now as she drew closer and focused her eyes, the fog of her breath dissipating as her throat tightened.

Dried yellow resin clung to the blackened edges of those ribs. Olivia gulped on air, took a step backward. In the shadows thrown by the tripod lights, her imagination might've tricked her again. What appeared to be clawed fingers jutted from the rock on either side of that crevice. Above the hole, a frozen black mouth, screaming.

"Olivia, are you done? Empty?" Lee called. "I'm ready to

light it up and run, if you are."

"Ah, yeah," she replied, voice thin.

"This close, if they sang to us, we'd be helpless," Ursov muttered, pulling an unlit flare from his coat.

"Best reason to torch 'em now, Yuri," Lee said.

"Yeah." Olivia pivoted, set the empty can on the tunnel floor, and stalked away from the hole in the wall.

Yuri snapped the flare, set it ablaze. With a smile on his face, his gold tooth gleaming in the red flame, he began to back away with great eagerness, waving his free hand. "Let us finish this."

They reached the bulkhead, and he chucked the flare at the eggs. Immediately, they ignited, the fire a bright flash before it erupted, flooding over the piles, and engulfing them.

"Hell yeah!" Lee exclaimed.

Olivia smiled, elated at the sight. Sweat that had begun to cool on her brow warmed as the heat of the fire spilled out onto her. She walked backward toward the bulkhead, wanting to watch.

A tiny, fizzy squeal keened in the crackling fire. Then another and another. A chorus of miniscule shrieks filled the cavern. The little black eggs began to roll, bounce, and hop about like corn kernels on a hot plate.

"Uch!" Lee cried.

The first of those black eggs erupted and a tiny dark shape squirmed free, dove from the flames. A small insect, silverfish-like, wriggled and skittered away from the fire.

A second egg burst, another creature skittering out. Another and another and another. More tiny shrieks. Within seconds, there were dozens of the things fleeing, creeping about. Three creatures dashed across the floor toward the bulkhead, charging right at them.

"Fuck!" Lee shouted. "Run! Run for it!"

Olivia spun, forgetting the stinging soreness in her legs from the arduous journey down to the drill chamber. The sudden white-hot shock of adrenaline flooding her veins had numbed her to the pain and she pivoted on her heel.

Breath caught, she broke into a run behind Ursov and Lee, terror and desperation stabbing at her guts as she watched them easily outpace her, leaving her behind.

"Hey!" she called.

They did not turn back.

Tears blinded her, her feet flying, the shrieking tinny and pitched behind her. "Don't leave me! Please don't leave me!"

She heard a rolling thud from behind her. The chamber bulkhead had been shut. And yet those shrill, tiny cries were growing louder. She stole a glance backward and saw a mass, a mist, a swarm of those black, silverfish-like creatures sweeping the tunnel in her wake.

They were chasing her.

Facing forward, pushing herself harder, she saw no sign of Ursov or Lee. She was alone in the tunnel, running, sweating, panting as her heart pounded, her lungs burned. "Don't leave me, please!"

Ahead, the next bulkhead was open. She ran through it, slipped a little on the flooring, and continued onward. There had been a tunnel to the right of her and she prayed that she hadn't made a wrong turn somewhere. It had been a straight shot, hadn't it? Had there been any turns in the path?

She couldn't remember having made any turns either time they'd traveled to the dig chamber. Olivia gasped, struggling to breathe, and ran into the next area through another bulkhead, those things close on her tail. On the right, the drill control room, empty.

In front of her, Ursov and Lee, beckoning her onward.

"Come on, Olivia!" Ursov hollered.

He was a lighthouse. A beacon. His thick accent was the most beautiful sound she had ever heard. That gold tooth sparkled as he smiled reassuringly, waved her on. She ran to him, shouted as loud as she could. "I'm coming! They're right behind me, Yuri! They're hundreds of them!"

"Hurry! Bulkheads close too slow! Must make it to the control room, to the chamber, close the door as soon as we get in!" Ursov cried.

They ran up the steps, down another corridor. Olivia felt that her heart might burst at any moment. When she saw the doors to the chamber, another wave of frantic relief passed through her body.

Somewhere distant, deep, something exploded. The ground shook, her footing unsure as the world around her crumbled to dizzying shambles.

They spilled into the chamber room and Lee turned, jogging to the sweeping computer desk on the left. He pressed a few buttons and pointed at the chamber. "Get in!"

Olivia nearly crashed into the glass as the doors began to open. They moved too slowly for her liking. Whirling about, she saw the massive horde of black insects at the end of the corridor, sweeping like a broiling curtain over the walls and ceiling coming toward them. They skittered, unaffected by gravity.

"Close the bulkhead!" she screamed.

Lee pressed another few buttons. The bulkhead whirred, began to close, and then stopped. "Fuck! It's jammed."

"Figures," Ursov said, leaning close to Olivia.

"What do we do?"

"I shut the door myself." He patted her shoulder with a large hand and sprung toward the door. Getting his fingers onto the metal edges, he began to wrench the door downward, pulling hard. The muscles in his arms stood out like steel cords.

The glass tunnel doors had opened enough for Olivia to step onto the inner platform and access the pressure chamber. It slid to the side immediately, welcoming her in. She spun, saw Lee jumping in beside her. Her eyes widened at the sight of Ursov stomping on a black, skittering insect. "Yuri, get in!"

"Close the door and go!" he hollered.

Another rumble shook the walls. A hiss approached. A sizzling, frothing, furious hiss that, as it grew louder, turned into a sloshing roar that echoed in her skull. Olivia clutched her throat. "What is that?"

"Breach! The tunnels are flooding!" Lee cried. "Yuri, for the love of God, get in there and let's go!"

Ursov stomped on another bug. Then, the swarm swept in through the bottom of the open bulkhead and covered him. They engulfed him, the writhing horde of bugs slithering, skittering, swallowing up every part of him where he stood in the doorway.

Olivia screamed.

"God dammit!" Lee slammed his fist against the panel and the glass doors closed, leaving Ursov and the creatures on the other side, sealed off from them.

Ursov did not fall or flounder. He continued, completely enveloped in the swarm, to pull down on the bulkhead, closer and closer to the floor. The things must have been attaching to him or were trying to, fighting to find his spine, wrestling with one another for ownership of his massive, powerful body. His blood splattered and dripped on the linoleum.

Olivia sobbed, backing toward the pressure chamber. "Yuri!"

"We've gotta go. Get in!" Lee gave her a shove.

Frothy, dirty water flowed into the room from under the

bulkhead and Ursov staggered slightly from the strength of the surge. He fought against the current briefly before stepping away from the door. The creatures thrashed, massed up, fled from the water and up his legs to his torso.

As Lee forced her into the chamber, his body partially blocking the scene in the control room, Olivia saw many of the small, insect bodies wriggle in the water, contorting madly, their shells seeming to disintegrate.

She fell against the chamber floor and Lee shut the door. Staring up at him, her jaw worked soundlessly for a few seconds before her lungs swelled. "Yuri!"

Lee engaged something and the air grew lighter, thin. "I'm overriding the initiation sequence. We don't have time to wait. S1 is flooding. Just hold tight... hold tight."

The chamber hummed loudly and jumpstarted upward. Not bothering to strap himself in, Lee stood at the closed door with his forehead pressed to the metal. Olivia couldn't move; her aching body had shut down. She clung to the floor and sobbed.

Chapter 12

The silence was heavy in the mess hall as Olivia sat slouched at one of the long tables. She'd barely noticed the bruises on her arms or the cut on her face. Frank had taken care of the latter for her, the bandage pulling at the skin of her cheek. Her body ached from the expedited trip up from S1.

No one seemed interested in their dinner.

Finally, Timmons grunted, ran his fingers through his hay-colored hair. "It's too fucking quiet. Someone say something."

"Like what, Joe?" Mitchell asked.

"I don't know. Anything. I can't stand this."

"It's done. Yuri did it. He got the job done," Wert said.

Lee coughed. "He always did. It didn't go the way we'd planned, but he got it done."

"I'm sorry. Those creatures moved too fast for us to close the doors in time," Vazquez said, cleaning his glasses with a small cloth. His eyes were tired, the lids raw. "We couldn't risk sealing anyone in."

"It's not your fault, Vazquez. Not you, not Sok. It was the damn door. That one always got hitched and needed a swift kick," Timmons said, lighting a cigarette. "Criminy, cheap ass company."

"I didn't know they'd activate like that," Olivia said. "I thought it was just body heat. I didn't think the fire would-"

Frank cut her off. "No one knew. It's okay."

"It is what it is and it's over," Wert stated.

"With the eggs gone, maybe Wilcox will regain his humanity." Frank shrugged as the others glanced his way.

Timmons balked. "Whoa, we're not lettin' him out, are we?"

"Well, no, but we could check on him…"

"I don't want to risk it," Wert said. "The MedBay stays sealed. He's still got one of those creatures on him, and that makes him dangerous enough."

"He'll die in there," Olivia breathed. "Alone. In the dark."

"Good riddance," Timmons spat.

"Three days 'til pickup," Petry mused. "Just need to wait it out. The storm'll have passed the day before the boat is due, so the waters'll be nice and calm. It'll be a sunny day, I know it."

"They died in the water," Olivia said.

"Hmm?" Wert turned her way.

"The seawater. It hurt the hatchlings. Like it melted them or something. I saw it down in the control room."

"Interesting." Lips parting, Wert seemed to ponder.

Timmons eyed her, exhaled smoke. "Maybe we can toss our good friend Wilcox overboard and see if it works the same on him."

She sniffed. "I wasn't suggesting that at all."

"Small ones aren't built as tough, I'll bet. That's why they need a host," Frank said.

"I know… we could fill some buckets, cut open the MedBay, run in together, and dump seawater on him like one of those, eh, what're they called? Ice-bucket challenges? Yeah, like one of those. That'd be a time, eh!"

"Quiet, Joe," Wert warned.

"I'm just makin' conversation here. I'll take this over the dead silence any day."

"I think I preferred the silence," Mitchell stated.

"You prefer a'lotta things over talkin' it out, Mark." Timmons took in a long drag from his cigarette, bared his teeth.

"If you say so."

"How's that coffee? Smells a little strong."

"Fuck you, Joe."

"Don't talk to me like that, Marky. No way. Not you."

Wert sighed. "Stop it."

Olivia stared at the food on her plate. The yellow of the eggs had a sickening hue to them. She swallowed back bile, thinking about the shell that had to crack to release the yolk.

Timmons laughed dryly. "Sure thing, boss man."

"I wonder," she began, eyes heavy lidded. "...what they were. Where they came from."

"I'm sure they'll do all kinds of tests on the one the suit is toting around," Vazquez said.

Timmons exhaled smoke. "My money's on aliens."

"It's an aggressive parasitic organism, that's all we know. Maybe it is a damn alien," Petry muttered. "At least we're only dealing with one now."

Timmons scowled. "A big one."

"The eggs came out of a pocket in the rock, right?" She paused, saw that the others were looking at her, and cleared her throat. "I got up close and I swear it looked like the inside of an animal infected with a bigger version of that parasite. There was some kind of residue leaking from the cavity. It was still alive somehow, holding the eggs. Maybe it was in stasis like the eggs were, trapped in the rock until the drill turned on a second time."

"You think Big Tooth killed it?" Wert asked.

"Maybe," Olivia replied. "You woke up after that. Right after that. The drill punched through, spilled her eggs."

"Her?" Petry asked.

"Their mother," she said.

Petry grimaced. "Mother? What now?"

"Maybe it wasn't the eggs calling to you..."

"Jeeee-sus," Timmons exclaimed, grinning widely at Frank. "Rob, what're the symptoms of decompression sickness again?"

"The entire point of going down there to burn those things was to destroy them before they called us again," Petry snapped. "What are you suggesting, Ms. Nelson?"

"I'm not… I'm just saying, the song stopped when you killed it, so, I'm…" Her chin lowered. "It could have been her, or the eggs, so no matter what, we needed to burn them."

"Fuck, d'yah think Wilcox is gonna lay a bunch'a eggs?"

"No, Mr. Timmons, I don't," she replied.

"And why's that, Ms. Bug-Expert?"

Olivia flinched. "Because the eggs were inside of the creature down there. She wouldn't have been very mobile, not at her size. They spilled out when her body was ruptured. Also, if the species could reproduce asexually, it wouldn't have compelled Wilcox to drag Spencer Hersch down to the drill chamber, to the other eggs waiting for hosts."

"Right, of course…"

She continued. "They have to breed somehow. Maybe the species is sexually dimorphic, or maybe they need male and female hosts. They use the host's body, obviously. If it was trying to take one of us down there, it might've been because it needs a mate."

"Gross." Timmons exhaled smoke.

"What do you base any of those assumptions on, Ms. Nelson? Last I checked, you're the OcSaf rep, not a deep-sea biologist," Petry said. "Unless you have some credentials you're hiding somewhere."

"I studied zoology for years – obsessively. I was fixated on it. That's what I base my assumptions on, Mr. Petry."

"Isn't that nice? Well, that's still a whole lot of speculation about a new species we've only seen a glimpse of, Ms. Nelson," Petry said. "We'll let the scientists pick Wilcox apart on their own time, and happily move on with our lives knowing we'll never hear about it again."

"Amen," Timmons quipped.

"I think I'd like to go lie down in my room now," Olivia said, getting out of her chair. "I'm very tired."

"I think we're all tired, Ms. Nelson." Wert nodded.

"I know I am." Lee sighed, eyed his cup of coffee. "Not that I could sleep if I tried. A few more days. Just a few more days."

As she walked toward the door, Olivia turned back and saw Vazquez watching her, his brows knit. She waved weakly at him, and he waved back.

The time on her useless cell read 9:16PM and she couldn't sleep. She imagined him there in the darkness, alone in the MedBay. In the darkness of her cabin, on her bottom bunk, she stared until the swirls in the shadows of her vision adjusted to the low light and allowed her to see the shapes of things in the night. She wondered if his black eyes let him see those shapes better than her human eyes. If his senses were keener somehow, changed. If the pressing isolation hurt, as tight as the chains around him.

She remembered the black swarm that had flooded over Ursov's body in the control room. Each of those small things had been just as hungry, just as desperate to live as the one on Wilcox's back. It had started small, like its siblings, but had grown large on its host.

Rubbing her palm, she looked at her skin, white to her straining eyes. The puncture wound from the bug's sting had faded some. A bruise marked the area of trauma. It must've taken a bite out of her. Would Wilcox had done the same if she hadn't escaped from the MedBay in time?

She clenched her fist.

Outside, sheets of rain continued to pummel the rig. Thunder rolled, shook the room. Olivia forced herself up and dressed.

She walked down the steps to L2, exiting through the doors at the landing. The elevator was closed now, the panel alight. Forgetting that it had existed at all, Olivia chuckled softly to herself.

The storm's rage filled the hall with shivering echoes, and she continued down, passing the left that would have taken her to IT or the meeting room, until she reached the fortified doors of the MedBay. For a moment, she hadn't recognized it at all. They'd bolted down planks of wood and welded rebar into place like a gridded cage across the doors. They'd done one hell of a job, for sure. Nothing would get in; nothing would get out.

Swallowing, she inched closer, leaned to the side, and waited. Rain sputtered and hissed from outside. A low rumble of thunder passed overhead. Olivia pressed her ear to the only part of the glass door still accessible, having to twist slightly to reach it.

After a few seconds, she pulled away and folded her hands in front of herself. "I'm sorry for what's happened to you, Astor. I don't know if you can hear me, but I'm sorry."

Wind howled along the sides of the rig.

Olivia frowned, chin low. "You're not alone, okay? Maybe we didn't exactly… hit it off, but I'm here, and I'll visit you whenever I can, until help arrives."

A muffled clicking surprised her, the source hard to place. The skin along the nape of her neck prickled icily.

She sat by the door, back against the wall, and stared at the scuffed, linoleum floor – the harsh lighting from above made the tiles look as pale as her skin in the dark.

Olivia cleared her throat and began to sing.

Beautiful Dreamer, wake unto me,

Starlight and dewdrops are waiting for thee;
Sounds of the rude world heard in the day,
Lull'd by the moonlight have all passed away!

Beautiful dreamer, queen of my song,
List while I woo thee with soft melody;
Gone are the cares of life's busy throng

Beautiful dreamer, awake unto me!
Beautiful dreamer, awake unto me!

Beautiful dreamer, out on the sea,
Mermaids are chanting the wild Lorelei;
Over the stream let vapors are borne,
Waiting to fade at the bright coming morn.

Beautiful dreamer, beam on my heart,
E'en as the morn on the stream let and sea;
Then will all clouds of sorrow depart,

Beautiful dreamer, awake unto me!
Beautiful dreamer, awake unto me!

On the last verse, she choked on her own voice and clapped her hand over her mouth, tears running down her face. Eyes shut tightly, Olivia shuddered, held it in, held it back.

The rig trembled.

"Don't let it get yah down, Livvie. Don't let it get yah down," she whispered into her palm.

"Olivia."

Her eyes opened and through hot tears she saw Vazquez standing at the end of the corridor. She hadn't heard the chime of the elevator announcing his arrival. He must've taken the stairs as well.

"How long were you standing there?" she asked.

"Long enough." He approached and took a seat beside her in the hall, his back against the wall. "You're visiting him again?"

"It's different this time. I just feel so awful for him. It's dark in there, Austin. He's alone in the dark. Starving to death."

"You feel sorry for him. Wanted to give him some company."

"Right, but I couldn't think of anything to say."

"So, he gets a song."

"Yeah."

"It was a pretty song. Familiar. Can't place it though."

"It's 'Beautiful Dreamer'. My mother used to sing it for me, and at the end, I sang it for her," Olivia said, wiping her eyes.

"It must have a lot of emotional significance."

"I told you I was in an accident a few years ago. That's where I got this plate in my head." She lifted her hair away from above her ear and showed him the scar along her scalp. "I almost died."

"Yeah..."

"After the accident, when I was in the coma... somehow, I remember her singing it to me in the hospital room. Like a dream, I heard her voice... singing that song to let me know I wasn't alone in the darkness. I followed her voice all the way home, and when I woke up in that bed, she was there beside me. She was diagnosed a few months later. After they took her off life support, kept her morphine drip high, she just lay there sleeping. I sang to her to let her know that I was there. To call her home." She paused in reflection, lips parted and eyelids heavy. "No one deserves to suffer alone, in silence, in darkness."

"You're a good person, Olivia."

"I'm having a hard time believing that right now."

Vazquez touched her shoulder. "You are. We're going to make it, okay? Help'll be here in a few days."

"I should try to sleep."

He smiled gently. "So should I, but that ain't happening. Gotta love that insomnia, right?"

"So, you're going to be up for a while is what you're saying?" She searched his eyes, her face growing warmer the longer she stared at him. A small smile appeared on her lips as well.

Vazquez nodded, stood, and offered her his hand.

His mouth tasted good, like she imagined it would. Her fingers glided over the smooth skin of his back, over his shoulders. They kissed hard, tongues meeting, lips meshing. Those kisses turned softer, slower. He pushed his hips against hers and the bunk bed began to creak in rhythm with his movements.

After a particularly loud screech of grinding metal echoed in the cabin, he paused so they could both laugh together, their noses brushing.

"L4 is a ghost town. I think we're good," he whispered in her ear before squeezing her hip. His own began to move again with a slow and determined purpose.

Olivia wrapped her thighs around him, arching on the bottom bunk. His body felt good. He felt good. She moaned through parted lips and shivered when he moaned back at her.

They lay nude on the bed, curled up close together. Her cheek on his chest, his arm around her, cradling her. Idly stroking her thumb across his shoulder, Olivia exhaled, pleasant endorphins still coursing through her veins.

"Well, that happened," he said.

"You didn't see this one coming, did you?"

"I had hopes." Head tilting, he offered her that warm smile of his, eyes sparkling. "Why do you think I was trying to invite you to my room the other night?"

"You lied to me."

"Sorry, I hope you can forgive me."

"I might be able to, given time." Sliding her palm down along his stomach, she stopped at the blankets, where they pooled at his pelvis.

"I should ask where you're from, seeing as how we'll both be blowing this popsicle stand soon. I'll need to come visit you. Oh, yes, I will be visiting you."

"I'm from West Virginia."

"Ew."

"Hey!"

"Sorry, I'm from Cali. I just didn't think you'd be out that far. Wow. I bet it's... nice there, yeah? I didn't mean 'ew' like gross. I meant like, wow, that's far. Huh."

She sighed. "I guess no visits then."

"What? Are you kidding? I might move there."

"Move there? Why?"

He wiggled his eyebrows at her. "To be closer to you."

"Slow it down, Romeo. Darn, we literally just met."

"Oh you," he said, reaching over the side of the bed for his glasses on the floor. Vazquez put them on and blinked at her as if testing the lenses. "Ah, good, still beautiful. Just making sure."

"Goofball," she muttered.

Her door cracked, she stood partially in the hall with him, her nightclothes hanging off of her slender frame. Vazquez had dressed and, besides the bed-messy hair, looked put together, his shirt tucked in. He smiled and they kissed on the lips, him bowing and her pushing up on the balls of her feet.

"You sure you don't want to sleep here tonight?" she asked.

"The bed's too small and I kick. Like a donkey – a literal donkey. I mean, I really roll around. I also can't sleep, so I'd just be lying there with my eyes open for hours and hours. But maybe I could come back if I get tired and take the top bunk. How about that?"

"That would be nice."

"Then that's what I'll do."

"You'll knock softly until I answer and let you in?"

"Or, I mean, you could give me the key…"

"And if you lose it, I won't be able to lock my door."

"I won't lose it."

"You can knock softly. I'm a light sleeper."

Vazquez rolled his eyes. "Fine."

"If you don't come back, I'll understand," she said.

"I'll come back."

Again, they kissed. He gave her a squeeze and walked away, turning at the end of the corridor toward the elevator.

Chapter 13

Though her eyes were tired, her pulse refused to slow, and her skin felt like it was on fire. A good kind of fire. Warm. Alive. Olivia lay in her bed with the reading lamp clamped onto the side of the wood frame, the little bulb bright in the dark room. The book was one she'd read many times. She smiled softly.

A strong crash of thunder shook the entire rig, her room shivering, and, for a moment, she imagined a shriek sounding from below. That smile on her lips faded, her thoughts drifting to the darkness again, where she would float alone, lost.

With the rain thrashing the windows and the wind howling, Olivia found it easy to believe that she'd have heard a cry. A mournful wail joined the roar of the storm, continuing as it lowered, raised, whipped around the platforms outside.

She took in a breath.

The cabin phone rang.

Her pulse jumping, Olivia swung her feet off her bed and darted over to the wall phone. She picked it up in the middle of the second ring, held the speaker close to her ear, the receiver to her lips. For a moment, she merely listened. "Hello?"

The rain pelted the window harder.

Olivia's face twisted up. "Hello, who is this?"

A click. She'd been hung up on.

Head spinning, she blinked at the phone before placing it back on the wall, in its holster. Back to the bed she went, picking up her book from on top of the blankets.

Nestling into her reading position, her expression still vexed, Olivia stared at the words within her book and couldn't, for the life of her, focus on what they were saying. And then, they disappeared into blackness when the reading lamp went out.

"Ah!" She sat up again, reached for her phone and saw that it was no longer charging. Luckily, she had a full battery. Pulling the plug out, Olivia brought up the flashlight function from the main screen and shone it about her cabin.

Grabbing the wall phone, she prepared to call comms but heard nothing through the receiver. It was dead.

She dressed quickly.

Out in the corridor, the emergency lights had kicked on. The facility shuddered, the storm really beating down on her now. Lightning cracked so loud that Olivia felt it in her bones.

She ran down the corridor until she reached the door to cabin 11 and knocked softly. After a few seconds, she knocked a little harder. Wringing her hands in the hall, Olivia looked back and forth, shining her cell light down to send the shadows running.

Sighing, she abandoned his doorstep and stalked back the way she'd come. A cold hand had taken a firm grasp on her heart, her insides churning, and Olivia opened the door to the stairwell.

She'd reached the landing for L3 when she heard the footsteps, saw the lights above her. Stopping, she looked up. The spotlights of several flashlights searched the walls above her.

"Hello?" she called.

"Oh, Olivia! The power's out!" Sok replied.

"Dennis?"

"Some IT team we've got here, eh?" Timmons barked from up there, his laugh dry.

"Could be an RME problem. We don't exactly know yet," Sok said.

Olivia waited for them to join her on L3. "It's no big deal, right?"

"It's pretty typical to lose the power, especially during a storm as powerful as this one," Sok explained. "It's nothing to worry about, Ms. Nelson."

"Olivia, Dennis. You can call me Olivia."

"Ah, yes, Olivia."

"Were you already investigating?" she asked.

"Um, no. I was in my room, finishing some data entry on my personal computer when the power went out. Ah, Austin, he kicked me out of the IT room. He said I needed to rest and took the helm from me. He wasn't tired, you see, he's…"

Olivia nodded. "He's got insomnia."

"Exactly."

Mark Mitchell stood behind them, his flashlight blinding them all temporarily. He swayed, the beam of light moving with him. "We heading down to RME or what?"

"I'll go to IT, see if Austin's already looking into it," said Sok. "Ah, you guys, you could go down to RME, check the breakers."

"I'll go with you, Dennis," Olivia said.

"Oh, okay. Yes, that's fine!"

"Before you go anywhere…" Timmons raised a walkie-talkie to his lips. "Check, check…" His voice echoed on Sok's belt, from his own walkie-talkie, and from the device in Mitchell's hand. "Good."

Sok and Olivia went to L2 while Mitchell and Timmons continued down to L1.

The IT server room was empty. Sok searched around incredulously, walking one end of the room to the other. He turned to Olivia, his glasses shining. "He's not here!"

"Where would he have gone?"

"If he decided he wanted to take a break, maybe he went to his room. He could be in there."

"I already knocked earlier. He didn't answer."

"Oh, well, then, maybe he's up on L3. He could've been playing on the arcade machines. That's a possibility."

She frowned. "He would have come down by now."

"Oh, yes. I don't know!"

"Does he carry a walkie?"

"Austin never carries his walkie." His demeanor shifted, a small bit of attitude having slipped into his tone. Sok tensed, looked down. Guilt appeared on his face. "He's probably in the bathroom."

"Maybe," Olivia said. "Do you think we could help the guys down in RME?"

"We could certainly try. Not much we can do up here."

They exited the IT room and walked together to the main corridor. At the junction, Olivia shone her cell flashlight to the right, toward the elevator, and then to the left, toward the MedBay.

The light didn't travel very far, the darkness too thick down that way. She frowned, not liking how cold the air had become in the corridor. Something clucked its tongue, the sound distant, muffled, hidden in the shadows.

"Dennis, turn your flashlight down there," Olivia whispered.

He did.

The MedBay had exploded out into the corridor, the rebar twisted, and the wooden planks snapped and jagged. The pieces of the cage were strewn about, pulled, and ripped into strange shapes on the floor. Broken glass sparkled, mixed with the sawdust and metal brackets.

Her insides clenched. "Oh my God."

Sok was on the walkie. "Timmons, Mitchell, he's out! He's out of the MedBay!"

"Who? Wilcox? What?" Timmons replied.

"Wilcox is out!"

Olivia swung her phone around, looking for any sign of movement. "We need to get out of here, Dennis."

"We're coming down to RME, Timmons," Sok spoke into the walkie. "We'll be there soon."

Sok opened the door to the stairwell and peered in, shining his flashlight up and around. He ushered Olivia in, stepping to the side as she pushed through, not having wanted to wait out on L2 by herself any longer. They stood on the landing and Sok nodded, collecting himself, breathing deeply. Together, they carefully traveled down to L1, down two flights of stairs.

On the L1 landing, Olivia sprinted toward the door. A wet glob of something warm and sticky slapped across her shoulder, where her neck was exposed. She reached to it, felt it in her fingers. The putrid smell of it burned her sinuses, made her wretch.

Sok's flashlight lifted, the spotlight moving up to the bottom of the previous flight, the beams dull and rusty. He began to shake, his bottom lip trembling. Slowly, her guts twisting around inside of her, Olivia pivoted on her heel and looked up at what Sok had caught in the bright spotlight.

Vazquez hung spread eagle above them, his corpse suspended by thick, worm-like ropes of segmented resin. It looked like dried spit, bubbly and creamy and yellow. Like pus from an infection had wrapped itself around him in viscous tendrils – the sort of drainage that clumped together, retained a shape even as it dripped. The kind that hardened into nasty, clear scabs. His guts dangled from a ragged tear in his belly, the blood a vivid red in the stark light. One eye remained, the other a dark and bloody hole. His jaw had been ripped out, his tongue hanging. Maroon, syrupy pulp marked where his groin had been. Some of that gunk, that disgusting discharge that held him captive, dropped from above and smacked against the floor around her feet.

Olivia screamed.

Sok opened the door and pulled her onto L1, running with her, their hands clasped, forcing her to keep up. He was a tall, slender man, with long legs and he nearly dragged her to the RME area, past the ruined lab doors.

They spilled into the RME area and Sok stumbled to a halt, releasing Olivia's hand. He struggled to speak, face twisted up and teeth bared. "Austin is dead!"

"What?" Timmons asked.

"Austin is dead," Sok repeated, heaving. "Oh, he's dead. He's back there in the stairwell. I can't…"

"Hold up, shit!" Timmons spun around, gestured wildly at Mitchell. "Grab whatever'll double as a weapon. Yeah, that crowbar'll do. Grab that rebar too. Lady, put that wrench down."

Olivia staggered blindly toward them, the heavy metal tool falling from her hand to clang against the floor. Despite having been holding it tightly only seconds before, she didn't remember picking it up. She let out a low, warbling wail and shook her head from side to side. "What do we do?"

"First, we get the fuckin' power on," Timmons hissed. "Then we hunt this bastard down and smash his fuckin' head in, just like I wanted to do earlier, before ya'll stopped me!"

Mitchell lowered his head, his tired eyes lost. In the glow of the emergency lights, he looked very pale. "We should stick together."

"Yeah, of fuckin' course, we should," Timmons said. "The generator is in the back, further in. We can check on the power grid, make sure the breakers are reset."

When her knees buckled and she sat on the floor, Sok grabbed her arm and attempted to pull her back to her feet. He stared at her with his intense dark eyes, the lenses of his glasses flashing in the light. "Ms. Nelson, you have to get up. We're about to leave. You can't stay here all by yourself. It wouldn't be safe."

She nodded weakly, sniffling, and allowed him to help her. Olivia stood beside him, grimacing. "Right, yeah. Stand back up."

"Come on, let's go." Timmons waved at them and, flashlight trained ahead, left the RME area, stalking toward a dimly lit hall to the left. Each step he took was faster than the last.

Mitchell, Sok, and Olivia rushed after him.

The sputtering sparks were bright and violent, the breaker box on the floor, torn wires strewn every which way. Thick cables had been wrenched from the walls and ceiling, their inner coils of copper filaments exposed and frayed. The generator lay on its side, the bolts having held it to the cement blocks smooth and stretched. To Olivia, it looked like a gutted animal on the Sahara.

Timmons ushered her out impatiently, giving her a shove into the hall when she refused to comply right away. "It's dangerous! Out! Out!"

She wavered on her feet, numb and silent.

Inside the generator room, Timmons cursed and muttered. "Son of a bitch. Fuck. Fuckity-fuck-fuck."

Olivia hovered in the doorway, glancing down the dark hallways on either side. In one hand she held her phone, the flashlight pointing around randomly. In the other hand, she clutched a large hammer. She swung it, preparing her strength, eyes moving over the shadows as she watched for any sign of movement. "What's going on in there? Talk to me. Please."

"A bad fuckin' time, that's what," Timmons replied. "Mother-fucker knocked the generator over and tore out the breaker box. He killed the power."

"I thought he was mindless, an animal," Mitchell muttered. "Thought the bug ate his brain."

"There must be some sort of rudimentary intelligence left in him if he's capable of that level of foresight," Sok stated, licking his lips. He shrugged, head low. "I mean, that isn't something an animal would do, is it?"

"A smart animal would," Olivia said. "I think… it's in his brain, controlling him, accessing his memories. He knew the layout of this facility, so now the creature does too. Whatever's left of him in there serves the parasite now."

"Wow, that's great." Timmons burst out of the cramped generator room, Sok and Mitchell behind him. "We're going upstairs to wake up the guys. Lee's on 4 – the others are on 5. I say we grab some more shit to use as a weapon on the way, so they're not helpless."

The others nodded in agreement.

They stopped at the RME cage and stocked up, grabbing wrenches and prybars. Olivia traded her hammer for a long prybar, the heft of it unbalanced in her hand. She rolled her shoulders, feigned confidence in her grip, and gave Sok a terse nod when he eyed her. He showed off a long piece of rebar.

"I've never struck anyone before," he told her.

"Neither have I."

"I've never even yelled at anyone."

Timmons snorted. "Well, it's time you learned, kid." He stepped out of the RME cage and glanced back and forth, assessing the scene. Shooting Mitchell a sharp look, he waved at him. "Come on, yah bum, you're supposed to be watching out for me."

Mitchell, a flashlight in one hand and a crowbar in the other, jogged to catch up with Timmons. Soon, all four of them were trekking down the corridor, passing the lab on the right.

"Y'don't think he tried to go back down there, do yah?" Timmons asked, pausing to look toward the lab.

"No, it's flooded," Olivia replied.

"Huh, that's too bad…"

As they entered the stairwell, she kept her flashlight trained on the steps. Olivia heard their reactions to the sight of Vazquez's corpse but did not look. She couldn't. She didn't need to. That image of him was burned into her brain. So too was the rancid smell that filled the landing.

"Jesus," Timmons breathed.

They began walking up the steps.

Sok let out a soft exhalation. "I was supposed to be in the server room, not him. He was supposed to be in bed. I let him talk me into leaving so he could take over. If I'd stood my ground, he'd still be alive right now."

"But then you'd be dead," Mitchell stated, voice low.

"Oh…"

"You don't know that it happened that way, Dennis," Olivia said quietly, walking beside him up the steps to L4. "Only you guys have the code to those doors and Wilcox didn't break into the IT room. He didn't get him there."

"He would have been in his room," Sok said.

Mitchell stepped behind them both, bringing up the rear. He pointed his flashlight the way they'd come. "So, the

155

creature would have come for someone else. He would've hunted in the halls. Found another one of us."

Timmons, leading the way, whirled on them, and snarled, his top lip raised. "Would you guys keep it down? I'm pretty sure that thing is hunting right now, and you're makin' a ruckus. It's probably watching us, waiting to pounce."

They continued their journey.

"What do you suppose it eats?" Mitchell asked.

"Fuck man, it eats us," Timmons hissed. "Shut up and keep walking. Only one more flight. I want Lee up first."

"Didn't look like it ate Vazquez."

"Mark, what the fuck did I just say?"

Olivia swallowed thickly, cell shaking in her hand as she pointed it up the steps. Her wrist ached from carrying the prybar. She ignored the pain, her mind elsewhere.

Spencer Hersch had been on the floor, his neck broken, and his guts spilled out. The creature – not Wilcox – had killed the man right there, in the lab. After whisking the hapless victim away in an attempt to bring him to the eggs, the creature had hit an obstacle. An insurmountable snag in its plan. A tantrum had ensued with Hersch absorbing the brunt of its wrath. Perhaps it was furious that it didn't know the code to access the pressure chamber. Had it even known it would need a code? Did Wilcox himself know anything about the chamber, other than its location? Was he paying attention when Petry used the access panel the first time they'd gone down to S1? Or had it been something else entirely that sent the creature into a blind rage?

Her jaw tensed.

Why had it killed Austin? Her eyes burned, her lungs empty and sore. Mitchell was right; his body hadn't been chewed on. Nothing meaty was missing, unless you counted his… She tasted hot vomit and took in a sharp breath. He'd been brutally murdered, mutilated, hung up on display. The creature wanted the body to be found. It wanted to send a message. Was it taking its revenge on them? Had the creature been angry over its captivity? They'd rolled it in chains and snapped on a padlock. They'd confined it to a dark room to dehydrate or starve to death. Sure, that would make it mad. That would make anyone mad, right?

Mad enough to kill its captors.

But was it the creature seeking revenge, or Wilcox himself? She wondered quietly, senses trained on the stairwell, listening for any sound, looking for movement in the shadows.

They reached L4 and Timmons opened the door, peered out cautiously, and slipped into the corridor. He waved at them, nodding, eyes flitting back and forth.

Sok appeared at her side, signaled that he was going ahead to scout, pointing first at his eyes, then forward toward the open door. Mitchell's flashlight trained around the darkness in the stairwell, cut a swath of light through the deep black. She felt paralyzed, cold. Lingering on the step closest to the landing, Olivia felt Mitchell give her a little push, his dense palm pressing on the small of her back. Then, his fingers swept upward through her hair. With no time to react, she simply jogged the rest of the way, unsettled.

The door shut and they were on L4. She turned to Mitchell, unsure of what to say. He blinked at her, a flashlight in one hand and a crowbar in the other. Olivia's throat tightened.

"What?" he asked her.

"Nothing."

"Lee's down this way," Timmons said. "Stick together, guys. Keep your heads on and stay frosty. This thing is fast and strong, but its bones can still break. Trust me, I know from experience."

They knocked on Lee's door three times before he answered. He let them in, the room small. Putting on his jeans and boots right in front of them, Lee listened to what they had to say.

His eyes closed. "Austin? Austin's gone?"

"I'm sorry, Casey," Sok said.

Lee raised his hand to his own face and gripped his mouth, sat on his bed. He rocked slightly on the bottom bunk, shaking his head. "No. Are you sure? Austin can't be gone, man."

Sok frowned deeply. "He's dead. The creature killed him."

"Wilcox you mean? Wilcox killed him?" Lee scowled.

"I don't think that's Astor Wilcox anymore," Olivia said. "Not really, not with that thing controlling him."

"We should kill it." His eyes twin flames, Lee stood and grimaced. "We outnumber it. If we can flush it out or corner it…"

"Slow your roll, buddy," Timmons said. "We still need to go up to L5 and get the others. We'll need all hands on deck if we're gonna gang up on this bug."

"You didn't want to come down with us to S1," Lee stated, eyes moving over Timmons' face. "And now you're on board with forming a posse? Hunting it down and killing it?"

Timmons glanced away. "Hey, shit's changed, y'know? It's loose on the rig now. Told those guys we should've left that chump down there, didn't I? Didn't listen, did they? Now look what's happened. And as usual, I've got to clean up the mess."

Lee stepped closed to him, their heights matched. "I noticed you weren't heading out there to do it alone."

"No, because I can't do it alone. I need my team. My team fixes shit when it breaks." Timmons offered a little smirk. "And right now, shit is one-hundred percent certifiably broken."

"Gimme that crowbar," Lee said, hand extended toward Mitchell.

Pulling the second crowbar he had strapped to his belt, Mitchell handed it over and nodded slowly when Lee took it.

"Got your flashlight?" Timmons asked.

"Yeah, of course I do."

"Great, then let's go."

Without hesitation, Lee slipped out into the corridor first, teeth bared as he searched back and forth. Olivia came out next, followed by Sok, Timmons, and Mitchell.

Chapter 14

Relying more on their flashlights than her cell, Olivia traveled up the next two flights to L5 with the others surrounding her. It didn't go unnoticed that the men had formed a loose circle around her, and part of her resented the protection as much as she appreciated it. She wanted to tell them that she didn't need the special treatment. Yet, she couldn't shake the memory of that odd sensation, the stony hand against the small of her back and the fingers brushing through her hair. She cursed her vivid imagination, preferring to blame that over the alternative.

Mitchell would have seen something, alerted them. He was there too, one step behind her and to the left. He would have seen if Wilcox – the creature – had been that close to her.

L5 was silent, save for the ambient hiss of the rain pummeling the rig and the occasional roll of deep, throbbing thunder that rattled the foundation. The emergency lights glowed dimly along the corridor, still and serene.

Timmons whispered to them, "Wert first."

They woke Wert and he dressed. Though he asked many questions, Timmons held up a hand, grimaced. "Larry, just hurry up and get ready to move. I'll explain it when we're all in one spot, man. Don't got the time to tell every single one of you the story."

Wert seemed to understand that he had to wait, and as soon as he was ready to go, out they went, traveling as a tight group down the corridor to Frank's cabin.

Frank was already dressed, answering his door immediately. "I was about to come out and start looking around, but, ah, something told me to stay put."

"Good instincts, guy," Timmons said. "Mitchell's got a wrench for you. It's the long wrench. Take it."

They hurried down the corridor to Petry's room and, before Timmons could knock, the door opened a crack. Petry stared out with his one good eye, made a sound in the back of his throat, and ushered them in with great zeal.

Olivia was one of the first to walk into the large room, the same make and model that Wilcox had been given. To her eyes, the cabin might as well have been unoccupied. None of the man's personal effects were staged anywhere on any of the dressers. The large single bed was made, sheets taut across the mattress. A faint scent of cologne hung in the air, the only sign that a person had spent any amount of time in the cabin.

Petry's face had an ashen quality to it as he spoke. "What's going on out there? I heard weird noises from the hall…"

"Weird noises?" Timmons asked.

"Tapping and thumping."

"When?"

"Maybe thirty minutes before you showed up."

"I didn't hear any tapping or thumping," Wert said.

Petry eyed him. "You must have been sleeping."

"I didn't hear it either and I was awake," Frank stated.

"What's going on?" Petry repeated his question.

"Yes, please, now that we're all here, Joe…"

"Right, so Wilcox is out," Timmons replied, holding up a hand to curb any questions before he'd finished. "Not sure when he busted outta MedBay, but… he took out the generator, tore the breaker off the wall. And… he killed Vazquez."

Frank grimaced. "What?"

"Vazquez is dead, torn up and glued to the wall in the L1 stairwell. No man did that. It's just a monster now. It's out there on the rig somewhere. Could be anywhere. I figure it's time we take care of it before it takes care of us."

"Are you kidding?" Frank stood up straight. "You want us to go out there? Hunt it down?"

"Yeah. I do."

"We should just stay right here!" Frank exclaimed. "Help'll arrive in a few days, and we've got access to water in the bathroom. We're together. I doubt it'd attack us all at the same time."

"We don't know that," Timmons said. "Thing could bust down a door no problem, remember? It might not wanna come charging in and try'n take on all of us, but then again, it might not give a shit. I don't want to wait and find out."

Rushing to the long dresser beside his bed, Petry yanked a drawer out and rifled through the contents, digging for something under a pile of folded shirts. He produced a small pistol and a box of ammo, his eye alight. "It'll regret busting into this room!"

Wert's jaw dropped. "You've got a gun, Bill?"

"Sir, yes, I do. Do you think this is the best time to give me a rash of shit over it?"

"No, I don't…"

Loading the gun, Petry squinted. "We can't stay here, Frank." He glared at Timmons. "But going after it is a stupid idea, Joe. Maybe you got in a few good licks a day ago, but it's changed since then, and you all know it. We have to assume it's wholly hostile, and a lot stronger."

"And smart," Mitchell muttered.

Petry grunted. "Exactly, we can't stay here."

"What's your suggestion then?" Wert asked.

"I say we head to the mess hall and lock it down. We'll have food and water, plenty of space to move around. Hell, there's a restroom in the kitchen. We can ride it out there, sleep in shifts, until help arrives."

"I like that idea better than camping out in your cabin, Bill," Frank said, brows knit. "But we have to get there first, don't we? We need to get down to L3."

"You guys made it all the way from L1 to L5 without any trouble. If it tries anything, there's seven of us versus its one. And one of those seven, well, he's got something a little better than a metal pipe to swing around." Petry held up the pistol and grinned mirthlessly.

"It's got to have a survival instinct. Most animals do," Olivia chimed in, clearing her throat at their sudden stares. "If it sees us as a threat, it might hide from us now that we're together."

Petry brightened, his smile stiff. "Oh, I forgot the resident expert on the newly discovered species was here. Ms. Nelson, maybe you can explain why destroying the eggs didn't work, hmm?"

"Well, I…"

Lee took a step forward, placing himself between Olivia and Petry. "We've all been theorizing, Petry. Back off of her."

Petry lifted himself on the balls of his feet to meet Lee's stony gaze. "It's a valid question, isn't it? We sent three people down there to do a job she said needed done and only two people came back up. It would make me sick to know that Yuri died for no fucking reason. Let me ask the question, Lee. If she can't answer it, she can't, but let me ask the goddamn question."

"What the fuck is wrong with you, man?" Lee asked.

"I don't feel so well, Lee. I don't feel so well," Petry said, head low. "And I'm tired of people being wrong, costing us our lives."

"The eggs needed to be destroyed or it would've either

dragged you down to them or brought them up to us," Olivia said.

"So, instead, it's just going to eat us. Good to know."

"That's why we've got to kill it first, Mr. Petry."

"You were beggin' for its life a day ago, Ms. Nelson. You were singing to it. Yeah, I heard about that."

"That was when I thought there was still a person in there. Before that creature killed Austin, the way it killed him…"

"It killed Spencer first, Ms. Nelson, don't you forget that."

"Bill, leave her be," Wert said. "As for your plan, I'm not for it. I think Timmons is right. I think we need to go after the creature and kill it – together."

Petry balked, shoulders squaring. "Huh? Why in the hell would you want to do that for?"

"Because I don't want to hide while that that son of a bitch creeps around on my rig. It's killed twice and I am for damn sure it'll take another crack at us before you know it. It might even go after the folks who show up to check in on us, and that just doesn't sit well with me, Bill."

"Storm'll pass and we can call them-"

Wert shook his head. "How? Who's gonna reestablish the satellite link if we're all cowering in the mess hall? Power's out, so the server room is down. Doubtful any cell could pick up a signal – not without a goddamn miracle. You had the right idea about the thing being outnumbered. I say we stick together, sweep the facility, flush it out, corner it, whatever… We kill it. Hell, we do that boy Wilcox a favor. We end his suffering."

"Ayup," Timmons agreed.

"Who knows what'll happen if we corner it, Larry!" Frank exclaimed. "A cornered animal is a dangerous animal. And it's dark. You didn't see how fast that thing moved."

"I guess we've got to have a vote then, eh?" Wert asked, glancing around at the others in the cabin.

"Guess so, Larry," Petry said.

"All in favor of hunting it down and killing it?" Wert asked. He raised his hand.

Olivia, Lee, and Timmons raised their hands too.

Petry scowled, raising his free hand proudly in the air. "All in favor of waiting it out in the mess hall?"

Frank and Mitchell raised their hands as well.

"Dennis, you aren't voting?" Lee eyed him.

"I, uh, I don't know... I'm trying to think of which plan is more logical. Which one makes the most sense."

"Don't matter. Four to three, we win," Wert said.

"Oh no," Petry said, waggling his finger. "That one, she doesn't count. She's not one of us, boss. Her vote doesn't count."

"Like hell her vote doesn't count," Wert snapped.

"Every say she's had has landed us in hotter water. No, she doesn't get a vote. It's us, your crew, we get the vote. It's three to three, Larry. Dennis, whose side are you on, kid?" Pivoting on his heel, Petry narrowed his one dark eye and glared at the tall young man fidgeting in the cabin. "You want to go get picked off one by one hunting a monster in the dark, or do you want to wait in the mess hall where it's safe, where you have food and water?"

"Ahhh..."

"Come on, Dennis, it killed Austin," Timmons said. "It'll keep killing until there's no one left. We need to do something."

"I mean, the most logical thing..."

"Dennis, don't be an idiot. Aren't you a vegetarian? You ever killed something bigger than a cockroach, kid?"

"Technically, no. However, it's noteworthy that-"

"Come on, Dennis, for Austin..."

"Let him choose, Joe. Same for you, Bill. Stop badgering him," Wert loudly interrupted, his hand in the air.

"Yeah, Dennis, make up your own mind. Don't listen to them, right?" Lee said, offering a patient smile.

Sok licked his lips, looked around the room. "I, uh…"

"Maybe he's okay with going out there in the dark. He's got that rebar. He knows how to use it," Petry muttered.

After biting his bottom lip for a few long seconds, Sok adjusted his glasses and studied each face in the cabin. "Um, it would be the most logical choice to lock ourselves in the mess hall and wait for rescue. We can fortify the doors with the tables. Take turns sleeping. There's food and water…"

Lee deflated. "Huh. Yeah."

"Four to three. It's done," Petry said.

Wert nodded slowly. "Alright, vote's done. Guess we're heading down to the mess hall and setting up camp."

Timmons groaned. "Shit."

"Hey, man, if you want to go out there and take it on, be my guest," Petry said. "But me, I'd rather live. And I think these good folks feel the same way."

"Right," Lee scoffed.

"Real easy to be brave in here, son," Petry said.

"Guess we'll head down the stairwell to L3. It's real dark in there, so watch yourselves," Timmons said.

When each had been given a weapon, they readied themselves to exit Petry's cabin into the corridor. As soon as the door opened, Timmons gave Petry a small shove.

"Hey, watch it…"

Timmons grunted, growled in his ear. "You're the guy with the gun. You go first, brave leader."

Begrudgingly, Petry slipped out and glanced around. Timmons came out right behind him, followed by Wert and Lee.

Frank, Mitchell, Sok, and Olivia, in that order, joined them in the corridor, the emergency lights dim but functional.

"Maybe it is hiding," Frank whispered.

"Or waiting for us in the stairwell, where it's dark," Timmons hissed, grumbling as he studied the hall.

With Olivia in the center of their pack, they walked quietly, carefully, to the stairwell door and paused there.

Again, Petry hesitated.

"Go on," Timmons muttered.

"Everyone got their flashlights ready? I want every inch of that stairwell lit. I don't want that son of a bitch sneaking up on us," Petry said, his eye narrowed.

Olivia, only armed with her long prybar, swallowed thickly. "I don't have a flashlight."

"Should'a grabbed one down in RME. Too late now. Just keep low. You're the smallest one here, Ms. Nelson. If it's going to go after any of us, it'll be you," Petry stated.

"I've got your six, dear," Wert told her.

She nodded briskly.

Petry opened the door to the dark stairwell and shone his flashlight in, illuminating the cold steel and cement along the walls. The shadows shrank. Timmons and Lee went in after him, their own spotlights dancing across every surface. Once they'd all gathered on the landing on L5, Petry, with Timmons close beside him, descended the first flight of steps.

Thunder rolled, the sound softer than earlier. While the rain continued to beat the rig, the roar had faded considerably.

Olivia thought to herself that the storm was indeed passing, the relief a tiny beacon of light in the oppressive darkness.

Petry opened the stairwell door on L3 and exhaled shakily, the pitch-black void out in the corridor stopping him in his tracks. He recoiled, hissed, "Give me a moment." Gulping on air, he exited the stairwell, flashlight first and ushered the others out.

Timmons shoved his way to the front of the line, brushed past Petry, and swung a hard left by pivoting on his heel. The entire performance reminded Olivia of one of those cop-shows during a home raid – anything could be waiting on the other side of an opened door. She smiled even though it wasn't funny. His execution had been so precise, so theatrical. Timmons swept his flashlight over the small corner of the hall behind the door, across the closed elevator doors to his left, poised to strike with his crowbar or jump back to retreat into the stairwell.

Finding nothing of note, Timmons grunted, moved aside. Only then did he direct the others to leave the landing and step out. Lee slunk out followed by Mitchell. Olivia and Sok slipped out at the same time. He murmured an apology for bumping into her. She dismissed it politely and, as she left the landing, got a glimpse of Petry's sullen scowl.

"Why's it so dark?" Olivia asked, her voice low.

Timmons answered in a rough whisper, "Bastard must've knocked out the e-lights."

"Smart animal," Mitchell mused.

"It's a straight shot at least," Frank said, exiting last and blinking at the deep shadows ahead of them. He swallowed, sucked in a sharp breath. "Just walk. It's not that far. We're almost there."

Their flashlights cut bright white trails through the corridor, caught the sparkling bits of broken glass under the emergency lights along the way. A strobing flash of lightning casted an eerie glow on the white linoleum closest to the windows.

Olivia heard Wert beside her, his breathing heavy. She looked over at him, frowning at his shuffling limp. Turning to face forward, she listened to the wind and rain, focused on the empty echo of the corridor. Her ears strained to filter out the sound of the storm and her own heartbeat.

Sok was at her right, Wert on her left. Mitchell and Lee were directly in front of her with Timmons and Petry leading the way. Their pace had quickened, the mess hall visible on the left, only twenty feet ahead.

That was when Frank, who had wound up bringing up the rear after leaving the stairwell, cried out suddenly, the scrape and scuffle of his boots on the linoleum frantic. He screamed, his voice pitched.

Olivia spun on her heel, the prybar throwing her off balance as she attempted to raise it. Multiple spotlights fell onto the corridor behind them, caught the image of a pale, shrieking Frank as he slid away from them, back the way they'd come, across the floor on his belly into the black mouth of the open elevator doors.

"Fuck!" Timmons shouted, spinning around.

Petry held his gun up, aiming his flashlight. "Rob!"

Before he could plunge into the elevator shaft, Frank hooked himself between the cracked doors with his elbows, the bottom half of him swallowed up. He clamped his palms down on the metal surface, held on with spread fingers and screamed again. His eyes bulged, the whites seeming to glow in the spotlights trained on him. "Help me!"

Unable to move, Olivia stared as Timmons bolted past her toward the elevator, his crowbar swung over his shoulder. "Bill! Bill, come on!"

Another scuffle of feet.

She turned slightly, peering over her shoulder. Petry had broken into a run too – in the opposite direction. The smaller man went sprinting for the open mess hall door, nearly tripping over his own little feet. And then, Mitchell, his jaw hanging open and his sweaty face twisted up in terror and confusion, took off like a madman after Petry.

Lee lunged, grabbed for Mitchell's shoulder, and missed. "You cowards! You fucking cowards!"

Frank shrieked, convulsing in arrhythmic undulations to steel himself against whatever force wrenched on his bottom half. With Timmons three yards from the elevator, a white-hot urgency flared in Frank's terror-stricken eyes. He disappeared, pulled bodily into the black shaft.

"Rob!" Timmons shouted.

"Help me!" Frank cried, the sound echoing.

Wert loped to Timmons, frantic. "Good God! Good God, it got him! Joe, where'd it take him?"

Shining his flashlight down the shaft, Timmons choked. "I don't see him! Fuck!" He shined his flashlight upward, head cocked. "I don't know! Jesus, I don't know! Frank?! Frank, can you hear me?!"

Somewhere above them, Frank called out, his voice muffled, quieter, and yet just as desperate. He called for help.

"We've gotta go after him!" Lee hissed, running over to the elevator to join Wert and Timmons.

Olivia stumbled that way as well, Sok seemingly rooted to the spot in the middle of the corridor. He trained his flashlight back and forth indecisively.

"Where?" Timmons asked, "What level? What fucking level? Jesus, Frank! Frank!"

The response was a faint cry, pleading for help.

Swaying behind them, Olivia glanced back at Sok. He still hadn't moved. A firm grip took her upper arm and she gasped, spinning about to face Wert. A few words spilled weakly from her numb lips. "What do we do?"

"We get the hell out of here," he replied.

"No!" Lee declared. "He's still alive! Listen!"

Indeed, buried under layers of other, ambient noise, another low, distant wail for help echoed through the corridor.

"We'll never find him, Lee," Timmons said, forcing the elevator doors shut. "Wert's right. We've got to go. We need to get to the mess hall and barricade the door."

Lee growled, gripped his long crowbar. "We could take it. Only two ways onto L3 and we're lookin' right at 'em."

"I'd rather have that popgun if we're gonna try that," Timmons said, backing away from the closed doors.

"Then I kick Bill Petry's lily-white ass and take it from him," Lee's lips curled, one hand holding the crowbar and the other balled into a tight knuckled fist.

"Guys, do you hear that?" Sok asked.

Wert turned to the left. "What's that, Dennis?"

"Listen."

Olivia strained to hear, head tilted, and teeth bared. For a moment, she imagined Frank's screaming growing louder, closer. Except, it wasn't screaming. Not human screaming. No, that sound was distinctly inhuman. A pitched, staccato shriek like grinding gears in an old, abused car. Flanged. Agonized. It cut off suddenly, right at the crescendo.

Silence.

Rending metal squealed from above them, a quake in the flooring sizzling up through her feet. Roaring air blasted the closed elevator shaft, the crash shaking the walls, rattling the windows. Timmons leapt down the corridor, cursed.

She grabbed Wert's wrist. "What was that?"

"Thing just cut the elevator cables and let it drop. That's what that was! Timmons, Lee come on!" Wert pulled Olivia along as he limped toward the mess hall doors.

As if summoned, Petry appeared there, staring down at

them with his one wide eye, ducking away a split-second later.

Lee jogged ahead, was the first to enter the mess hall. As Olivia and Wert stepped in, Timmons and Sok close behind, the room exploded with frenzied, furious voices.

"Not now!" Wert hollered, giving Olivia a gentle push toward one of the tables. "Dammit, knock it off! Petry, Lee, stop it!"

Lee had Petry cornered, the shorter man trembling, pointing the gun at him. Both glared at the other, hovered in place. Lee swung his crowbar toward the ground and cried out, stalked back toward the entrance. He shoved by Mitchell, completely ignoring the other man's weak attempt to get his attention.

Working together, Timmons and Lee closed the doors, fortified them with a table laid flat against the wall. Without any real tools in which to do the job properly, they instead relied on whatever they could find close by. Sok brought them a reel of cabling he'd found by the TV. This was woven around the door handles, through the folded table legs.

Timmons and Lee dragged both arcade machines over next, one at a time, adding them to the barricade until the set of doors was entirely hidden.

"There's candles in the kitchen," Sok stated. "I'll get them. We need to conserve the flashlight batteries."

Olivia nodded. "I'll help you."

Using his lighter, Timmons set each of the fifteen long white candles aflame in their glass holders. Spread out across the four remaining tables, each little light cast a meager but warm glow on their faces. Outside, the rain had slowed, the thunder muted.

Mitchell wrung his hands, head low.

Many minutes had passed before Lee, jaw working soundlessly, finally looked up from the floor. "Thanks for the help back there, guys."

Wert cleared his throat. "This isn't the time…"

"Then when is?" Lee asked.

"It was too late for Frank," Petry said. "The thing, it had him. You knew he was done-for, Lee. What were we gonna do?"

"Anything! We could've tried. He was right there, man. You ran, Petry. You too, Mitchell. How could you do that?" Lee started to stand. When he caught Wert's stoic gaze, he sat back down. "He was our friend."

"The plan was to get to the mess hall, not fight the creature. Defend against it, yeah, if we had to. Not fight it. You wanted us to go jump down the elevator shaft after it?" Petry scowled.

"I wanted us to try to save Frank," Lee said.

"I was scared," Mitchell muttered.

Lee twisted around, glared. "You think we weren't?"

"No, but…"

Timmons lit a cigarette, exhaled smoke in the candlelight. He sat at the end of an empty table, hunched and pale. "Quit it."

Olivia held onto a cool bottle of water, leaning over the table. Though she could hear their every word, her mind was elsewhere. Dryly, she swallowed back a sick burp. "How safe are we in here?"

"I mean, if it wants in, it'll get in." Timmons shrugged.

Petry nodded, presented the gun. "It won't get far."

"Nowhere to run in here, Petry," Lee whispered.

Petry shook his head, made no reply, and turned away.

A thud, heavy and sharp, reverberated through the closed, barricaded doors. The arcade machines vibrated. Each person in the mess hall sat up, eyes and ears trained on the front of the room.

"It's here," Olivia breathed.

It tapped a few times. Then came a quick double-rap, more akin in sound to a gentle knock at a front door. A friendly, lighthearted knock, like a neighbor coming by to ask for a cup of sugar, Olivia thought.

A long moment passed while they waited, listening, until it knocked again. *Hi, neighbors.*

Mitchell's face glistened, bleached, and sweaty in the low, flickering light. "What is it doing?"

"I think it's fucking with us," Timmons replied.

"What?"

"Marky, it's smart, ain't it? Smart like a man because it used to be one. It's an asshole too for the same reason. It's fucking with us because it's a goddamn asshole."

As if in response, the thing knocked on the door again. There was a cadence to that series of timed knocks, and she recognized the beat immediately as the first part of '*Shave and a haircut*'. Her nose reflexively crinkled.

Knock-knock. '*Two bits*!'.

"Prick." Timmons blew smoke. "Just kick down the doors already, you piece of shit."

They sat and waited, listened while exchanging cautious glances. The quiet air grew heavy. Timmons let out a low, mirthless chuckle, his smoldering cigarette mostly ash.

"What's so funny, Joe?" Petry asked.

"Maybe it was trying to be polite. 'Let me in please', it just said. Jeeee-sus." Timmons covered his face, shook his head, body shaking from repressed laughter. "Or, better yet, 'Candygram!'"

Lee slouched at the table. "Shit, man."

"Wilcox is out there with his briefcase, checking the time on his Rolex. Did we have an appointment? Not that he'd show on time, right? Give him a few and he'll knock again."

With a snort, Timmons burst out into hysterics.

"Get a'hold of yourself, Joe," Wert snapped.

Timmons, sobering with chilling speed, sat up, flicked his cigarette to the floor, and offered a wide grin. "I got a tight hold, boss, trust me. Shit's broken bad and I'm holdin' it tight."

Wert sighed. "We sleep in shifts. I'll take the first of 'em if you'll give me the gun, Bill."

"I'm not handing it off to anyone. I'll take first shift with you, Larry." Petry stiffened. "I'm not giving up my gun."

"Fine," Wert said. "I suggest you all see what towels and tablecloths you can scrounge up in the kitchen cabinets. Makes for a better bed than the cold floor."

"I'm good," Lee stated.

Olivia folded her arms under her head, her cheek supported against her arm, suddenly too exhausted to keep her eyes open. Her pulse slowed like the rain beating softly against the rig. The sensation of a blanket being laid over her shoulders caused her to stir, and a soft voice instructed her to 'rest'.

It was a bright sunny day, the breeze pleasant and the sidewalk relatively free of other pedestrians as she swept out of the corner store, the doors jangling behind her.

A heavy plastic bag in each hand, Olivia walked along the side of the road. Cars passed, stopped at the red light up ahead, and continued along Main Street when the light turned green.

She passed many little shops on this stretch of Main, the intersection of Pine a block away. The bakery smelled good, as always, and she paused to gaze in on the cakes in the large front window display. It was worth standing there for a few extra moments just to ogle the desserts. She heard laughter.

Some of the local kids were fast approaching on their bicycles, foolishly weaving in and out around the parked cars lining the street next to the coffee house. A blue sedan came to a sudden stop and honked at the kids, eliciting a round of excited hoots from their little gang. Curse words were exchanged, more hoots.

Five teenagers, all boys, all on rugged dirty bikes, flew past Olivia. One whistled at her, another hooted.

"Hey babyyyyyy!" a boy cried.

"Show us your tits!"

"I got somethin' sweet for you!"

She ignored their comments, waited for them to finish passing, and stalked off with her head low and face hot.

Skirting around bright orange road cones, Olivia stepped over cracks in the sidewalk, careful not to trip over the uneven terrain caused by tree roots. They'd broken up the cement, pushed it apart. The offending trees had been cut down recently, the smell of sap and raw lumber still fresh. Soon, they'd tear out that entire section of sidewalk, remove the stumps, and make it look nice and new for the boutique set to open in a month.

Across the street, two old women cackled outside of the antique store, sharing secrets, and smoking stinky cigars.

At the next intersection, Olivia saw the lights turn yellow along Main Street and, after hitting the corner, made a right at Pine to cross over. She might've paused, her pulse elevated.

The little white pedestrian light flashed.

She'd made it most of the way across when she caught motion in her peripheral and looked to the right to see the huge, black Buick barreling toward her.

The blare of a horn deafened her.

A crash, loud, clattering. Men were screaming.

Olivia sat up, nearly fell out of the seat and onto the floor. Her stiff neck ached, and her ears rang. That loud crash still reverberated inside of her skull, her scalp on fire along that scar above her right ear. As the world flooded in around her, she realized, horrified, that the crash and the screams had not been part of the dream. The others in the cafeteria were shouting back and forth.

Timmons screamed, "Jesus Christ!"

She wrenched herself to her feet, saw the candles struggling. Flashlight beams searched the ruined drop ceiling, Sok and Lee falling back toward the blocked doors.

There were sections of the ceiling missing, the panels smashed on the mess hall floor. Petry raised the gun, aimed at something above them within the empty spots, and fired off a few loud shots, the sound sharper and more painful than she'd imagined. The men called back and forth, shouted, scrambled.

Black arms with grasping hands reached from the ceiling, dug long talons into Petry, and hauled him up in the air. He squealed, dropped the gun, kicked, and flailed. In the strobing, chaotic lights, Olivia stared as blood rained down across the floor and tables, splattering every which way until Petry stopped screaming. A wet, crackling, ripping sound ensued.

His body fell to the floor and lay still. His head followed, clonking thickly, teetering to a stop.

Another figure, lanky, long, dark, descended from the ceiling onto a tabletop, the movements fluid and yet mechanical. A piece of humanoid machinery posed partially crouched in the candlelight, the spotlights falling onto its shining black carapace, highlighting trace bits of pale skin that glowed with an alien bioluminescence. Something whipped back and forth behind it. It was a tail – a long, segmented tail.

Strong arms sheathed in faceted layers of dark shell moved in the light, the long sharp fingers curling. A second set of arms moved separately under the first, the hands deformed, their shape that of long, scythe-like pincers.

The face.

Olivia gulped on air, frozen at the sight of it. Black eyes shined. The mouth opened, exposed gunmetal gray fangs. His hair, where visible, was damp and dark. The thing had once been human, hadn't it? Those features were still there, buried, mixed in. A horned crest flared back along his temples. Along his jaw, on either side of his mouth, the mandibles flexed. The way it moved, it seemed to pose, to let them get a good, long look at it. To awe at its glory. It basked in their paralyzed fascination. Oily yellow sap oozed from a bullet wound on its shoulder, the shell cracked at the entry point.

She fell back, hugged the wall. The creature leapt from the table, landed on the floor, and made a straight line for Timmons. The man swung his crowbar at it, the creature ducking under it and veering off toward the side of the room.

Lee ran to Petry's body, gagged, and frantically searched the floor with his flashlight. Hissing, the creature dashed toward him, swerving away at the last moment when Wert appeared with his weapon raised.

"Where's the gun?" Lee asked.

Wert stood by his side, held his flashlight in one hand and his long piece of rebar in the other. "Keep looking for it! I'll cover you!"

Mitchell heaved, scrambled to the doors, and began to yank on the first arcade machine on the left.

Sok ran over to him, tried to pull him away. "Mitchell,

stop! They need our help. Come on!"

"Fuck you! I'm getting out of here!"

With a grimace, Sok whirled, sprinting over to Timmons' side with his piece of rebar in the air. He bared his teeth, obviously frightened. "I'm here! What do we do?"

Timmons watched the creature, his chin low. Smiling, he nodded slowly, taking a step to the side. When he stepped to the side, the creature took a step to the side as well. "We fuck with it, that's what. Hey, you! Wilcox! You in there, you braindead prick?"

The thing tilted its head, blinked its black eyes.

Timmons went on. "You heard me, you stupid, self-centered Ken Doll. Told yah not to touch it, didn't I? Now look at yah. You're a big ugly bug. How's it feel? You can be honest with me."

The creature clicked at him.

"If you're suffering, we can help yah, buddy."

It crouched, tail thrashing. Both sets of arms moved at once, its humanoid hands flat on the ground as its pincers wiggled in the air around it upper belly.

"Found it!" Lee exclaimed, holding up the gun.

The creature zipped across the floor, lunged at him. From the right, Wert brought down the rebar across its shoulder, knocking it off course. That whip of a tail cut through the air, slashed at Lee's hand and sent the gun sliding across the floor toward Olivia.

Narrowly avoiding another swing from Wert, the creature let out a warbling click, darted toward the shadows, and wove in and out of view as the men tried to catch it in their flashlights. It seemed to revel in its own speed and agility.

Transfixed on its motions, Olivia licked her lips. It *was* fucking with them. She saw intelligence in those black eyes, a malevolent self-awareness beyond the simple need to survive she'd witnessed in the swarm of parasites. That mouth, that horrible bestial mouth, curved strangely in the light – a grin. It must have sensed her gaze and turned toward her, the right corner of its top lip tugged upward in a familiar way. It paused its macabre frolicking to focus its entire attention on her, then wagged its tail back and forth like an overexcited dog.

'*Play?*' she imagined it crooning.

Timmons took his chance and finally got a whack in, cracking his crowbar across the thing's skull. It staggered slightly, spun, and let out a hiss. Receiving a whip-strike across his side from the creature's tail, Timmons fell back before attempting to land another blow. The creature dodged and skittered away, slipping closer to the front doors. Mitchell bolted as soon as he saw it coming, rounding the long tables on the other side of the room. The creature had closed in on her.

"Hide, Ms. Nelson!" Sok cried. "Please hide!"

She bent and picked up the gun. "Astor!"

A click, a whirr. It paused, tilted it head.

Olivia swallowed, pointing the gun at the creature. As it approached her, its movements oddly tentative, she tried to take aim. The thing did a little weaving motion, its mouth emulating that plastic smile she'd seen before. She cleared her throat. "Hello, Astor. Can you hear me?"

It trilled.

While the creature was distracted, Mitchell returned to the process of dragging the arcade machines away from the door, the sound loud and low.

Lee, Sok, Wert, and Timmons came up behind it to form a loose circle, their steps cautious and their weapons raised. A knowing gleam flashed in the creature's eyes, and it paused, peered over its armored shoulder at the men surrounding it.

"Astor, look at me," Olivia said.

In the low light, those black eyes shifted. It did not turn toward her, though it did appear to look at her, its head tilting ever so slightly to the side. The tail lashed back and forth, forcing the men to keep their distance.

Her finger felt at the trigger. In that instant, the creature dove for her. Another body appeared, threw itself into the fray, blocking her. It was Wert, his arms wrapping around the thing. He tackled it, grabbed for its neck with his elbow, trying to hook it.

A blur of bright red sprayed outward and flecked her face with hot blood, the thing slashing Wert open with the sharp protrusions jutting from its top set of arms. And yet, Wert held on.

"Shoot it!" Timmons cried.

The creature bucked, twisted Wert around, and dug its claws into his arm. That second set of hands, the pincers gnashing, gutted Wert in one fell motion, spilling his intestines to the floor as the thing pulled the man's right arm so hard that it tore from the socket, the sound of the meat tearing and the bone breaking wet and crunchy, echoing in the room.

Wert screamed weakly, the sound cut off.

Olivia fired the gun, unsure of her aim. The creature shrieked over the sound of the ringing in her ears, tossed Wert like a ragdoll, and shimmied backward, that tail nearly tripping Timmons. It kept its head low, reached up to touch the deep gouge along its cheek. Examining the yellow blood on its hardened claw fingers, it chirped sharply.

She bit her lip, the world around her muffled. Still, the sound of its curious trilling emboldened her to take a step forward, the gun warm in her hands.

Timmons and Lee hovered close by, weapons drawn and ready. They circled the thing on the other side, worked their way closer as it backed up against the wall, allowed them to corner it. It seemed oblivious to their movement, preoccupied with the wound it had just received on its face.

Sok scrambled away, running to find Wert in the shadows beyond the reach of the remaining candles. Somewhere in the darkness, he called out for the other man, voice cracking. "Mr. Wert? Mr. Wert, I'll find you, sir. Say something, please. Sir?"

Mitchell dragged the second arcade machine away from the doors and fought with the table next, throwing himself backward to wrench it free from its binding. Gasping and gulping, he at once began to unwind the cables connecting the table to door handles, his sobbing audible.

"Mark, you piece of shit, get over here!" Timmons hissed, keeping the creature in his periphery.

Lee licked his lips, held his crowbar tight. He inched forward, raised it, and then fell back when that tail lashed close to his face. When he spoke, it was in a hushed tone. "Olivia, shoot it."

She heard him, nodded, focused on aiming the gun at the creature's head. That yellow gory path along its cheek was proof of her luck. Side stepping, her breath caught in her throat, she lifted the gun, fought to keep it steady.

Fluttering candles shed a feeble light across the creature, a wayward flashlight on the floor nearby half-turned toward them offering an unsettling backlight. As Timmons passed, his shadow fell across the wall, across Olivia. He worked his way around the creature, closer to her.

Not bothering to track on either Lee or Timmons anymore, the creature faced her, its form close to the floor. Those black eyes met hers. Licking her lips, she found her finger floating over the trigger, locked in place above it. For some reason, she was unable to pull it a second time. Perhaps it was the way the creature knit its brow, shrank closer against the linoleum. Or maybe it was due to the parted lips, the little frown on its face.

"Come on, girly, shoot it," Timmons said, edging closer to her, his grin tight and forced. "It's right there."

Bile burned in her stomach. Olivia's hands shook, her gaze moving over Wilcox's face, those eyes imploring her. Her finger touched the trigger. "I've got it."

"Jeeesus, just gimme the gun!" Having slid up close enough, Timmons grappled with Olivia, wrestling the gun from her hands.

She struggled briefly, let him take the gun, and shrank against the wall behind her. Face hot, limbs tingling, Olivia found herself staring at the creature – it had bristled and advanced on them in only a second. With a shriek, its bottom jaw unhinged, the blackness within that mouth unimaginably deep. She saw multiple rows of gunmetal gray fangs. It lunged.

A strong arm, the creature's, shoved her to the side as it pounced on Timmons before he could get a shot in. Both pincer hands punctured his stomach, drove deep into him, soaking his shirt with dark red blood. Just as fast, the pincers withdrew, bringing with them loops of frayed gray guts and bits of tattered, dripping meat. The stink of raw sewage filled the air.

The gun fell to the floor.

Screeching, the creature skittered back, let Timmons drop, and leapt back into the ceiling. A few tiles dropped, smashed on the floor, its heavy movements rattling the walls.

Timmons burped up blood, on his back, hands on his stomach. Trying in vain to scoop himself back together, he gagged, looking down at the damage. Lee ran forward, dropped down beside him, hunting for the gun.

"Ah, shit!" Timmons' face twisted up.

Mitchell flung open the doors into the corridor, panting as he stared out into the shadows. He turned to the others and his eyes widened. Clumsily, he rushed to Timmons, stood above him. At the sound of chittering, he ducked, searched the ceiling. "Doors'r open! We need to get out of here now!"

Timmons choked. "Oh yeah, just drag me out, right?"

"Where do we go?" Olivia asked.

"The processing area. Safest place here. Big metal doors. No access in once you close 'em, lock 'em," Mitchell said, sweat streaming down his face.

She shook her head. "Why didn't we go there first?"

Sok appeared. "No food or water. Oh no, Mr. Timmons."

"Jesus, boy, called me Joe. For godsake."

"Where'd it go?" Lee asked.

"Back up into the ceiling. I don't know. But we've got to get out of here now," Mitchell said. "Need to get down to processing and lock the door."

"Larry?" Timmons asked, growing paler by the second.

"Ah, he's, um, he's dead," Sok replied.

"Well, shit."

"Come on, get his arms," Lee said, hooking Timmons under his armpits. "Mark, I need your help. Come on, man!"

Mitchell fretted, glanced around, and then took Timmons by his boots, lifting up gently.

Timmons groaned in pain.

Olivia picked up a flashlight from the floor as they traveled to the open doors. Her prybar was by the table, but she chose to grab a fallen piece of rebar, finding it lighter, thinner.

Off they went to the stairwell, Olivia leading.

Chapter 15

They'd made it to the landing on L2 when Timmons let out a cry and began to twist and flail. "Put me down! Put me down, dammit! Ahh!"

Mitchell and Lee immediately complied, placing him on the ground.

"Lean me up, don't leave me flat on my back like this..."

Working together, the two men helped Timmons sit up and pulled him closer to the wall where he could lean. Burping up red and pink froth, Timmons winced, bared his teeth.

"Ah, shit... shit..."

"Joe, we don't have time for this," Lee whispered. He glanced up and around. "We're almost there. You can rest soon. And there's a med kit in Processing, I know there is."

"Oh, yeah, just need a band-aid," Timmons said, smirking. He licked at the blood lining his lips and then, groaning, dug inside of his jacket for his cigarettes. "Help me light this, would'ja?"

Lee guided the cigarette into Timmons' mouth and flicked the lighter. He swallowed thickly turned back to Mitchell. "Did anyone grab the gun?"

Sok stepped forward. "I did."

"Let me get that." Lee held his hand out.

"Sure thing, of course." He gingerly drew the gun from his back pocket, offering it Lee with the trembling precision of a layman performing guided surgery.

Lee took it, checked the ammo. "Couple shots left. I saw it bleed, which means we hurt it. Aim for the head and I'll bet it'll drop. Olivia, keep that light pointed up."

"Sorry..."

Mitchell frowned. "We gotta keep moving, Joe."

185

Timmons exhaled smoke and coughed. "I think I'll just …stay here if that's okay."

"What? No way," Lee said.

"My… guts are out, Case. I'm dying. I can feel it. Fuckin' prick …jacked me up. Jeee-sus, he sure did." His grin spread, his teeth bloodstained. "Can't do much for me now."

Lee grimaced. "I'm not going to leave you here."

"You have to… I'm dead weight. That, and I, hah, I… don't want yah to have to stare at my corpse for the next two days." Smoke trailing from between his lips, Timmons tilted his head back. "Just… lemme get that rebar."

"Rebar won't do much good."

Timmons grunted. "Well, shit, I know that."

"You're hurt and it'll come right for you as soon as we're gone, man," Lee said. "Don't do this. Please, don't."

"Hell, I'll buy you some time, right? Thing'll have to get personal… close quarters… I'll get in a few good whacks…"

Lee grimaced. "Only a couple shots left…" His jaw tensed, he held out the gun to Timmons. "Take it. Make it regret getting personal with you."

His hand weak, Timmons took the gun. "You sure?"

"I'm sure. Dennis, give him your flashlight."

"Um, right…"

Timmons lay the flashlight in his lap, gave a weak chuckle around his cigarette. "I'll give him what for, lads."

"Timmons," Olivia said. "I'm sorry…"

"No time to apologize. Just… get the hell outta Dodge."

Lips numb again, she nodded.

"Go on then, get," Timmons said, less gruff than earlier. In fact, speaking took more effort and he had to take in a shaky breath. "Marky, you take care of these kids, you got it? They're kids, Mark. You don't… let anything happen to them."

Mitchell winced, head low. "Right, Joe."

They continued down the next flight, and the next, until they reached the landing of L1. Olivia accidentally scanned her flashlight up and caught part of Vazquez's leg. Her throat burned and she grabbed for the door to open it.

Olivia studied the smashed glass doors on the left, shook herself. They turned down a short corridor on the right before the hall opened into the open RME section of L1. At the end of that corridor, they found a single steel door. PROCESSING, the label said. Five inch by six foot foggy glass panels framed the door on either side, barely letting Olivia get a peek inside. She could only see vague shapes on the other side. Surveillance cameras pointed down at them as they gathered and Sok took the lead.

"With the power out, the security system runs on the back-up, which is fine, really." He flipped open the panel and it lit up. "See? Still working."

"Good. Hurry, Dennis," Mitchell said.

Sok typed in a password and the locking mechanism within the door sighed, clicked, and released. He opened the door, let the others in, and shut it tightly behind them. The door locked as soon as he pressed another button on the inside.

The e-lights glowed dimly in the room, Olivia turning to look at the long rows of metal tables covered in equipment, hand-held tools she didn't recognize, and protective gear – goggles, face shields. Counters lined the large room, a swinging door in the far back labeled 'LOCKERS'. There were no windows, no drop ceiling, only girded iron, and riveted plates. Above them, in a grid of piping, the sprinkler system blinked, sensors always on.

"Are you sure it can't get in?" she asked.

"Not easily. It'd have to rip that door off," Lee said.

"But the glass…"

"Unbreakable," he said. "'Sides, I doubt it could squeeze in."

"Why is this room so heavily secured?"

Lee shrugged. "Rare minerals are processed here. Some of them are worth a lot of money. Company doesn't want anyone stuffing their pockets."

"Only a few people have access. IT and the lab techs. Site Lead. Safety Manager," Sok said.

Her chin lowered. "And there's no food or water?"

"There's a, um, a sink in the bathroom."

"Better than nothing…" She bit her bottom lip and began to explore the room, studying the strange equipment on the counters. Wrapping her arms around herself, she slowly walked the perimeter of the large room.

There were collections of broken rock segments in glass cases along the one stretch of counter, measuring tools left out between the displays. A giant rock tumbler of some stripe had been installed into the wall. Curious, Olivia neared one of those glass displays and peered in. Within, bits of vibrant blue crystal poked out from gaps in black chunks of stone. Her eyes widened at the lovely, rich colors. Captivated by its beauty, she shivered.

The others were silent behind her until Mitchell began to gag and whine, leaning against the far wall closest to the door. Olivia turned, expecting to see something upsetting at the foggy glass panels on either side of the steel door. Instead, she only saw Mitchell quaking, eyes closed, running his fingers over his face, through his greasy, thinning hair.

Relief flooded over her despite the state of him. Guilt gnawed at her stomach soon after. Mitchell rubbed his sweaty brow and grimaced, head low. Her attention shifted from his despair to the dark, blurry movement behind the fogged glass and her heart fluttered in her chest. Something upsetting had indeed wandered up to the door outside.

"Oh!" Words failed her and she pointed.

"Shit," Lee said. "Mitchell, get away from the door."

Mitchell didn't need to be told twice. He skipped away, gasped at the sight of the black hand pressed palm-down on the glass. "It's here. Holy shit, it's here."

An undefined silhouette, a shadow, drew closer and pulled away. It pressed right against the glass next, the details a bit easier to see. Part of its face, a black eye, became visible. A muffled trill sounded from outside. A curious little sound met her ears as it tapped its claws on the glass. It backed away. A loud crack, a heavy, thick impact – its fist against the glass. Not even a sliver appeared in the opaque surface. It punched the glass again, shrieked.

It disappeared from view. A thud, metallic. The steel door didn't budge. Another thud, another shriek. It howled, the cry metallic, as serrated as a rusty bone saw.

Sprinting to stand only a few yards from the door, Lee shouted, teeth bared. "Yeah, fuck you too!"

The creature threw itself against the steel door one more time and let out a pitched wail, the tone vaguely human. A warped voice, uncanny in its resemblance to what had once belonged to another man, cried out in frustration. Astor Wilcox, junior partner, had himself a tantrum out in the corridor. Then, the cry faltered, trailed off into a heavy, eerie silence.

Olivia waited, breaths shallow.

After a few minutes had passed without incident, Mitchell began to cry again, bracing himself against one of the tall metal tables. He quaked and shuddered.

"It can't get in," she whispered.

Mitchell sobbed. "And we can't leave…"

Lee fell against the wall, slid down along his back,

slumped over on the floor. "Son of a bitch. I don't want to die here."

"We're not going to die here," she said weakly.

Lee shot her a deadly glare. "You don't think that thing won't attack the rescuers? What'll happen after that? They won't come looking for us. They'll just firebomb the whole damn rig."

"Ah, Site Decimus has a net worth of over 1.5 billion dollars, Casey. I doubt they'll destroy it," Sok said.

"We shouldn't have left Joe," Lee muttered.

Mitchell coughed. "He wanted us to leave him."

"You didn't argue, did you?" His eyes turned accusatory, Lee's lips pulling back. "Back in the mess hall, all you wanted to do was get away. First, you left Frank behind, then Joe…"

"Now com'on, that ain't fair… I was scared…"

"You were so scared you were ready to leave us all to die as long as it meant you got to slip away."

"I'm sorry."

"At least you're goddamn sober now," Lee hissed, gritting his teeth. He shut his eyes. "Thought I was going to get a contact high off you earlier. Made me sick."

"Now look here, kid…"

"No, you look here. We stood up for you, man. After the accident, we stood up for you. We all kept our mouths shut for how many years? Been two for me. Two years since I started on Decimus. Two years of watching you fall all over yourself. And how about Joe? He fought for you, said you were better. Wert let you stay." Lee's brown eyes opened, and he stared up at Mitchell. "How many times did Petry threaten to walk you down to Safety to get swabbed, man?"

Mitchell swallowed thickly, looked away. "Stop it."

"I don't want to die here because I don't want to die next to you, Mark. I don't deserve to die next to you."

"I wasn't thinking straight," Mitchell muttered, rubbing at his face. "Dammit, I wasn't thinking straight at all. My feet moved on their own. I ran. I couldn't think. I just ran."

"Which time?" Lee asked.

"Frank was screaming. I couldn't see him die. I couldn't see someone else die. You weren't there. You didn't see what I saw. You didn't see Dave's body. What was left of him."

"So, you up and ran?"

"I did. But I didn't want to leave Joe. I just knew he was too stubborn to be talked down. He chose to stay."

"Right."

"I blame myself well enough. You go ahead and blame me too. I don't even care anymore," Mitchell said. "Blame me for every single one of them."

Lee shook his head. "No one blamed you for Dave."

"Thing is, I blamed myself." Pausing to look at his hands, Mitchell turned them over, studied the lines and the creases, the dirt and the callouses. He blinked, licked his lips. "When Joe called me in that night, I was three sheets to the wind. I mean, I was gonzo-gone. Should'a said no. It was after hours and I was off, so it wasn't like I broke a rule by having a drink, but I'd told Joe I was dry again. Didn't want him to think I'd fallen off the wagon, so I showed. Made myself stand there, pretended to be okay. Next thing I know, Dave's… and I thought I'd blacked out. Thought I'd blacked out and let my best friend die."

Lee nodded slowly, exhaled through his nose. "It was those things calling to us the first time. Not you."

"I didn't know that. Not then, at that moment. Not when I was staring down at that heap of bones and meat. The harness was soaked in blood. That was the only thing that clued me into what I was even looking at, y'know. The harness. Signaled Norris to shut her down as soon as I realized. Threw my guts up over the side of the platform. God, I thought I'd done it. For days, I thought I'd done it." Choking on those last words, Mitchell raised his arm, stifled a sob. He bit down into the fabric of his jacket, cried weakly.

"Man…" Lee sighed, shook his head.

"I shouldn't 'uv run away when Frank needed me," Mitchell wept, shaking his head.

"Look, let's just move forward. No use dwelling now. I just want to live through this. We've all made mistakes."

Sok wrung his hands nearby, glanced over at the closed steel door. He fixed his glasses on the bridge of his nose. "I couldn't even move when Mr. Frank was in danger. I just stood there, frozen to the spot."

"I hesitated. I should have shot the creature," Olivia said, wrapping her arms around herself. "It's just that I thought I saw something in its eyes – something human."

Lee shrugged. "I guess I could've done something different somewhere in there, but I can't think of it. Maybe I could've stayed in my room, let you guys knock and knock."

"We all should've stayed in our rooms," Mitchell said.

"Hell, I should've hopped on the boat and gone ashore." Lee sat up, lifted his chin, and nodded sagely. "But no, I decided to stay, didn't I? Thought it was the right thing to do. Not that I had anywhere to go yet."

"I feel that. Definitely don't have anywhere else to go." Mitchell coughed, wiped at his eyes. "She got the house and the kids in the divorce."

"I didn't know you had kids, Mark," Lee said.

"Two girls."

"Wow."

"Haven't seen them in years. She couldn't take the drinking. Truth is," Mitchell said, smiling sadly, "I stayed on

Decimus after the accident because I had nowhere else to go."

"You can get a little one-bedroom real easy an hour from shoreside. I know a place," Lee said.

He nodded. "I might ask for more details later."

Lee turned his attention to Sok and Olivia. "Since we have the time, what about you two? Got any tragic backstories, or what?"

"Ah, well, no…"

"Come on, Dennis. This is the part where we share shit. You're so secretive, man. Quiet and polite. Everyone knows you're the smartest person onsite – I've heard about your degrees." Leaning back against a set of drawers, Lee tilted his head and regarded Sok with cool, curious eyes. "Petry blabbed."

"Oh, hah-hah."

"Tell us something. Anything."

"Ah…" Sok considered his next words. "I'm one of seven children."

Lee's brow raised. "Whoa, that's a lot of kids."

"It was hard growing up without a space of my own. We had to share rooms, after all. They all moved away eventually. Ah, except for me. I mean, I work on the rig every few months, but in my off time, I'm home, with my mother," Sok said.

"Aw, what a good son."

"Hah, thank you, Casey. Someone had to stay. She's older, you know. She needs my help. It's rough for her when I'm away for extended periods of time. The goal is to find a high paying job closer to home. Something less dangerous." Finding something amusing, he pressed his fist to his smiling mouth.

"I'll take that. Olivia, what about you?"

She sniffed. "One of three. Two half-brothers. I never

see them. My Dad didn't really come around much after he remarried. It was just me and my Mom for the longest time, until she passed from cancer a couple years ago. Been on my own since."

"Did you care for her during her illness?" Sok asked.

Olivia gave a short nod. "I did."

"It's a lot for one person."

"It was. But when it's for family, it's what you've got to do."

He nodded. "I completely agree. I wish my siblings felt the same way, honestly. It's fallen onto me to be the responsible one and while I don't resent them for that fact, it would be nice to have some assistance, or at least be recognized. Not that I need recognition! Oh, that sounded selfish. It's just very difficult to do it all on my own."

"You could ask for their help, Dennis," she said.

"Ah hah, I've tried. The response tends to be, um, 'you've got this, Dennis'. 'If anyone can do it, it's you.' I don't want them to think it's too much for me. I don't want my mother to feel like a burden either," he said. "Family is complicated."

"That it is," Mitchell agreed. "Case, how 'bout you?"

"Me?"

"Yeah, we've all opened up. Your turn."

Lee rubbed his face. "Hmm, I don't really do the whole family thing. Close friends, yeah. Those I got a few of."

"You don't have a family?" Mitchell asked.

"My family doesn't have me. Haven't spoken to either of my parents for years. They disowned me, threw me out onto the streets when I was sixteen, all because I told them who I am." Lee smiled a little, rolled his shoulders. "As I said, I got a few close friends and that's all I need."

Mitchell frowned. "They kicked you out for being yourself?"

"They sure did."

"Their loss. You're a great man."

Lee eyed him, nodded. "Thanks."

Olivia searched the cabinets and lockers in the back room until she found protective gear. It wasn't a soft fabric, but it would suffice as bedding on the hard floor. Sok had helped her, and they both offered the protective suits to Lee and Mitchell.

It occurred to her that her cellphone was still in her pocket. She pulled it out and woke it up, frowning at the cracked screen and the low battery. The bar situation hadn't changed yet. Still no service. Looking around at the metal walls, her brows knit.

"Say, Dennis, would you get reception in this room?"

"Doubtful, even if the link were up."

"Damn."

"Sorry."

"Not your fault," she said, shutting down her cell.

Piling up a few hazmat suits on the hard floor, Olivia curled up in the corner furthest from the steel door and closed her eyes. Exhaustion had again caught up with her and she felt a tug at the back of her eyelids, urging her to drift down into the dark waters of sleep. She hoped not to dream.

A few musical notes played somewhere far away, dancing in the stagnant air along that long, deserted street. It was night, the sky black and starless. The streetlights were out of order, the green and yellow bulbs dead. For as far as she could see along Main Street, each traffic light shined red, at every intersection. Olivia held herself tightly, stared at the eerie glow.

No cars. No people. No sound, save for the tinkling warble of a distant piano, the plunking drawn out, out of key. The song was lost, needing to be found.

Storefront windows sat empty, devoid of light. Dry tree stumps lined the road, the gnarled roots growing up through the crumbling sidewalk. She walked toward Pine St, stepping over huge cracks in the concrete, her foot rolling over thick tendrils.

Gradually, the music grew louder. She was headed toward the source, apparently. Her chest hurt. The melody was familiar. As she stumbled over higher mounds of cracked concrete, she began to hear the lyrics, a woman's voice singing.

Beautiful dreamer, the woman whispered, *wake unto me.*

"Mom?" Olivia called.

Pine Street seemed no closer as she hurried her pace, the sidewalk broken and raised in her path. Shops tilted, slanted over, their windows cracked and doors bowing.

Beautiful dreamer, out on the sea…

"Mom?!"

Beaauuuutifullllll dreee-

She climbed over a heap of broken concrete, fingers digging into cold, wet soil. The roots here were shiny and segmented, intricate swirls embossed into them. Just as she reached the top to look out onto Pine St, a shadowy figure on the next corner waving her onward, one of the tendrils closest to her hand slipped around her wrist, snagged her.

In an attempt to wrench herself free, Olivia staggered backward and almost toppled down. The root did not give, held on tight, dug into her flesh. She pulled on it, eyes wide. That tendril had hundreds of little legs, each sharp, each segmented. It wasn't a root at all, but a centipede – an awful, slithering centipede.

She screamed, yanked on it, drawing more of the

creature from inside of the mound of rock and dirt.

The red lights glowed brightly, closing in around the corners of her vision. No music, no song. Only her screams.

A hand on her shoulder, shaking her softly.

Olivia started, gasped.

"Shh." It was Sok's voice. "Sorry, Ms… Olivia. Wake up."

"What's going on?"

"Listen…"

She turned onto her side, leaned on her elbow. Lee and Mitchell were awake, their attention trained toward the door, both men held enraptured to a low fluctuating tone emanating from the other side of the steel door.

"Do you hear that?" Sok asked.

Her mouth was dry. "I do. What is it?"

"Sounds like a voice, doesn't it?" Mitchell asked.

Olivia crawled to her knees, strained to hear, to separate that monotone, wavering sound from the strange, hollow echo of the processing room.

A male voice, almost inaudible, moaned. "Help me."

Mitchell grimaced. "Who is that?"

"Wilcox?" Olivia suggested.

"No," Lee stated.

The voice called again, strained. "Please, help me. Please."

Sweating profusely, Mitchell swayed, caught himself on the metal table on his right. "Holy shit, that's Frank."

"Impossible," Sok muttered, licking his lips.

"Help me. Please, please help me."

"He's right outside the door," Olivia said.

Mitchell gulped on air, spun around to stare at the others, his eyes bulging. "Shit, he's alive. He's still alive…"

"It didn't kill him?" She scowled incredulously.

"He must've crawled away after it left him to come after us. Frank, you crazy son of a bitch…" Eyes gleaming madly, Mitchell grinned, approached the door. "We've got to let him in."

"Dennis, open the door," Lee said, running over to join Mitchell at the entrance. He pawed at the controls, peered over his shoulder at the slender young man. "Come on, he's out there. We need to drag him in before that thing comes back."

"It isn't logical."

"What? Get over here…"

"No, it… it isn't logical. Mr. Frank was taken on L3. We heard him above us. There's no conceivable way that he not only survived the attack, but managed to crawl down every flight of stairs, avoid the creature, and find us," Sok said, his lips tight over his teeth. His chin dropped. "I'm, uh sorry – it's a trap."

"A trap? You think it dragged him down here?" Lee asked, expression horrified.

"I don't know but opening that door… is unwise."

"I agree with Dennis," Olivia said.

"Help me… please, please help me…"

"He's right there." Mitchell bent and peered through the foggy glass. "I think I can see him, guys. There's a little light out there, and I think I can see him."

"If it dragged him here, we should go out and get him. We have weapons. We could fight the thing off, pull him in, shut the door. We can't leave him out there, even if it is a trap," Lee said, exhaling raggedly. "It'll kill him if we don't do anything."

Clearly frustrated, Sok rolled his shoulders and stalked over to the steel door. He glared at Mitchell first, then Lee. His hand hovered over the panel on the right, dropped to his side. Lips close to the glass, Sok called out, "Mr. Frank, is that you?"

"Help me. Please."

Sok swallowed thickly. "Mr. Frank, is the creature out there?"

"Help."

Shoulders tensing, Sok shook his head. "What's your name?"

"Please, help me."

With the weight of the pyrrhic victory evident in his tired eyes, Sok again turned to Mitchell and Lee, gesturing toward the glass. "Something's wrong. We're not opening the door."

"He's confused, in shock. Probably lost a lot of blood. Dennis, you can't leave him out there," Lee hissed.

"I'm sorry, Casey, but… I'm not opening that door."

"Open it."

"No."

"Dammit, Dennis, open the door. Please. I can see him too. He's only a few feet away. One of us can grab him, pull him in…"

"No."

Mitchell charged at Sok, grabbed him by his collar, and swung him around to slam his back against the door. "Dammit, Dennis, open the door! I'm not going to ask you again."

"But…"

"I left him to die once!. I sure as hell ain't doing it again, you hear me? I'm tired of running. I'm going to save my friend's life. Open. The. Damn. Door."

Taking in a sharp breath, Sok closed his eyes and nodded anxiously. As soon as Mitchell released him, he flipped the panel open and typed in a code. The lock whirred.

"This is a bad idea," Olivia whispered, hanging back and clutching her piece of rebar again.

Sok refused to pull the door handle, dropping back as Mitchell did it instead. With a creak, the corridor appeared before his eyes, Lee squeezing in beside him to peer out.

The e-lights directly outside glowed dimly, shadows swelling just beyond their reach. Ugly red streaks on the floor led to him. A set of pale white hands splayed across the tile, the sleeves stained a deep rust brown. Frank's hair clung and stuck in congealed, stiff tufts, his head turned to the side. He lay on his stomach, twitching, half of him in the light, the other in shadow.

"Frank!" Mitchell hissed.

"He's further out than I thought," Lee said. "Hey, can you cover me? Dennis, keep the door open."

"Don't…"

Dismissing Sok with a wave of his hand, Lee cautiously stepped out in the corridor, eyes flitting back and forth between Frank and the deep shadow many feet ahead. When Frank twitched again, Lee quickened his pace.

He'd nearly reached him when Frank's head turned, exposing his face. Both milky eyes stared off dreamily, his mouth hanging open. His chin was coated in dried blood.

"Help me."

Those words hadn't come out of Frank's gaping mouth, from between those frozen dead lips. His head turned a bit more, exposing the black, segmented cord wrapped around his neck, guiding his movements.

The creature lowered from the ceiling onto his back, that long, whiplike tail extending down, under, around Frank's throat. Lifting Frank up slightly, like a marionette, the tail flipped him over, tossed him into the light. Only the top half of Frank's body rolled out, his entrails hanging out from under his torn shirt, cleaved off just under his exposed ribcage.

The creature lighted gently, daintily on the floor, both

sets of arms supporting it as that mouth, that toothy, horrible mouth, opened. Frank's voice came out. "*Help me, please.*"

"Fuck!" Lee kicked his feet, propelled himself backward toward the door. He slammed into Mitchell, the other man frozen in terror only a foot behind him.

It lunged, landing on Lee, sent him hurtling through the open door with its full weight on top of him. Lee slid along his back, the creature shrieking, grabbing at him.

Mitchell leapt close, brought down a crowbar against the creature's skull. The resounding crack of its shell – or bone, or whatever it was made of – reverberated through the processing room. The thing spun on him, bared its fangs. Mitchell swung on it a second time and the creature caught the crowbar with one of its humanoid, clawed hands. The pincer hands lashed out, swiped at Mitchell, its tail lashing.

Olivia rushed in, swung her rebar. Its tail knocked her feet out from under her, sending her crashing to the floor beside it. Staring at her with its black eyes, it regarded her coolly before driving one of its pincer hands down against Lee.

Struggling under it, Lee grabbed that arm, fought to hold it back, his screams loud and unhinged.

Sok grabbed her arm, helped her to her feet. He too ran in, swung his rebar at it. Its other human hand grabbed it, attempted to yank it from his grip.

The creature straddled Lee's kicking, flailing body, a pincer aiming for the man's throat. The other pincer hand balanced itself against the wall on the left. That tail undulated, serpentine, cut the air sharply. Both human hands were occupied, holding onto Mitchell's crowbar, Sok's rebar. It clicked and trilled, the noises almost… euphoric.

Peering over at Olivia, it beamed, pride written on that

horrid hybrid creature's alien, yet oh-so-human face. Wilcox's face. The mandibles along his jaw flexed inward, clung close to the bone. He grinned with gunmetal gray fangs, let his long, hideous tongue hang out, and panted loudly. He grinned at her, at Olivia. He wanted her to watch.

No, not he. It.

She swallowed, geared up for another swing. "Astor, let him go. Do you hear me, Astor?"

At hearing that name, the creature began chirping like a baby bird, the grin widening.

"Stop it, Astor."

It trilled excitedly, gave a hard shove on both weapons, and threw both Sok and Mitchell back to fall to the floor. Its hands free, it grabbed Lee's head, twisted sharply to the side, and snapped his neck.

Olivia cried out, stumbled forward, raised the rebar. The tail caught it, wrapped around the length of the metal bar, slid around her wrists. It yanked her close, turning its body to catch her with splayed, open arms.

Shouting incoherently, Mitchell dove in and drove his crowbar into the creature's back, just under the chitinous, armored shell covering its shoulder blade. It shrieked, let fly a hand, and sliced Mitchell's throat wide open with the blade-like protrusion growing out of its arm.

Gagging, clutching at his neck, Mitchell staggered to the side, the blood bright red as it flowed over his fingers.

Olivia wept, slammed her fists against the thing's chest. It held her near, held her tight, and glanced over at Sok.

He stood many feet away, shaking, holding the rebar in the air. Licking his lips, he let out a whimper. His voice held no weight when he choked out three words. "Let her go."

It clicked at him, bared its teeth, and turned its back dismissively. The creature carried Olivia to the open door, chirping, tail lashing, its hands holding her against its chest.

She thrashed, struggled. It held her tighter.

"Stop! Let her go!" Sok cried a little louder.

A low chirp left its lips. Olivia felt it tense. It angled itself in the corridor, pivoted, and she got one last glimpse of Sok in the Processing room, the door hanging open. His thin face was all twisted up, the rebar swaying in his slender, shaking hands.

"Dennis," she breathed. "Dennis, help me."

His bottom jaw worked loosely; he stood frozen.

That self-aware malevolence sparkled in the creature's black eyes, and it caught the door handle with its tail, pulled it shut with an audible click – Dennis still inside the Processing room.

The next minutes were a blur as it took off running, Olivia in its second set of arms. It kept those pincer blades tilted almost flat to avoid cutting into her as it carried her into the shadows.

Chapter 16

All she knew was rocky, disjointed motion and swirling darkness, the creature's shallow, wet breathing crackling in her ear. Its scent, sickly sweet, reminded her of sunbaked roadkill and day-old sweat. Strong, diamond-hard fingers held her firmly against an equally rigid chest. The flat side of oppressive pincers dug into her sides, kept her body pinned.

Her head spinning, she took note of the dim light, and the blur of the world became clearer, taking shape. The creature had stopped running over the walls, along the ceilings, up the stairwell. Slowing to a crawl, it carried her a bit further and set her down, crouching in front of her.

She kicked her feet, pushed herself back against a wall. Nearby, a flashlight on the floor shone into the corner of the small room, reflecting backward. The exam table had been knocked onto its side, the cot torn to shreds. Swallowing back bile, Olivia realized where it had brought her.

Her eyes returned to its face.

Both sets of hands touched the floor, and it crept up to her, observed her with inky eyes. The wicked grin faded, became an awkward, toothy smile. It blinked, overtook her, and grabbed for her hand with one of its own.

As much as she wanted to fight, it was too strong. The creature forced her palm against its hard cheek. Where her flesh met the shell, the colors shifted, turned bright red and yellow. It trilled deeply, obviously elated.

"Astor," she breathed. "Can you understand me?"

Top lip tugging upward on the right side of its mouth, it nodded slowly, mechanically.

"Can you talk to me, Astor?"

The thing blinked again, drew closer. The deformed

pincer hands trailed down her shoulders, its humanoid fingers tenderly cupping the sides of her face. Mouth working, it clucked, let out a low, grinding sound. It croaked painfully.

"What was that?" she asked.

Its jaw opened, lips forming words, and Olivia's own voice spoke back to her. "*What was that?*"

"That's my voice."

"*That's my voice,*" it replied, still copying her.

She closed her eyes. "I want to hear your voice, Astor."

Another low grinding sound escaped its throat. "Ah-iv."

"Can you talk to me?"

"Iss."

"What do you want?"

It ran its long talons through her hair, studied her face. Closing in on her, the creature nuzzled her throat. "Oo."

Heart pounding, she nodded. Her insides felt cold, a chill running up and down her spine. "Oh, I don't think I'm good enough for you, Astor. I don't deserve a guy like you."

Pulling back, the creature gazed at her face and forced her hand from its cheek to its chest, over its heart. The colors swirled along the black tendrils delving into the flesh, the remaining skin ghost white. It leaned in close, smiled at her, implored her with its black eyes. The parasite hadn't swallowed Wilcox's face in its entirety. Those lips were still human, even if the teeth were not. It smiled again. "Wee-ah. Wee-ah… ah-red-ee… wan."

"We're already one?"

"Yeh-ess."

"Why did you kill them all, Astor? Why did you do that?"

"Nah breed. Threat. Threat." Those brows knit, irritation flashing on the thing's face. It bared its teeth. "Kill threat."

"They were afraid of you."

205

"Good." Wilcox's tortured, shredded voice rasped from the creature's mouth. The more it spoke, the easier it became to understand. Intelligence blazed in its eyes, concentration screwing its face. "Tied me. Left me. Took you."

"You didn't need to kill them if you just wanted me," she said, twisting in its grasp. It slid its pincers downward, slipped them under her shirt and began to pry it up. Olivia grabbed the fabric, yanked it back down.

"Killed them for you." It searched her face. Clawed fingers wrapped around her wrists, forced her hands above her head even as she began to thrash in protest. It continued to lift her shirt with those pincers.

"Stop it, Astor." Olivia controlled her volume.

It bared her bra, clicked excitedly. One pincer held her shirt in place while the other slid between her breasts, under the band. The creature licked the front of its teeth, leaned in closer until its forehead pressed against hers.

The ridges along its skull dug into her skin. Olivia writhed. "I said stop, please. Astor, I said stop."

It paused. "Lie with me."

"I don't think we're …compatible. I'm sorry."

"No?"

"No, Astor. You're not human."

"No?" Blinking, its nose crinkled in confusion and it arched its back, angling its hips to peer down at the chitinous scales of black carapace covering its pelvic region. It trilled, lashed its tail.

"Let me go."

Frustrated chirps broke from its lips as it released her hands and felt at itself, claws running over the intricate, embossed surface of its shell. When the creature cupped its enclosed groin, it whimpered and croaked.

"The doctors can help you, *Astor*." She emphasized his

name, spoke it clearly, loudly. Eyes shining, a tear broke along her lower lashes and trickled down her cheek. "When we're rescued, you should let them help you. I'll be there with you too."

Taking her shoulders with its top set of arms and holding her in place with the bottom, it attempted to mount her, undulated twice. It gave up, growling as it pawed feebly at its own body.

"Astor, are you ...tired?" She'd wanted to ask if it was hungry, but the word stuck in her throat. Images of corpses being gnawed down to the bright white bone ran through her mind like a macabre stop-motion picture. "I would lie down with you if you wanted to sleep. We could rest together."

It stared at her, head tilted.

She placed her palms on that hard chest, heard it inhale sharply. At her touch, the shell changed colors. It took her right hand by the wrist and, to her horror, forced it down along its belly. She fought desperately. "Astor, no."

It continued, slipping its claws under her fingers, molding her hand. Olivia grimaced, shut her eyes as it reached the destination. She felt textured furrows in the shell shiver. At once, its hips gave a start, began a slow thrusting motion. The ridges under her fingertips parted and something slimy, hot, and ribbed slid across her palm.

"Oh God," she choked, eyes still shut tight.

A low, staccato moan – jagged but human – tore from the creature. It squeezed her hand, forced her to hold that stiff, mucous drenched thing. Ooze slurped in her grip. Not human in shape or feel – thick at the base, long, corrugated, the tip swollen and bulbous. It pounded like a heart, the creature's moans and motions growing frenzied after only a few seconds.

It bucked, barked in ecstasy, and caught itself before it

could collapse on her. That long wet tongue slid across her throat.

Numb, Olivia's shallow breaths hitched, her lungs tight. Disgust twisted her mouth, her eyes open but staring off blindly. She lay slack, her hand falling to the floor when released. Whatever it had fouled her palm with tingled, burned her skin.

"Nyuh." It nuzzled her affectionately.

"Astor, let me go," she whispered. A muffled little crackle met her ears. The creature trilled, rubbed its cheek against her shoulder. She swallowed, collecting herself, and studied the way it moved. Its eyes were closed, its arms sliding around her middle. A series of loud clicks left its throat.

Lifting her right hand, she stared at the viscous product of the creature's passion, the stuff yellow and oily like congealed chicken fat. Her stomach turned and she scowled, wiping her palm on its armored back. At the touch, it chirped.

"What happens now, Astor?" Her head tilted back as she felt it sink lower to rest its head in her lap. Olivia absentmindedly stroked its hair, ran her fingers over the horned crest sweeping along its temple. The other horn dug into her thigh, causing her some discomfort.

The long, chitinous knives that ran the length of the creature's spine flattened against its body as it relaxed. "Marry."

Unable to stifle an anguished bout of laughter, she slapped her clean hand over her mouth, shuddered. She felt the creature stiffen, looked down to see it staring at her, the expression on its face one of great offense. Olivia swallowed, fighting to regain composure. "Astor, what about your, ah, your fiancée?"

Subtle acceptance smoothed its brow. "Mm, no."

"Will we live in your house?"

"Condo."

It was with great difficulty that she fought off another wave of hysterics, tears streaming down her face. Grimacing, she nodded quickly and wiped drool from her chin. "Ah, of course. Right. So, we're going to get on the boat? Go with the rescuers?"

It stiffened again. "Kill."

"Can't kill them, Astor. We need a ride home to your condo. How can we get married and live happily ever after if you kill them?" Olivia smiled mirthlessly, petted the side if its face.

"Kill," it repeated.

"Then no marriage. No condo."

Shifting in her lap, the creature appeared to concentrate, bumpy brows furrowing deeply as its black eyes searched the floor. It licked the front of its sharp teeth. "No?"

"No, Astor. We need to get rescued first. You have to see the doctors. They'll help you. We can get married right after that. We can be happy together. Isn't that what you want?"

"Ucht-t-t…"

"That's what you want, right?"

"Children." It blinked. "Have children."

"Well, right. Of course. Once we're back on land, and married, children. Right."

"Many children."

"Yeah, yeah, as many as you'd like – once we're rescued."

"Hungry."

She squeezed her eyes shut, throat tight. "Me too. Do you want to go to the kitchen, Astor? Do you want me to make us something to eat?" Acutely aware of the warble in her voice, Olivia bit her bottom lip, controlled her breathing.

"Bring food. I bring." Sliding off her, its two sets of arms worked together to support its weight, the tail lashing back and forth. Its deformed pincer hands clacked on the floor.

"Food for me?"

"For you."

"Oh, that's so sweet, honey." She forced a warm smile. Opportunity knocked; she answered. "You'll go get me something to eat, yeah? Up on L3, in the kitchen?"

"Yes."

"In the pantry, there's, ah, there's little plastic containers of cereal. In the… the kitchen pantry. Do you know where that is?"

"Yes."

"Honey, that's what I'd like. I'd like one of those little plastic containers of cereal. Maybe a boxed milk. A spoon?"

"Food?"

"Yeah, honey, milk and cereal."

"Meat?"

"No, no meat."

It studied the floor. "Acht-t-t-t…"

"I know you'll bring me exactly what I want, Astor. I am so very hungry. I don't feel well. Kind of weak and sick. Haven't eaten for a day, I think."

The creature trilled, searched her face. In a distorted human voice, Wilcox's voice, it muttered. "You did that to yourself, you know. It didn't have to be like this."

"What?"

"I bring. You stay." The spikes along its back raised and it took a mechanical step away from her, talons clacking against the linoleum. "Stay, don't move."

"I'm not going anywhere."

Regarding her with narrowed eyes, its suspicious grimace

turned to a slight smirk. A slow nod followed. It lowered its chin, mandibles spreading and separating from its jawline. The creature convulsed once, a thin belch escaping it, and a putrid glob of amber colored sick gushed from its mouth.

Olivia let out a cry, scrambled to get away before the creature grabbed her with its humanoid hands. It coated its second set of appendages in that ooze, belched up another fresh batch, and slathered it in thick ropes across her arms and shoulders, attaching the cords of sticky resin to the wall behind her. While it looked wet and stretchy leaving its mouth, it held her fast, tightening as it hardened.

Lips shining, it bared its teeth and leaned in as she squirmed, unable to loose herself from the webbing. It pointed a single clawed finger at her face and smiled. "Stay."

Panting, she nodded frantically. "Yes, right."

It gazed at her, head twitching, movements reptilian, and then hopped out of the light into the shadows, disappearing from the MedBay. For the first few moments, Olivia merely breathed, chin lifted, eyes closed. Biting her lip, she began to struggle in the net of corded resin, the stink of it making her sick.

Whatever it was made of, it refused to give despite her thrashing and, after a few minutes, she went limp in its hold, sweat on her brow and tears in her eyes. The urge to scream overcame her. Olivia cried out, kicked, flailed.

A shuffling sound out in the corridor met her ears and her weeping ceased, her lungs emptying, clenching in terror. She'd drawn the damn thing back with her wailing. Hot contempt flooded through her veins. Hatred not for it, but for herself. It had heard her and come running right back to check out the noise, as an animal might do.

Another shuffle of feet.

In the low, reflected glow of the wayward flashlight in the corner of the MedBay, a figure appeared. Sok, shaking, his piece of rebar clutched tightly in his slender hands, stared at her from behind his shining glasses.

"Dennis," she whispered.

"Olivia, I found you."

"I'm stuck, help me out of this…"

He dashed over to her and dropped to a crouch, began pulling on the cords. When that didn't work, he jumped up, searched the cabinets, and drew out a pair of medical scissors. With those he was able to cut through the ropes of sticky webbing. "Can you walk?"

"I think so," she said.

"You're not injured?"

"No. Hurry, please."

"It's really tough," he said, snipping away.

Once freed, Olivia took his hand, standing. "It's up on L3. If we can get back down to the Processing room, we can lock ourselves inside again. It can't get in."

"We'll have to go now. Are you ready?"

She nodded.

The ambient light from the windows along the corridor was more than enough to guide their way toward the stairwell. However, as soon as Sok opened the door, Olivia winced at the deep dark black greeting her.

"Flashlight's too bright," he whispered. "It'll see, I'm sure."

She reached back to her pocket, withdrew her cellphone, and turned it on. A softer, less obnoxious glow emanated from the screen. Not wanting to see how low the battery was at that point, she immediately turned it over in her hand.

Holding the cell out to cast the light across the landing, she brought into full view Timmons' slumped, eviscerated body, tangled up and stuffed into the corner beside the door. Covering her mouth and shutting her eyes, she spun away from the sight.

He had to take her phone from her for only moment, searching the floor around Timmons' corpse for the gun. When he didn't find it, Sok swallowed thickly, held back a retch, and shuffled over to her to place the phone back into her hand.

Sok took her arm, gently guided her away from the scene, and nudged her when they had reached the steps., Finally able to open her eyes, she glanced at Sok and the two nodded, descending.

Quickly but carefully, they slipped down the steps, doing their best to keep each footfall silent.

They had reached the L1 landing when a loud, shimmery melody began to blast from her cell speakers. Shocked, Olivia nearly dropped the thing, flipping it over to see an incoming call – George Leblanc's name and icon appearing in the center of the screen. "Oh shit, we have reception!"

Metal crashed, echoed loudly from somewhere above them.

"It heard! Silence it!" Sok exclaimed.

Olivia dismissed the call, every fiber of her being screaming at her for not answering, for not begging, crying out for Leblanc to send help, to send a warning to the boat already on its way. In the silence that followed, the creature shrieked.

"Hurry!" Grabbing her arm, Sok tugged her along, rushed out into L1, and looked back and forth. "It's clear."

They ran together, turned at the corner toward Processing lab. Olivia dodged Frank's shredded corpse, gasping when again confronted by it. As Sok slammed against the steel door and flipped the panel open, a metallic thud boomed from their level. It came from the direction of the stairwell, down the corridor.

Typing in the code with fumbling fingers, Sok unlocked the door and opened it. Another shriek, this one very close. They slipped inside, shut the door. At the same time, something heavy rammed into it.

The creature raged on the other side, punched, and kicked. It tested the glass again, over, and over. It howled, it wailed. Something wet and thick smacked the foggy glass next, the creature holding Frank's half-body up by the hair and pounding the dead man's face into a broken, bloody pulp.

Olivia hugged herself and watched, thankful for the opaque nature of the glass. She couldn't see more than vague shapes. Still, she knew what it was doing. The skull eventually cracked and caved in, pulverized. The creature tossed the body aside, roared.

Rather than look behind her and see the two bodies she knew would be there, lying still and mangled on the floor, she checked her phone. The battery was dying, the reception gone again. Olivia choked back a sob.

"It's okay."

"No, it's not." Leaning on the closest metal table, she rubbed at her raw eyes. "Dennis, this room is a dead zone, and we need to get a call out. We need to warn them."

He wrung his hands. "I'm sorry."

It slammed its forehead into the glass twice. A slivering crinkling pop noise tinkled from the frame.

Shuddering, she stole a glance and saw the first signs of tiny cracks in the glass spiderwebbing around the point of impact. Her insides went cold. "The glass…"

"It can't fit through."

"It could try."

"Not without critically injuring itself."

Tearing her gaze away from the door, Olivia pivoted on her heel, slid her phone back into her pocket. "Dennis, we

214

need to think of a plan. We can't stay here."

He frowned. "Staying here is the safest, most logical option."

"Casey was right." Peering back over her shoulder, Olivia gazed at Lee's corpse on the floor. Beside him, Mitchell's leg was visible from around the tables. "It'll attack them. They'll send out a team to kill it. Even if they do, we'd still be trapped in here for another week, maybe more. If we want to survive, Dennis, we have to get out of this room."

"Olivia..."

"I have to call George. He'll know how to contact the boat. We can get in one of the escape rafts along the side of the rig – I saw them, I know they're there. We can float out at sea, wait for the boat to come. It'll be here in another day, won't it?"

"Olivia, please…"

"We can wait for the boat. The creature won't follow us out there. Seawater kills them. It killed the smaller ones. I watched it happen. They melted."

"We don't know if that will work."

"We still need to get out."

"Well, of course, but…"

"That's the only way to contact them, to tell them what's here. They'll walk in blind. The creature will kill them."

He grabbed her shoulders. "Slow down. You're right, but we need to form a plan. We have to figure out a way to get out of here, warn them, and get to the life rafts. I don't know about seawater killing it, but I'd feel a lot better not being trapped here on the rig with that thing. The problem is… we're in here, and it's out there – outside the door."

"Is there another way out of this room?"

Scowling, Sok glanced over at the door just as the creature slammed its forehead against the glass. "No."

"We'll die in here…"

"No, we won't." He turned to her, waggled the rebar. With a stiff nod, he squared his shoulders. His voice dropped to a whisper, and he leaned toward her. "There's only one way in or out, so the obvious, most logical thing to do is to switch who is out and who is in. Once the door is shut, that's that."

Her eyes widened, she whispered back. "Dennis, what are you suggesting? Trapping the creature in here? We're in here."

"We wouldn't be in here once the door shut."

"How?"

Biting his lip, he looked around the room. "We'd have to trick it into coming in, first. Ah, then, we'd need to find a way to incapacitate it somehow, just for long enough to escape and shut the door behind us. It doesn't know the code."

"I don't think that rebar is going to do the trick this time," she breathed, teeth bared.

"Maybe not, but we have other tools at our disposal. Brute force isn't always the answer, after all. Look around, there's got to be something in this room that we can use to restrain the creature, or at least slow it down."

Olivia and Sok separated, began to look through the cabinets and drawers. She found a small electric chisel and a face shield. He found cables and brackets. In the corner of the room, a heavy-duty hoist system with a massive set of grabbers swayed, rock dust visible on the tray underneath.

"What is this?" she asked.

He shrugged. "Ah, well, they'll bring up big chunks of rock, right? They'll need to lift it, transport it to the big tumbler. The hoist runs the whole length of the room, see? That's the track along the ceiling there."

"Ah…" Her face lit up. "If we grabbed the creature with

this, we could hold it, at least for a few seconds…"

"I doubt it'd stay still long enough for that. The hoist lifts and lowers pretty slowly. Ah, sorry. It was a good idea!" An apologetic smile appeared on his lips. Sok glanced at the door as the thing outside thudded at the steel, evidently taking a break from slamming its head against the glass.

She deflated. "Damn."

He adjusted his glasses, studied the track along the ceiling. Chin lowering, he scanned the room, looked over the long metal tables. Sok blinked, perking slightly. "Ah, but… um… it could release something else."

"What are you thinking, Dennis?"

"Olivia, how are you with tying knots?"

"Good, I guess, why?"

"Because we're going to need a strong one," he said.

The long metal table was heavy and her arms and back burned, muscles straining as she helped him lift the free end up. They had to climb on top of one of the other tables, positioning themselves where the track ended, ten feet into the Processing room, the door directly in front of them.

Dangling from cables looped around its leg, the other end of the table hung from the hoist, elevated as far as it would go. There was a good five feet between the top of the door and the ceiling, so Olivia hoped that the creature wouldn't notice the table hanging up there.

Sweating, panting, she tied the best, tightest knot she could with the cables, fastening the table leg to the ceiling, along the hoist track further back. The brunt of the weight rested on Sok as she did her work, his breaths shallow, pained.

When she had finished, she nearly fell to the floor. Stumbling to her knees, she suppressed the urge to vomit, her stomach tumbling and rolling. The cramping in her shoulders and wrists was almost unbearable.

"Are you okay?" Sok asked quietly.

"Yeah," she lied.

He looked toward the steel door. "This will only give us a few seconds. We'll need to run for it as soon as it's down."

"Got quiet," she whispered. "Do you think it's gone?"

"No, just waiting, I think."

"Waiting for what?"

"For our next move, I'm sure." Sok took off his glasses and cleaned them with the bottom of his shirt. A shaking hand placed them back on the bridge of his nose. "It has to know we're planning something, smart as it is."

"I'm scared."

"So am I." His eyes moved over the hoist above them. Turning to the tabletop beside him, Sok picked up the small controller and bit his lip. "Honestly, I'm just hoping it swings hard enough to knock the creature down. It also needs to be standing right there, ten feet in."

"I'll make that happen."

"Are you sure you want to do this?"

She choked out a laugh. "You ask me that after we tie the two-hundred-pound table to the ceiling?"

Sok smiled. "Hah."

"I'm ready if you are, Dennis." Arms wrapped around herself, she gave a short nod, sucked in a breath of air.

"I am."

Chapter 17

She stood ten feet from the door, swallowed thickly. Cautiously, Olivia approached until she stood inches away from the cold steel, her eyes traveling over the smooth surface. On the right, the foggy glass had been cracked deeply, wet with something dark and thick, but remained unbroken. Clearing her throat, she counted to five.

"Astor?" she called.

Silence.

Looking further to the right, she saw Sok waiting there in the corner, his lips taut across his teeth, the controller in one hand and the piece of rebar in the other. The door would open inward when the time came. As long as the door stayed open or the creature didn't decide to peer around it, he would remain hidden from view.

She stared at the door. "Astor? Are you there?"

Silence.

"Astor, I want to apologize. Please, answer me."

A series of clicks, a shadow at the glass.

Olivia's throat tightened. Already nervous, the astringent fumes from the massive amount of aerosol disinfectant they'd sprayed throughout the room burned at her eyes and nostrils, made it harder to breathe. "I've made a mistake. I want to come back out and be with you."

It trilled, the shadow moving back and forth.

"The thing is," she said. "I don't want you to hurt my friend. I want to open the door and come out, but I don't want you to hurt him. It's not his fault I was so stupid."

A dark hand pressed against the glass.

Olivia placed her palm against the glass too, the two overlapping. "Before I open this door, you have to promise me that you won't hurt him."

From the other side, a distorted, metallic voice. "No."

"Then I won't open the door, Astor."

"I will get in."

"Or I can come out willingly. We can be together, just like you want. That's what you want, isn't it?"

"Ucht-t-t-t... I could have you. Doesn't matter. We are already one. Already... one. I know... why. Why your blood..." The creature croaked, pawed at the glass. "It is me ...I am it... but before it was me... it was you."

"What?" she asked.

"Blood. Your blood. It takes the blood to know its host. Attaches. Digests. First blood, yours. My blood second. Before it was me, it thought... it thought it was you. Now, you are in me."

"Astor, how do you know that?"

"It... told me."

"The parasite?"

"Not a parasite. It is me. I know because it is me. You are... part of me. I want to be... part of you. Be one. Olivia. I could have you, already have you, because we are... we are one."

She rubbed the small, sore spot on her hand, her eyes on the floor. "It bit me. It was digesting my blood, preparing to attach to me. Instead, it ended up on you. You have my DNA in you."

It clicked and trilled. "Trace... enough. It is why... why only you... you cared. You... you knew."

"Ah, yes. I sensed it, I really did," she stammered, searching for the right words. "Of course, Astor, I knew that we were connected after that, ah, creature, attached to you. That's why I'm begging you, right now, to forgive me and to let my friend live. You let him live before, didn't you?"

"Yes."

"You could let him live now."

"Threat now. Not threat before."

"He isn't a threat, Astor. He's terrified of you. Forgive me and promise not to hurt him, and I'll open this door. I'll be sweet and loving. What do you think?"

"Ach-t-t-t…"

"Astor?"

"Yes."

She exhaled shakily. "Okay, I'm going to open the door." She turned to Sok, grimaced.

Sok's eyes widened, and he nodded, sweat glistening on his brow. He straightened, sucked in a breath.

One step at a time, Olivia walked backwards until she stood ten feet from the door. Sok, hidden in the corner next to the panel, typed in the code and the locking mechanism hissed and whirred.

"Go on, Astor, open it. It's unlocked!" she shouted.

The handle clicked and the door slowly swung open. Crouched, cautious, the creature stepped in, holding the steel door with one of its left hands. Head low, black eyes searched the room immediately in front of it. The fumes must have burned its nostrils and it cringed, shook itself like a dog. Those eyes fell on her next, and it proceeded forward, walking on its hands and feet, its second set of arms drawn up against its chest. The tail slithered in the air.

"Astor, did you mean it? Your promise?" she asked.

"Where is…?"

"He's hiding because he's scared. Did you mean it?"

"No, will kill."

She tensed, hugged herself. "That's not very nice, Astor."

It took a few more steps, closing in on her. Tilting its head, it showed off its sharp teeth in a snarl. "Nice?"

"Not nice."

Another step. The creature glanced back and forth,

sniffed at the air. The spines along its back stood up straight, its tail lashing. With a reptilian twitch, it focused on her once more. Then, it stood. At its full height, standing over six feet tall, the thing flashed a plastic grin and seemed to pose for her viewing pleasure. It croaked, snickered, dark amusement twisting its features. It spoke in Olivia's voice. "*Not nice.*"

"This again?"

"*This again?*"

"Astor, stop that and come here."

It feigned coyness, chittering through parted lips. Taking a few more steps toward her, a foot from the spot she needed it to reach, the creature paused, let its tongue loll out. After licking its teeth, it glared at her openly, his voice returning. "Where is he?"

"I told you. He's hiding."

"Can't smell anything."

"Because I helped him hide."

It narrowed its eyes. "I… am not stupid, Olivia."

"I know."

"Do you?" it asked contemptuously.

"We're already one – how couldn't I?"

The creature tilted its head, took another step closer to her. Its jaws opened and, from its mouth slipped her voice, perfectly replicated – it sang. "*Beautiful dreamer, wake unto me! Starlight and dewdrops are waiting for-*" The heavy metal table slammed full force into the creature, knocking it off its feet straight into the countertops ten feet to the right.

"Go!" Sok screamed.

Pushing off against the floor, Olivia ran for the door, her entire body like a spring, the tension exploding into her, through her, carrying her forward.

Sok was already on the other side, rebar swinging in his hand. She jumped over the creature's lashing tail. It was fighting to get on its feet. The table twisted loose, her knot coming undone, and dropped on its legs, momentarily trapping it against the countertops. With a serrated shriek, it shoved the two-hundred-pound table off and into the air.

She skidded, pulled the door shut behind her. Her efforts were stopped dead, throwing her off balance. The creature had grabbed the edge of the door, held it open, its jaws hanging wide, teeth shining as it let out a deafening, staccato scream.

The rebar in Sok's hands came down. In one fluid motion, letting out his own battle cry, Sok javelined the rebar right into the thing's chest, in the center where the chitinous, armored plating had yet to join. Yellow blood spurted out, an agonized wail rattling Olivia's skull. It staggered back into the room.

Sok shut the door, locked it, and slipped to the floor to lay on his side. He blinked, fixed his glasses, panted.

"Oh my God!" Olivia dropped to her knees. "Oh my God, it worked! It really worked!"

Gulping, Sok nodded. "Ah, yes. Yes, it did!"

The creature roared, banged on the door from the other side. It slammed its forehead against the foggy glass over and over, the slivering cracks deepening, forming a ring.

"Come on," Olivia said, pulling herself to her feet. "I don't know how much longer the battery is going to last."

Sok stood, exhaled roughly. He watched the glass splintering as the creature raged against it. "Of course."

She hurried down the short corridor with the tall, slender man at her heels. They'd made it to the end when the thick, foggy glass shattered. Spinning around, Olivia stared, nearly petrified to the spot. The creature had two of its arms out through the broken glass and was pawing at the steel door, searching for the panel. It found the panel, ripped at it, and withdrew its arms.

Nothing happened.

Both arms came out again and it continued to paw and stretch, shoving its head through the five-inch gap, twisting its shoulder in next. It shrieked, black eyes on her.

"It can't fit," Sok assured her.

She swallowed, took out her cell. "I know."

Gunmetal gray fangs bared, it let out another pitched wail, shoving itself into the gap, broken glass cutting into the flesh not yet fused to the black shell of the parasite. Yellow blood dribbled out. It had locked onto her, all energy now focused on escaping. Using its two free hands to hold the outside of the frame, it wrenched part of its broad shoulder through the gap, the carapace cracking, bleeding.

Olivia frowned deeply. "Oh shit."

"It'll get wedged in there. Let's go."

"Right, yeah." She turned, reached the end of the corridor and looked left. One last time, she glanced back at the steel door and let out a soft cry.

Sok took her arm. "Life raft first. Call second."

The creature had torn nearly half of its body out from the gap, the shoulder of its top arm dislocated, the shell fractured with exposed yellow and brown viscera visible within. It screamed at them, the sound both alien and frighteningly human. Wilcox's shriek mixed with the creature's serrated roar. With a hard yank, it pulled another few inches of its body out into the corridor, its armor crunching as yellow globs splattered on the floor. A flanging howl reverberated down the hall.

They ran.

The platforms they needed to reach were accessible on L2. They ran up the stairs, flew out into the corridor, and sprinted toward the exit outside. The windows allowed trace bits of early morning sunshine to filter through.

Throwing open the doors, Sok held up an arm to shield his eyes against the sun and led the way. The rain hadn't stopped completely, a faint drizzle spitting on them from the few storm clouds left trailing across the sky. Where the sun shined through, Olivia saw the beginnings of a very lovely rainbow.

She might've tried to take a picture of it if the circumstances had been different. Instead, she had her phone clutched tightly in her hand as she followed Sok to the edge of the platform.

Together, they ran along the platform, crossed one of the metal bridges, and came down again along the front of the rig. He was drawing down the first life craft they'd come to, offering her a vest. She put it on, clasped it closed. He did the same.

The cables whined as they lowered the small, inflatable craft to the tumultuous waters. Her stomach lurched at the thought of sitting in the little boat, being tossed about out there while they waited for rescue.

From behind her, she heard a rattling growl.

Sok peered back first, let out a gasp, and flattened himself against the support rail lining the edge of the platform.

Olivia swallowed, stared at the creature poised on the metal bridge, many yards away. It had freed itself at a great cost. Parts of it were sheared off, the muscles and tendons exposed, the flesh underneath a sickly shade of yellow. In the unforgiving gray light, the carapace had a brown, greenish tint to its dark surface.

It limped, tail thrashing back and forth. Those black eyes watched her, its movements stiff. It vomited thick, yellow gunk, fell forward on the bridge, and held itself up with one hand. The ribs had been crushed, shards of bone protruding out. Some of its guts were showing from a gash in its belly.

"Astor!" she called. "Oh my God, what did you do?"

It trilled and clicked, forced itself forward, toward her. "Ah-iv… Ah-iv-ah…"

Sok grabbed her arm, tugged her to the right. There was another bridge there leading to a metal stairwell. He led her along, then up, moving quickly.

Chittering, the creature leapt onto the platform, skidding on the slick surface, and took chase. It was hindered by its injuries, pausing to pant on the ascending stairwell.

Olivia looked down over the railing, face twisting at the sight of it twenty feet below stuffing its bowels back into its abdomen. She saw the rootlike tendrils of the parasite snake around the opening in the creature's belly to help keep more of its innards from spilling out.

Those same tendrils were pulling the shattered fragments of its shell back together on its shoulder like a thread of stitching tightening along a wound.

It glared up at her, met her eyes. Letting out a shriek, the creature charged up the steps, grabbling the rails with both sets of hands and lashing its tail madly behind it.

Her ankle threatened to twist, her sneaker skidding on the slick scaffold. At the next stairwell, she grabbed Sok's arm, pointed to the set of metal steps going down. "Go that way. I'll go up. It's after me." Olivia gestured toward the ascending stairs.

"What? No!"

"You have to finish prepping the boat. It's hurt, moving slow. I can come around, meet you there. There's no time. Just go!" With a hard shove, Olivia sprinted up the steps. She heard Sok scramble down the next flight.

When she'd reached the midway point, traveling to the next level up, Olivia spun around, grabbed the railings. Her assumption had been correct; the creature was indeed following her and not Sok. It looked up at her from the landing, closer than anticipated. She yelped, ran up the rest of the way and turned left to run across a bridge.

A shriek, a scraping sound. Suddenly, it landed awkwardly on the bridge in front of her, having leapt from below. Horrified, her legs froze, stopping her dead. Yellow gunk leaked from its mouth, and it coughed, entire body shuddering. Pockmarks had appeared along the surface of its armored shell. To Olivia, it seemed that the ocean mist was to blame, the moisture beads caustic to the thing's biology.

Those small parasites, the hatchlings, they'd dissolved in the seawater. And now, the adult version shivered in agony from mere droplets carried in the breeze. It kept staggering away, shrieking, lunging forward, pausing to pant, staring at her the entire time. While part of the creature's intent was locked onto her, the other, the more primal side, desperately wanted to flee back to the safety of the corridors inside, away from the elements.

She took a step back, swallowed thickly. Sok called for her, his voice lost in the ocean waves, the wind, the pounding of her heart. Hands on both sides of the railing, Olivia peered over her shoulder then leaned to the left.

The ocean churned fifty feet below, just beyond a platform. A quick calculation ran through her head. She licked her lips, tasted the salt in the air.

It whined and clicked, pincer arms drawn up to its chest. The damp metal must have hurt it, for the creature walked upright and stiff, slouched ever so slightly. Black eyes blinked at its own clawed hands, studying the pitted burns forming along the shell covering its fingers. Chin up, it stared at her. "Olivia, help me."

"Astor?"

"Help." It staggered, hugged itself. "Ow… ow."

"Astor, stop. Look at me," she said.

Its mandibles flexed. A human sentience twisted its face up, the expression recognizable as a pained grimace. While it watched her, it took another step forward, bits of the shell covering its sharp toes flaking off. The tail lashed slowly. "Ow. Ow. Ow."

"Are you in there?" Olivia held her ground, clung to the railing to the left of her.

"Hurts. Hurts. Ow."

"It's the salt in the air, Astor. It's burning the parasite. You can feel its pain," she said, the breeze whipping her hair across her face. "If you go back inside, it will stop hurting."

A trill escaped its lips, the sharp teeth shining dully in the gray light. Again, it stumbled closer to her, the spark in its eyes fizzling, shifting to hatred. It spoke with her voice. "*Stop hurting.*"

Her insides went cold. At the sight of it crouching, tensing to spring at her, Olivia swung her foot onto the rail, both hands grabbing the bar, and propelled herself up to jump over the side. Before she could plummet to the water, strong hands got ahold of her, talons digging into her shoulder. The creature wrenched her back onto the bridge, growling in frustration.

Lightheaded, hands flailing as it attempted to throw her onto the grated flooring of the bridge, Olivia kicked until she slammed the ball of her foot against the opposite rail. The creature staggered under her, the smooth, crumbling shell along its feet slipping on the slick metal. Powerful as the creature was, it failed to maintain a grip and when she kicked the rail again, pushed off as hard as she could, the force shoved them both over.

Freefall sucked the breath from her lungs, the world spinning. Black shell, clawed hands, and a long whiplike tail whirled around her, Wilcox's grip on her shoulder so tight she could have screamed from the pain if she could draw in air. It shrieked for her.

She hit the water and everything went black.

Darkness swelled around her, enveloped Olivia in a cold void. Her hands moved, her legs kicked. She got no further, a crushing weight pressing against her insides, stealing the warmth from her skin, drawing the life from her body.

Alone, in darkness, she began to slow. Motion hurt. Muscles froze, went taut. No sound save for the muffled rumble of wind rushing past her ears, a muted roaring echoing around inside of her hollow skull. No thoughts.

A dark, empty town, the streetlights out. A sidewalk cracked and crumbled around black root systems. She walked unsteadily along, passing bent, vacant shops with dark windows, and tripping over gaps in the cement.

The ground under her feet grew steadily smoother, the sidewalk dissolving into a dull, black path. At the same time, the road and the town blurred, fell into shadow as she continued toward Pine St. All faded, all sank, all turned black.

In the void again, she hugged herself, felt nothing. Only cold. Only the crushing of her lungs.

'Beautiful dreamer.'

She looked up and saw a faint light, a sole, twinkling star in the deep black sky.

Her hand raised toward it, fingers spread.

Slender fingers wrapped around her wrist, pulled Olivia to the surface. She gasped, sucked in huge breaths of salty air. Blinded by the gray light of the early morning, she flailed as Sok dragged her up and into the escape boat.

Lying in the bottom, she gagged, drenched and cold. A

blanket found its way around her shoulders, and she watched with burning eyes as Sok stood up, peered over the side of the boat.

It took sheer will to sit up, crawl over to where he stood. The life vest she'd put on earlier was missing, her shirt torn. "Where's Wilcox? We… fell… where is he?"

"I saw you both go under," Sok replied, picking up a long, orange paddle. "You swam up. Just you. No sign of, ah, him."

Her head tilted forward, wet hair clinging to the sides of her face. "If it… the parasite dissolved…"

"He couldn't have survived it. Olivia, they'd, ah, merged. Perhaps completely. I don't think there was much of him left." He strained to propel their boat around the side of the rig, staying clear of the massive grid of support beams.

"I thought… maybe…" She nodded, made herself sit up again only to lean on the edge of the boat, lungs aching.

"We could board again, since it's dead," Sok said.

"Right, yeah…" Her eyes closed.

Every muscle cried out in pain as she climbed the metal rung ladder back onto the side of the rig. She dropped to her knees and crept onto the center of the platform before spilling onto her stomach to pant softly.

"Are you okay?"

She looked over, eyes bleary, to see Sok kneeling beside her. "I'm… I'm okay. Just tired. I hit the water pretty hard, I think. Side hurts."

"Let me see."

Twisted at the waist, she rolled over, touched her side. Traces of bright red came back on her fingers. "Oh, it must've… scratched me when it tore off my life vest."

Sok grimaced. "It's not deep."

"Good."

He managed a weak smile. "We made it, we ma-"

"Don't. Don't say that." Olivia laughed darkly, shook her head. "You never say something like that at a time like this, don't you know?"

"Ah… what do you mean?"

Her eyes grew tired. "You can't say you've made it before it's over, Dennis. That'll be your last line before whatever it is comes back and kills you off. Haven't you seen any horror movies?"

His brows knit. "Um, yes."

Another laugh broke from her lips, and she sat up, rubbing at her face. "Ah, shit, my phone." It was still in her pocket when she searched for it and she woke it up. "I guess it really is waterproof."

"Who are you calling?" he asked.

"George Leblanc. The boat's on the way, no doubt, but he needs to know what happened here. He needs to hear it first."

With a nod, Sok sat beside her, lanky knees drawn up and his arms around them. "I hope he believes you."

"He always does."

Something gurgled and spit. At the edge of the platform, where the ladder rose from the side of the rig, a yellow, sinewy hand reached, the gnarled, black encrusted fingers stretching to grab the curved rail.

Olivia scowled, thumb frozen over the call button. Beside her, Sok sucked in a sharp breath, sat up straight.

Horrendous, wet noises – cries, clicks – leaked from its open mouth as the peeled, slimy remains of its body clambered onto the platform and dropped into a heap of shuddering, oozing flesh. Bits of softened, jagged black shell hung to its muscle tissue, its face exposed, the skin blistered. Dark hair meshed with bits of frayed, withered husk. It wheezed, ribs shivering, and gathered its strength.

231

It dragged itself for another foot before crumpling, going limp, and deflating. Both black eyes stared dreamily into the void and what was left of its tail ceased its lashing.

"Is it… dead?" Sok asked.

"I don't want to check to find out," she replied, throat tight.

"We should… go back inside."

"Listen…"

Sok squinted through his scuffed, ruined glasses and tilted his head. He tensed, lips parted.

A thumping, sharp and fast, grew louder. Soon, the source cut through the air directly above and threw a shadow down on them as it crossed the sun.

It was Sok who saw it first and gazed up at the sleek black helicopter as it circled the rig. He jumped to his feet and waved his hands in the air. Olivia stared at it, eyes narrowed. The Samos-Barnes logo shone clearly on its side.

Somewhere, out at sea, a boat horn wailed somberly.

The large-screen TV flickered in the corner of the white room. A monitor beeped slowly, rhythmically. Wet, raspy breaths rose and fell as the camera zoomed in on the female newscaster at the desk, her attractive bust occupying the entire screen.

"Tragedy has struck a deep-sea mining facility owned and operated by the Samos-Barnes energy division, killing nine out of the ten workers onsite. The cause of the accident," the blonde newscaster said, her eyes focused on the camera, "was deemed to be a gas leak which led to an explosion when one of the workers inside lit up a cigarette."

A photograph of a young, handsome man in a suit appeared beside her. He had posed for the portrait, had a courtly smile.

She frowned. "Tragically, the accident also claimed the life of Samos-Barnes' newest junior partner, Astor Wilcox, who, at the age of thirty-three, was the youngest member of the company's board of directors. He had been visiting the site."

She turned, the green screen behind her displaying an image of the rig engulfed in flames. "Samos-Barnes' CEO, Brett Chambers, had this to say."

A man in a crowded board room appeared on the screen, his suit dark, his chic short hair a mix of brown and gray. His short beard was trimmed stylishly, his smile serious and yet charming. "We here at Samos-Barnes like to consider ourselves a family. That extends to every brand we own, every facility we run, and every person whose lives we touch. We are heartbroken to hear about this second accident at Site Decimus. On the heels of a preventable workplace death, this... calamity only solidifies our resolve to invest more time and effort into vetting and training our workforce."

The newscaster returned. "The OcSaf Rep assigned to investigate the previous death has declined an interview with GLL-5." She spun, smiled brightly, her blue eyes hollow. "Next up, what deadly cocktail of chemicals would you find if you tested your baby's formula? That, and more, at 11."

,

Other books written by P.J. Burgy:

Paladin 33: revival

When three young Rebels board a derelict ship looking for supplies to scavenge, they find something else entirely. Out in the deep, uncharted territory they find Riley, a woman frozen in stasis for ten years. They also find her companion, an alien creature which Riley calls her sister. Riley not so politely takes command of the Hijo, the Rebel's small salvage ship, and changes their plans. It quickly becomes apparent to the hapless youngsters that Riley isn't entirely human anymore.

The Plague Runner

Thirty years after the near extinction of mankind, small pockets of survivors hide away behind fortified walls. Only the Runner braves the world outside...In the wake of a viral outbreak, those who remain live in huge forts, guarded from the nocturnal Infected and roaming gangs of bandits. Kara, a Runner – an individual who travels by foot between the forts to deliver supplies – never wanted to settle in a walled community. To her, they are death traps, just waiting for an inevitable wall breach. She longs to return to the life of a Rover – a gun for hire driving a large, armored vehicle. When her lover's fort sends an SOS and is found empty the next day, Kara chooses to search for the missing people, alone. She encounters abandoned, crumbling cities, marauders, mindless infected, and cults of fanatical survivors. She also discovers that there is more to the Infected than she could have ever imagined. To stop moving is to die. To run is to survive.

Hello, Martin

When Lizzie Clay holds her first art exhibit, a charming stranger takes an interest. At first, Lizzie is thrilled at the man's proposal to fill his new home with her paintings, but it quickly turns strange after he offers to pay her full time. As she begins to work with him, odd—and bloody—events start occurring in the town of Puhtipstie.

Made in the USA
Middletown, DE
21 April 2023